THE HEART TO KILL

A DEAD COLD MYSTERY

BLAKE BANNER

RIGHTHOUSE

ISBN-13: 978-1-63696-007-4

ISBN-10: 1-63696-007-3

Cover design by: Damonza

Printed in the United States of America

www.righthouse.com

www.instagram.com/righthousebooks

www.facebook.com/righthousebooks

twitter.com/righthousebooks

DEAD COLD MYSTERY SERIES

ONE

It wasn't raining. It was a deluge. The raindrops exploded on the blacktop on Simpson Street, raising a mist of spray two feet from the ground. The early-morning crowds were bent and hunched under their umbrellas, not so much hurrying as fleeing from the downpour. I watched Dehan through the windshield as the wipers squeaked and thudded in their losing battle against the water. She stepped out of her apartment block, warped wetly as the wipers swept past, then regrouped and walked around the hood of my car. Instead of an umbrella, she had on an Australian leather hat and a long coat. She pulled open the door and climbed in with a self-conscious grin on her face.

"G'day, Bruce!"

I smiled, shook my head, and pulled away. "Bruce?"

She removed her hat. Her hair was tied in a knot behind her head and now she tightened it as she spoke. "Didn't you know that, Stone? Australians call all men Bruce, and all women Sheila. It's a thing. So I say, 'G'day, Bruce!' and you say . . ."

"G'day, Sheila. Never let me say you didn't teach me anything." We drove in silence for a moment, among the hiss, the squeak, and the thud, the wet noises of a January morning in

New York, and the warm sigh of the heater. "I was looking at the David Thorndike case last night," I said. "I'd like to review it."

She frowned. "Thorndike. Wasn't he the journalist?"

"Investigative journalist on the *New York Telegraph*. Found murdered in the apartment he shared with his girlfriend on Manor Avenue, at eleven a.m. on the eighth of March, 2008 . . ."

"Last seen?"

"The night of the sixth, Thursday, by his girlfriend, at about nine p.m."

"So no precise time of death?"

"Nope. Sometime between nine p.m. Thursday and eleven a.m. Saturday. Thirty-eight hours. No forced entry. Only access to the apartment was through the front door. He had been shot, once, in the head at short range . . ." I turned and smiled at her. "With his own 9mm Glock."

"He was shot with his own Glock? That's not cool."

"It's not polite at all, is it?"

"No. How about forensics?"

"Squat. The prints in the apartment were his, his girlfriend's, the landlord's, and a couple of others that got no hits on IAFIS. The only prints on the weapon were Thorndike's."

"Obviously, they ruled out suicide."

I nodded. "He was lying in the middle of the floor, on his back. Entry wound was center of his forehead. The weapon was left on the bookcase by the door. The slug, found on the carpet a few feet away, matched the weapon."

She snorted. "I guess that's pretty conclusive. So the killer was admitted voluntarily, got access to Thorndike's Glock, then shot him with it. One single, clean shot."

"It certainly looks that way, yeah."

"What about the girlfriend?"

"Katie O'Connor, she was out at a restaurant with a guy, paid with her credit card, tight alibi."

"Anything taken?"

"Yes, no, maybe. There were no signs of robbery as such.

Their money, his wallet, credit cards . . ." I made an "and so on" gesture with my hand. "All of that was untouched. In fact, it looked like the whole apartment was untouched. It was as though he simply arrived, shot him, and left . . ."

"Except he used Thorndike's own gun, so he was presumably there long enough to get a hold of it."

"That, and also his laptop and all his research were missing."

She sat frowning at her Australian hat, turning it around in her hands, like it wasn't the hat she'd expected to see there. "That doesn't make a lot of sense." She raised her frown from her hat to the windshield as I turned from 169th onto Franklin, among the ugly redbrick monoliths, made even more unlovely by the low gray skies and the broken lights on the wet blacktop.

"I guess we're not going to the station," she said.

"I thought we'd go and see his wife."

She gave one slow nod. "Okay, so this is not straightforward."

"No."

"Let me sum up what I understand so far." She hesitated a moment and glanced at me. "Are we headed for Manhattan?"

"Yup. 104th and Columbus. It is the apartment he shared with her, which she now shares with her new husband."

"Am I playing catch-up here? Do you already have an idea . . . ?"

I shook my head. "Ideas, I have a few, but then again . . ." I shrugged. "Too few to mention."

"Funny. So Dave is married, he's doing okay because he has a nice address on the Upper West Side. For some reason you will no doubt disclose in your own good time, he also had an apartment in the less desirable Manor Avenue, in the Bronx, which he shared with his girlfriend. He's an investigative reporter, you mentioned his research and his laptop were missing, so I'm going to go out on a limb and say he was investigating a story 'undercover' or whatever the journalistic equivalent of undercover is."

"That's my girl."

"Either as part of his cover, or because he's a real dawg, he shacks up with Katie O'Connor. Then one day, somebody turns up and rings at the door. It seems he knew the caller because it looks like he let him in. The caller got possession of Dave's Glock, apparently without a struggle, which adds to the impression that Dave knew his caller. The caller then very coolly popped a cap right between Dave's eyes, without leaving prints on the gun." She shrugged and pulled a face. "It was early March, he was wearing gloves." She shrugged again, only half satisfied with her own explanation. "He then puts the gun down on the bookcase, collects the laptop, and all Dave's papers, and leaves with them."

"That's about the size of it. We have to assume also that his killer knew that Katie would be out and Dave would be alone."

We crossed the Third Avenue Bridge in silence and followed it onto East 129th, toward Harlem. Then she started nodding and spread her hands. "Okay, so I'm going to state the obvious. It looks like he was killed for the article he was writing, or because of the article he was writing, or both."

I laughed. "You're covering all your bases, huh, Dehan?"

"Yuh. But things are not always what they seem. That's what you're always telling me, right? And it may also be that he was killed by his wife, or his girlfriend, or both, and the disappearance of his laptop and his papers is incidental to the murder itself."

"Agreed."

"Does she know we're coming?"

"Yeah. I called her last night. She's an editor on a fashion magazine. She said she'd be working from home today."

We followed Central Park North onto Cathedral Parkway and then turned left onto Columbus. I parked outside the deli, she shoved her hat on her head, and we made a run for the entrance to the block. In the elevator, as I shook the water from my hair, she grinned at me from under her absurd hat.

"Who's laughing now, huh, Sensei?"

She opened the door almost immediately and looked at us with angry eyes. She was tall, as tall as Dehan or maybe taller. It was hard to tell because of the huge mop of Afro hair on her head.

Her skin was dark, but her features were more Indian than African, her eyes were almond, and her nose was long and aquiline. The expression on her face was pure Latin American, but when she spoke, her accent was English. I guess it has become a small world, and almost all of it was present there in that woman.

"Yes?"

We showed her our badges and I made the introductions. She sighed and seemed to sag.

"Look, is this going to take long? I am really busy."

I raised an eyebrow at her. "I don't know how long it's going to take, Mrs. Thorndike . . ."

"Petersen. I married again. And it's Ms."

"Ms. Petersen. We only have a few questions, but we would appreciate it if we could come in."

She sighed again, with a little less irritation than the first time, and stepped aside. "I'm sorry. Come in."

The apartment wasn't big. There was an open-plan living room and dining room, with a kitchen separated by a pine bar. Most of the far wall was taken up by a large plate glass window that overlooked the gardens on West 104th. The furniture looked like IKEA. A door beside the kitchen led to a short passage where I guessed there was a toilet and a bedroom. She gestured us to a sofa and sat on the edge of an armchair. She didn't make herself comfortable.

"I honestly doubt there is anything I can add to what I told the detectives when it happened." She shrugged. "It's almost ten years ago. Since then I have remarried and started a whole new life. This really is *not* very welcome."

I nodded and made a face like sympathy. "But you understand, Ms. Petersen, we can't just let people get away with murder because our investigations are unwelcome to the victims' exspouses."

She looked embarrassed. "Of course." She sighed for the third time and spread her hands. "What would you like to know?"

Dehan came straight out with it. "Where were you when David was killed?"

She took a deep breath, held it, and puffed out her cheeks. She gazed at the rain-spattered window for a moment, at the heavy clouds, and then blew out and shook her head. It was elaborate, but it looked genuine. "It was ten years ago, Detective. I don't honestly know. Besides, from what I recall, they didn't know exactly when he was killed. Wasn't there a window of twenty-four hours or something?" She kind of winced. "I think I spent the evening with friends. They must have asked me at the time. Whatever I told them then holds true today."

I nodded. "Sure. When did you first realize that David was having an affair?"

Her face went hard. It may have been ten years, but the anger was still fresh.

"I was informed by the investigating detectives that he had been shacked up with some tart when they came to interview me. That was the same day they found him, in the afternoon."

Dehan was watching her carefully. "When was the last time you saw him?"

Again the long stare at the heavy, gray sky. She bit her lip and gave her head a couple of small shakes. "It's so hard to be precise. Even at the time . . ." She frowned at Dehan. It looked to me as though she was searching for some kind of female sympathy. "He'd be gone for weeks on end sometimes. I got used to it, the way you get used to an ache. At first it hurts, then it's annoying, and finally you just forget it's there."

I smiled like I understood. "Can you give us a rough idea?"

"It must have been a couple of weeks at least. We had this . . ." She made a face that was eloquent of everything along the bitterness, resentment, disappointment spectrum. "*Arrangement*, for what it was worth. He would often disappear for several weeks when he was investigating a story. He was a good journalist . . . He was a low-down piece of *shit*! But he was also a good journalist, very dedicated and very thorough. But we agreed that we would meet at least one day at the weekend during the periods that he was away . . ."

Dehan interrupted.

"So, excuse me, Ms. Petersen, when he was away, did he not tell you where he was going?"

"No! Good heavens no! He didn't even tell me what he was investigating. He was extremely secretive about his work. I didn't even get to see his articles until they were published."

I said, "Please go on."

She took a moment, like she was examining her memories and finding them wanting. "The first couple of weeks he'd come home on the Sunday and we'd do something. Then he would start calling instead, with some excuse. Then he wouldn't even call. In the end, I stopped keeping the weekends free because I knew he wouldn't show. I'd go out to dinner with friends, or to a show, visit my parents . . ." She shrugged.

Dehan said, "Your parents in . . . ?"

"Miami."

I smiled at her and glanced out the window. "That's one alibi I wouldn't mind checking up on right now."

She smiled back. "Yeah, I hear you."

"Ms. Petersen, is there anybody you can think of who might be able to give us a line on what he was investigating?"

"Like I said, he was very secretive about his work. The only person I can think of would be Bob, his editor on the *Telegraph*. I am guessing he had to tell him *something*, or they wouldn't have approved his expenses." Her face suddenly contracted with bitterness. "I don't know what he told his whore."

I studied the anger on her face. Ten years on and there was still rage and bitterness there. I wondered if it was enough to drive her to kill. I sucked my teeth and glanced at Dehan. She shook her head and I stood.

"Ms. Petersen, thank you for your time. We'll try not to disturb you again. If you think of anything . . ." I handed her my card. "Please give us a call. Have a good day."

Outside, the rain had eased to a drizzle, but the water cascading from the awnings and the gutters was loud and sounded cold and wet. Dehan raised an eyebrow at me and offered me her hat. "You want? It would suit you. You'd look like Indiana Jones."

"My brain cavity is larger than yours."

She snorted as I stepped out and ran for my car. She followed me at an easy walk. As she climbed into the car and slammed the door, she eyed me. "You sure about that, Sensei?"

I stared at her for a long moment. She stared back. Finally, I said, "I think she has enough rage and anger in her to drive her to kill, if the right provocation were there . . ."

"She finds out about Katie somehow, finds out where he's shacked up, goes to confront him . . ."

"It's feasible. But if she killed him out of rage, why was she so cool about it? Why the single shot? Why didn't she empty the magazine into him? Why did she remove the laptop and the papers?"

I watched her eyes move over my face as she pursed her lips. She gave a little shrug with one shoulder. "In some people, rage expresses itself as something cold and clinical. As to the laptop and the papers, like we said before, that might be something completely unrelated."

I grunted. "What d'you want to do now?"

"You know what? I'd like to see the apartment where he was killed. You think if we ask nicely, the new tenants would let us have a look around?"

I fired up the engine and winked at her. "I had a feeling you'd say that. I called the landlord last night. He's between lets. I said we'd be there just after ten."

She raised a laconic eyebrow. "Geez, Boss! You da best! You treat me *good*!"

"Don't you forget it, Little Grasshopper!"

TWO

By the time we got back to the Bronx, the drizzle had turned to the occasional freezing drop, carried on an icy wind that made even the bare branches of the trees shiver. Dave's block was a five-story redbrick with an orange fire escape. The main entrance was a small courtyard that had been barricaded with a large wrought iron gate covered in steel mesh and topped off with sharp iron spikes.

The landlord, Sammy Gupta, buzzed us in and we rode the elevator to the fifth floor. I had brought with me a folder with the crime scene photos in it. The door to the apartment was open and I peered in. It gave directly onto the living room. The floor was covered in a rough, gray carpet. On the right there was a window, and in front of the window there was a small dining table with two chairs. Against the wall there was a sideboard, and directly in front of us there was a sofa that might have looked new when the Beatles still had pudding-basin hairdos. In front of it there was a wooden coffee table with very thin legs and a glass top, and a lower level where you could put magazines. Opposite the sofa, against the wall on the left, there was a dresser, and most of that was taken up with a TV.

Beside the dresser, there was an open door that gave onto a

bedroom. From in there emerged noises of movement. I knocked on the door and shouted, "Mr. Gupta? NYPD. May we come in?"

His voice preceded him, "Oh, yes!"

He was short and thin, in pleated pants, a white shirt, and a tank top. He smiled a lot, kept his arms permanently bent at the elbow and his head cocked slightly at a constant "ah well" sort of angle.

"Yes, please, come in, how do you do? Hello."

We showed him our badges. "I'm Detective Stone, this is Detective Dehan. We are reviewing the David Thorndike case . . ."

"Yes, yes, goodness yes, poor David. I remember it well. Very tragic. Please, tell me how I can help you."

Dehan answered him. "We'd just like to have a look around. Has the layout changed much since . . . ?"

As she asked it, I opened the folder and took out the pictures, but Sammy was already answering her.

"Well, it was ten years ago, and I like to keep things up to date, you know? But, no, it hasn't really changed much. Not at all. As you can see from the photos." He grinned.

Dehan took the top photo. It was the same coffee table and the same sofa, in the same position. She pointed to the carpet, between the table and the door, about ten or twelve feet away. "The body was there, lying on its back. The head just missed the table . . ." She stepped over and turned to face me.

Sammy was nodding. "Yes, that is correct. I opened the door, came in, and there he was, just where you are standing. He looked very surprised."

Dehan ignored him and carried on. "Which means he was standing about six or seven feet from his killer. The shot was pretty much point-blank if the killer had his arm outstretched . . ."

She took a couple steps toward me and I stretched out my hand as though I were going to shoot her. It would have been impossible to miss. She kept talking.

"So the killer was standing more or less where you are

standing now, by the door. He has the door open or he has it closed, we don't know. He's either just come in or he's on his way out. Again, we don't know. But that's where he's standing, by the door."

Sammy was nodding a lot. "Yes, undoubtedly that is correct. He had to be by the door to effect that shot. No doubt."

I looked at him and asked, "Did you collect the rent in cash?"

"Always. I would come in the first week of the month, and he was never late. Always on time, no problem. That is why I was worried when he did not open, and no message, nothing. It was not like him."

"I know it was a long time ago, but can you recall where he worked? Where he kept his computer and all his papers?"

"Oh, yes! Always on the table by the window." He pointed to the dining table. "Always over there. Whenever I am come to see him, always he was at the table by the window, smoking cigarettes, drinking coffee. Always there."

"But it wasn't there that day."

"No, and I am pointing that out to the police. They are saying, 'There is no robbery!' And I am saying, 'Well, look here! They have taken laptop, and also all his papers! What is that if it is not a robbery?'"

"Quite right. How about his gun, Sammy? Did you ever see him with his gun?"

He beamed. "Oh, yes! Goodness, yes! He was very chatty, friendly kind of chap. He invited me in for coffee one time, and I ask him, 'You are no afraid of being robbed? With expensive computer and important work for the newspaper?' And he says to me, 'Oh no! I am always take out special insurance!' And he shows me a pistol in the drawer. 'I always take precaution!' He was a tough cookie, all right!"

"And where did he keep it, Sammy?"

He pointed. "Over in the sideboard. He said he wanted to have it close when he was working."

Dehan frowned. "Why was that? Did he feel he was in danger?"

"He told me he was an investigative reporter, and the people he investigated were very dangerous characters. He always wanted to have his insurance. Always he said it like this, 'I always have my insurance!'"

I walked over to the table and stood by the chair. I looked over at Sammy and Dehan by the door. "Here? This where he sat?"

Sammy nodded. "Yes, just there where you are standing."

I tried to visualize it. He'd be sitting at the table, writing, reading, smoking, drinking coffee. There would be a ring at the door, or a knock. The gun is in the sideboard. He goes to the door. He is careful, cautious, he knows he is in danger and likes to keep his insurance handy, so he asks who it is . . .

I said, "Was there anything else, Sammy, that you thought was odd that the detectives at the time did not think important?"

He danced his head around a bit. "Well, there was one thing, maybe it is nothing, but I thought it was odd."

"What's that?"

"It looked to me like he was going to leave. He didn't tell me anything about leaving, but in his bedroom, the suitcase was unzipped and open on the floor."

Dehan frowned. "What about his clothes?"

"No, they were all in the drawers and in the wardrobe. It was just the suitcase, which would be normally, you know, in the wardrobe or under the bed. But that morning it was out, on the floor, and open, unzipped."

I thought about it for a moment, but it didn't say anything to me. Dehan asked him, "Do any of the neighbors from that time still live here?"

He did his little dance with his head again. "Well, you know, people in apartment blocks like this one, they are mainly transient. They come and they go. But yes. Me. I live on the first floor. I have six apartments in this block. I live in one and I let out the other five."

Dehan rested her ass against the back of the sofa and crossed her arms. "Do you remember much about what happened that day, Mr. Gupta?"

"Sammy, please. Everybody is calling me Sammy. I always think, if you can bring a smile into somebody's life, even for a moment, you have done something useful. Isn't it?" He looked from me back to Dehan. We waited. He went on, "You know, Detective Dehan, I have a very good memory, because I am very observant. I am noticing the little details. And, of course, after poor David was murdered, I was thinking about what I had noticed that day, and also the previous days. I offered these observations to the detective who was investigation, but he thought they were not useful."

Dehan said, "We think they might be, Sammy. We'd like to hear them."

"Surely, I will tell you. Let me fill you in." He grinned at us, like he'd phrased it in a particularly enlightening way. "You know that he was here for just over two months, and for most of that time he was sharing it with Miss Katie O'Connor, a very pretty and lively little filly! Oh, goodness! She was very alive!" He laughed. "And she was often receiving visits from her sister and her boyfriend."

I frowned. "Her sister?"

"Yes. But about a week before he was killed, Miss Katie moved out. David was very upset because he was *most* in love with her. She was very charming! Very pretty! Really most nice. But they had a big argument and she went with her sister and her sister's boyfriend or husband, I don't know, I am sorry. Then!" He held up his finger, grinning at each of us in turn. "Two days before he is dead . . ."

Dehan said, "Thursday the sixth of March."

He nodded at her, as though he approved of her choice of date. "Exactly correct, yes, Miss Katie O'Connor comes to visit, to collect some things, at about nine o'clock. I am hoping, you know, that she will stay the night and maybe they will make up, because he is nice man, and he is very much in love with her. They don't fight, but she doesn't stay. She goes. Friday everything is very quiet, but in the evening a woman comes to see him."

"A woman? There is no mention of this in the police report."

"No! I know! Because the detective thinks I am making a mistake. I am hearing the buzzer outside—you know, the intercom—because my apartment is right by the gate. So I am hearing and seeing most people coming and going. And I am pretty sure that I am hearing a woman on Friday night. I am hoping maybe it is Miss Katie come back to see David. So I am going to the door and looking through the peephole. But I can't see properly. She does not put on the light. But she takes the elevator to the fifth floor. Ten minutes later, not more than fifteen, the elevator comes down again and somebody leaves. Next morning I go up to see about the rent, he is not answering his door, I let myself in, and, oh my god! He is dead."

Dehan held up her hands. "So, hang on a second there, Sammy. Let me see if I've got this straight. Did you at any point get a clear look at this visitor on Friday night?"

"No."

"Not when they arrived and not when they left."

"No."

"So what makes you think it was a woman?"

"Oh, the intercom. I think I recognize David's voice, so I am saying, 'Oh, goodness, maybe Miss Katie is coming back!' And I am looking through the window. I can't see her, but I can hear her voice asking to be let in."

Dehan pressed him, "And was it clearly a woman's voice?"

"To me it was clear. To me it was a woman. But she spoke very softly. Too softly to make out what she said, or to be sure who it was."

I said, "So you can't in fact be certain that this visitor actually went to David's apartment."

He looked apologetic. "I am certain that it was a woman, and

I am certain that she did. But that is only my own personal opinion. I did not see it with my own eyes, no."

I nodded a few times and looked at Dehan. She shook her head. "I'm good."

I turned to Sammy. "You have been very helpful. Thank you. We won't keep you any longer."

He wished us all the very best and begged us please to come again if we were ever passing by in the neighborhood. We thanked him and left.

Outside, the roads were wet and the air was cold and blustery. It wasn't raining, but the clouds were dark and sagging overhead and didn't look as though they were about to move on anytime soon. We climbed into the car, and I fired up the engine and turned on the warm air. Dehan rubbed her hands together and said, "Did you happen to talk to Miss Katie O'Connor last night as well?"

I smiled and pulled my notebook from my inside pocket. I flipped it open and handed it to her. "No. She's a Realtor working southwest Bronx. I figured you could give her a call and fix up an appointment. That's her number." I gave a small shrug and grinned at her. "There is no need for her to know we are cops until we get there."

She nodded and started dialing. "Less chance of her suddenly remembering a nonexistent dentist's appointment if she thinks she's going to sell us a house rather than get interrogated about her boyfriend's murder."

"That was the way my mind was working."

She put the phone to her ear and stared out of the window. "So, what? Are we married and looking for a place together, or what?" I gave her my expressionless face but she didn't look at me. After a moment she said, "Oh, yes, good morning, am I speaking to Katie O'Connor?" She laughed like they were sharing a joke and said, "Hello, Katie! Listen, when would it be convenient for you to see us . . . What are we looking for? Well, we were hoping you could point us in the right direction!" She laughed uproariously again. "One o'clock? Oh, really? Oh, that sounds *perfect*." She looked at me and blinked several times. "Darling, Katie will see us at one o'clock on Howe Avenue. She is showing a *gorgeous* three-bedroom semidetached house. Darling, are you listening to me?"

I raised an eyebrow at her. "Yes, darling."

"Katie, that sounds perfect. We'll see you there at one. Let's see if between us we can get the old dinosaur to make up his mind!"

She hung up and eyed me, suppressing a smile. I took my notebook back and said, "That was unnecessarily elaborate."

"What can I do? I'm creative. When a girl is creative, she creates, right?"

"I need to dry out, get some hot coffee and a donut."

She smiled. "All these years married, and you still say the most romantic things, honeykins."

"Cut it out!"

She snorted but remained silent the rest of the way to Fteley Avenue.

THREE

THE CLOUDS HAD BROKEN AND WERE HANGING, WHITE and wet, against a cold blue sky. An icy wind was whipping in gusts off the East River, flapping our clothes and dragging Dehan's hair across her face, forcing her to claw it back with her fingers so she could see where she was going. We leaned against the gusts and made our way up the drive, past the protruding garage, to the front door. It stood wedged open. I rested my hand on the doorjamb and looked in. Dehan rang the bell, then shouldered past me, muttering, "Door's open. We can go in." Then she called out, "*Katie? Katie O'Connor?*"

Katie O'Connor appeared in the kitchen doorway with a bright smile on her face. She had copper-red hair, deep blue eyes, and a cute spray of freckles. She was wearing a handsome tweed suit that made her look expensive. Her smile faded slightly when Dehan showed her her badge.

"Hi, Katie, I am Detective Carmen Dehan, and this is my partner, Detective John Stone. We'd like to ask you some questions about your relationship with David Thorndike."

It was a pretty brutal approach. Her whole demeanor seemed to collapse. She sagged, frowned, and said, "*What?*" Then, "No! I am working. I have potential clients arriving . . ."

"We won't take up much of your time, Katie, but it's easier if we do it here rather than at the station."

She picked up on the implied threat and sighed. "Fine, but please, make it quick. This is an open house. People could turn up at any time. What do you want to know?"

Dehan rubbed her hands and stamped her feet. "How about we start with why you two split up?"

A flash of irritation creased Katie's brow. "That was *ten years ago*!" She glared at Dehan a moment, then glared at me where I was still propped up against the doorjamb. "Can you come in, please, and close the door?"

I stepped in and closed the door behind me. Katie disappeared into the kitchen and we followed. We found her leaning with her ass against the sink and her arms crossed. Her face was flushed, and I couldn't make out if she was mad or scared. She was probably both.

Dehan rested against the door, and I went and sat on a pine chair at a pine breakfast table. I said, quietly, "Why'd you break up, Katie?"

She gave me that look women give you when they are seeing all men as one single, conjoined bastard. "Because he was a son of a bitch! Why are you asking me about this? It was . . ."

I interrupted her, "I know, ten years ago. We are a specialist cold case unit. David was murdered, so we aim to find out who murdered him. However much of a son of a bitch he was, murder is against the law. I hope you are going to cooperate with us."

It was like talking to an angry four-year-old. She stared at me with defiance in her blue eyes, and two red spots on her cheeks. Then she closed her baby blues and heaved a big, angry sigh.

"Okay, I understand, and yes, you are right, of course." She unfolded her arms, spread her hands for a moment, and then let them drop by her side. "We had been living together for a couple of months. He was a fun guy. He was very alive, dynamic, full of life and energy." She stopped and for a moment her eyes became abstracted. She looked out the window and into the back garden.

"You got the feeling sometimes with Dave that the world wasn't quite enough for him." She looked at me. "Do you know what I mean?"

I nodded. "Sure. He had an appetite for life."

"Oh, he sure had that. He was a good journalist. Tireless. He worked hard, very hard. A lot of women would have said too hard, but I supported him. I admire hard work and commitment in a person. I don't need some guy fawning over me twenty-four seven. I like to see a guy achieving something in life. So I supported him . . ."

Dehan narrowed her eyes. "Were you aware of what he was working on?"

Katie gave a lopsided smile. "No . . . Dave was super careful and secretive about his work. Nobody, and I mean *nobody* got to see it. Even his editor got the bare minimum of information."

I said, "Okay, so in what way were you supportive?"

She shrugged. "I made no demands on him—if I worked eight or nine hours a day, he would work sometimes twelve or fifteen, sometimes more. When he did, I would keep him supplied with coffee, food, whatever he needed until he was done." She shrugged. "We got up together, we went to bed together, and I was there at his side every step of the goddamned way. I believed in him."

I knew the answer but I asked anyway. "So what happened?"

"It's obvious, isn't it? I discovered the son of a bitch was married."

Dehan was chewing her lip. She said, "How'd you find out?"

She stared at Dehan for a long moment, then down at the floor. "He told me."

"He *told* you?"

She nodded without looking up. "It was about a week or so before . . . before they found him. I got home from work and he was kind of hyper. He wasn't making a lot of sense. He said the article was finished, it was going to be mega." She shook her head, still looking at the floor. "He was talking crazy stuff, about getting the Pulitzer, writing a best seller, making a fortune. At first I was right there with him." Now she looked up and held Dehan's eye. "I was as excited as he was. We were going to be rich, famous. It was going to be bigger than Watergate. Then, I remember it like it was yesterday, he took hold of me by the shoulders and told me to sit down. He sat next to me, on the sofa, and told me."

Dehan shook her head. "Son of a bitch."

Katie glanced at her. She looked grateful. "Yeah. He'd been married for five years, something like that. I don't remember exactly. I just remember going cold all over. The *betrayal*!" She stopped and studied Dehan's face for a moment, like she was searching for something there. "All the time we had been together I had thought I knew him, but he was a stranger. He'd been lying to me, using me. And what about his wife? If he was capable of doing that to her, what would he do to me in five years?"

Dehan nodded. "Suddenly, he was a stranger."

"Right. He told me he was going to come clean with her, tell her about us and get a divorce. Then we'd get married . . ."

She gave a sudden, startling yelp of laughter and leaned back, looking up at the ceiling, shaking her head in disbelief.

"Can you believe it? He had it all worked out. What he had done to his wife would just be swept away! What he was *going* to do to his wife didn't count. What he had done to me for the last two months, that wasn't important. None of that mattered anymore. Because he had decided we were going to get married. So now it was all okay."

I said, "So what happened?"

She glared at me. "What happened? I'll tell you what happened. I slapped his face and screamed at him. I told him we were finished, packed my things, and left."

"You packed your things . . . Did you have a zip-up suitcase . . . ?"

She shook her head. "No. I took most of my stuff, what I could fit, in a couple of holdalls. I left some books and CDs and went back a couple of days later to get them."

I scratched my chin a second, thinking. "Would that be the Friday?"

She raised her eyebrows. "Seriously? You expect me to remember the days of the week ten years ago?"

I managed to combine a sigh and a smile. "David's body was found on the Saturday morning. Your big bust-up would have been roughly the previous weekend."

She thought about it for a moment, then shook her head. "No. It wasn't the day before. Probably midweek, Wednesday or Thursday. I was there maybe ten minutes. Got my stuff and left."

We were quiet for a moment, then Dehan asked her, "He was found on the Saturday morning. Where were you the night before?"

Katie squinted at her. "It's got to be in the police report. Why are you asking me?"

"Could you please just answer the question?"

She sighed and raised her eyes. "Fine! I went out to dinner with a friend. They checked my alibi."

I looked out the window at the garden. The trees were nodding, and the sky had turned gray again. There were a few drops of rain on the glass.

"Katie, where did David usually work?"

She frowned, not understanding my question. "At home."

"No, I mean, where in the apartment?"

"Oh, we had a small dining table over by the window. He worked at the table."

I nodded. "I figure he had all his papers scattered around, taking up all the space, right?"

"I guess so, yeah. Why?"

"When you went to collect your books and your CDs on the Thursday, was his laptop on the table, with all the papers?"

Her face became serious. I could see she was searching her memory. I could tell it was a question she hadn't asked herself before. She frowned, then her frown deepened and she shook her head. "I'm not sure."

I nodded. "Yes, you are, Katie. Don't lie to me."

Her cheeks colored. "I don't think there was anything on the table. He'd finished the article. It makes sense."

"If that is right, where would he have put the article, and his laptop? Neither was found at the scene."

Her face was like a mask. It was as though she had climbed inside herself and she was now unreachable. She was still frowning, but no longer at my question. I had the feeling she was frowning now at her own thoughts. She said, "I don't know. I guess his editor . . ."

"Why would he give his laptop to his editor?"

"I don't know. You're asking me questions I can't answer."

"Well, what about friends? Did he have a close friend? Somebody other than you that he trusted?"

She thought, and when she answered her voice was almost a whisper. "No . . ."

"I think you're lying, Katie."

Her eyes flashed. "I am *not*! He didn't trust anybody! Not even me!"

"You're telling me he had no friends?"

"He had acquaintances. Some close acquaintances. But no friends. There was Bob, Bob Shaw. That was his editor. He was about as close as anybody ever got to him. And some guy he spoke about sometimes. I never met him. Guy called Lee. But I'm pretty sure the only person he would have trusted with his work, once it was finished, was his editor."

I thought for a bit, then sighed and put my hands on my knees. "Okay, Katie. I'm going to need an address and a number where we can reach you besides your work number. I'm pretty sure we'll need to talk to you again."

She reached in her purse and handed me a card. "Does that mean I'm a suspect? I have an alibi. It was checked."

I stood, took her card, and put it in my wallet. "Nobody has an alibi, Katie, because nobody knows at what time he was killed. Please, don't leave town."

As I opened the front door onto the icy, gray day, I heard Katie behind me. "Were you the couple who were due at one?"

I looked at Dehan, who turned to answer. She looked embarrassed, just shrugged, and shook her head.

I climbed into the Jag feeling vaguely depressed. Dehan climbed in beside me and we both sat staring at the bleak expanse of the sound, reflecting the cold gunmetal of the low clouds.

"Sucks," she said, and I nodded. "We need to eat and review what we have so far." I nodded again and fired up the old brute.

FOUR

I followed Castle Hill Avenue for a mile or so north, listening to the desultory squeak of the wipers, till we came to the Café Havana. In the cold and the rain, it looked like just the job. I pulled up outside, Dehan dumped her Australian hat on her head, and we loped across the sidewalk and pushed inside.

A bell clanked overhead and Julio, the bored-looking owner behind the bar, cheered up when he saw us.

"Hey, *parejita*! How you doin', man? You come to brighten up my afternoon?"

"It's what we live for, Julio, you know that."

We ordered a couple of beers and some chicken and black beans up at the bar, then found a table by the wood burner he had against one wall, next to a mural of a 1947 Chrysler Windsor with a half-naked Cuban girl leaning against the hood.

Dehan sat back in her chair and stretched out her long legs toward the fire. I took a couple of paper napkins and dried my hair with them. She said, "You like her for it?"

I stared at the flames a moment. "I don't know. We still have the same problem we had with Samantha. She's mad enough for it. David seems to have been a guy who knew how to make women mad. But I don't see the passion in the killing."

She was staring at her boots, like it was them talking to her. When I finished, she nodded at them and said, "I don't like her for it." She chewed her lip for a bit, then said, "There's something missing."

Julio brought over our beers and I took a long pull. As I set down the glass, I said, "I agree. And it's something to do with the laptop and his article. This feels like an execution, not a crime of passion."

She made a face like I'd just said two and two made four point zero one. "I don't know, Stone. I don't see it that clearly." She finally turned to look at me. "It's too much of a coincidence, isn't it?"

"You just said you didn't like Katie for it."

She sighed. "I know." She swiveled around and leaned her elbows on the table. "He finishes his article, decides it's going to make him rich and famous, decides to tell Katie about Samantha, and Samantha about Katie, Katie dumps him and moves out, his laptop and his papers disappear, and he gets executed—all in the space of a week. There is no way these events are not connected."

"I agree, but I'm damned if I can see how at the moment."

She gave me a lopsided smile and I was momentarily distracted by how extraordinarily beautiful her face was. "Oh, Mighty Sensei, a full morning into the investigation and you don't know the answer? You must be getting old."

She took a pull on her beer, smacked her lips, and examined the glass for a moment.

"How does this work? He finishes his article, and having put it all together, he realizes he has a bombshell on his hands. He's looking at the Pulitzer, a best-selling book, TV interviews—he's made the big time. Now, remember, this guy is security conscious, he keeps a gun next to his laptop, so what does he do? He puts his finished work somewhere safe . . ." She spread her hands and shrugged. "A safety-deposit box, his editor, a locker at the paper. Could be anywhere. Meantime, he decides to come clean with Katie. He has real feelings for her. After all, she is a rare woman who is prepared to support a talented, but very demanding man. So he tells her. She gets pissed and storms out."

She took another pull on her beer and examined the glass again, as though she was watching the end of the story play itself out on the side of her glass before she told me about it.

"Then, one of two things happens. Either he goes and tells Samantha the bad news, which seems unlikely if Katie has just dumped him . . ."

"He may have believed she would come back to him."

She nodded, then shrugged. "Or, Katie decided to tell her. Now . . ." She took a deep breath. "If Katie had killed him, you know what, Stone? I think she would have used a battle-axe. She has volatile emotions and she doesn't strike me as the ice-cold rage type. But Samantha, we don't know her well enough to be sure, but I could buy that. I could buy her judging him, sentencing him to death, and then executing him."

I thought about it for a minute. "What is it about Samantha . . .?"

"We know that they were married for at least five years, right? In all that time she was prepared to put up with him disappearing for weeks at a time, failing to show at weekends, broken promises. That's got to make you mad, right? But instead of confronting him, threatening him, or just dumping the son of a bitch, she swallows it and adapts her life to suit his. That is . . ."

Again she spread her hands, and I finished for her. "Cold anger."

"The final straw comes when, after all the sacrifices she has made, instead of getting her reward, some other dame gets it. She comes to see him. He lets her in. 'What the hell are you doing here?' She tells him she knows about Katie. She knows what he's like about security, she knows where he's likely to keep his gun, she takes it, and bang! Ice cold."

I did a lot of nodding. "It's neat, it's logical, it's convincing."
"But?"

Julio brought our chicken and beans, and we ate hungrily and in silence for a while. Finally, when I was wiping the plate with a hunk of bread, I said, "What would stop Katie from telling us she had spoken to Samantha?"

She snorted. "That's easy. The loyalty of two wronged women."

"Really? Good to know."

"You don't buy it."

I shook my head. "It's not that. It is a very credible scenario, and so far the most likely, but right now that's all it is. There is no evidence to support it. We need to find his laptop and his article. The fact that he was working on something that was apparently bigger than Watergate, the fact that he was apparently executed, and the fact that the article and the laptop disappeared without ever making headline news . . ."

I shrugged one shoulder and she nodded. "I hear you. It is pretty suggestive."

"At the very least we need to explore that angle. We start by talking to his editor, Bob . . ."

"Bob Shaw. You think he might have the article?"

"It's possible. But the *New York Telegraph* has always had a reputation for publishing high-quality, controversial journalism. It has been traditionally antiestablishment, whoever the establishment was. So you'd expect that if he had the article, and David was killed for it, he'd publish it. The added controversy of the murder and a posthumous Pulitzer wouldn't do the paper, or him, any harm at all. But . . ."

"If there were powerful enough interests involved, they might have taken out David and silenced his editor."

"Again, it's a possibility we need to explore. Right now, all we have is theories."

"So, the *New York Telegraph*?"

I stood and grabbed my coat from the back of my chair. "Appropriately located at Five Penn Plaza."

We took the Bruckner Expressway through steady, heavy rain, and for the second time that day crossed Third Avenue Bridge.

After that, it was left onto Columbus and a slow crawl south all the way to West 30th. We didn't talk much. We just watched a bobbing sea of colored umbrellas jostle each other and occasionally make suicide runs through the slow-moving river of traffic, lit up with red, green, and amber lights, like Christmas for fishes. Three more lefts found me a parking space outside the bank at 5 Penn, and we pulled up our collars and tried to dodge the raindrops in a hundred-yard dash to the big glass-and-brass entrance of the green marble lobby.

The paper had its offices on the fifth floor. We stepped out of the elevator into a sober mahogany-and-brass lobby that was as busy as Grand Central Station. I made my way to the reception desk and showed my badge to a pretty woman in a blue suit.

"Detectives Stone and Dehan. We'd like to talk to the editor in chief."

She winked at me with long lashes. "I'll see if she's available." She picked up the phone and pressed a button. "Usually it's attorneys who want to talk to her. Cops not so much. Yuh, Al, I got two cops here, Detectives Stone and Dianne, they want to see Ms. Pearce . . ." She raised her eyes to me. "He's just checking if she's free."

I frowned at her. "Ms. Pearce? What happened to Bob Shaw?"

"He retired, couple of years ago." Then, to the phone, "She's free? Okay, thanks, honey." She pointed at a large glass door in a long glass wall, through which we could see what looked like hundreds of people sitting in small cubicles, talking on the phone and typing furiously, often at the same time. "She says you got five minutes. Through that door, right to the end, you can't miss it."

We elbowed our way through the busy, noisy room till we came to a glass-fronted office at the end. Inside, there was an attractive woman sitting behind the desk in an elegant burgundy suit with a white blouse. She was talking on the phone and waved us in as I pushed open the door. She pointed at two chairs opposite and said into the phone, "Take responsibility, Emma. Just do it. If they sue, they sue. Just be damned sure of your facts. If they sue us, I want to eat them alive in court. So I need you to be right and I need you to *know* that you are right. Deal with it."

She hung up and we showed her our badges. "Detectives John Stone and Carmen Dehan, Ms. Pearce."

She glanced at the badges, then at our faces, and said, "Tell me you are here to arrest me and rescue me from this goddamn paper."

I smiled. "I'm afraid not. We just need to ask you a couple of questions. In fact, it was Bob Shaw we wanted to talk to."

She raised an eyebrow at the edge of her desk and ran her finger along it, like she was reading braille. "Bob? Bob's retired. Can I ask what it's about? If it's to do with the paper, it's to do with me."

I sensed rather than saw Dehan lean back in her chair and cross her arms. I said, "Do you recall the murder of one of your reporters, about ten years ago? His name was David Thorndike."

"Sure, I remember it. Dave was a damn good reporter. I covered the case for the paper. What about it?"

I looked at her with renewed interest. "Were you friends?"

She snorted. "Dave had no friends. Good reporters don't. We knew each other. I respected him. That's about as far as it went."

"You remember he was working on a story at the time . . ."

"That's why he was in that godforsaken apartment in the Bronx. If you ask me, it's what got him killed."

"Really? Okay, I'm asking."

"Dave had a real reputation. He and Bob were about as close as Dave ever got to anybody. Bob had a lot of respect for Dave as a reporter. He had proved himself time and again. But Dave was really jealous and really secretive. He played his cards close to the chest . . ." She paused and gave me a slow, deliberate once-over and smiled. "Real close to the chest, Detective Stone. You know what I mean? So Bob and Dave had come to a kind of understanding. Dave told him in very basic, limited terms the general area of his investigation, and Bob either approved it or not. If he approved it, that was pretty much the last he heard about it until the story was ready. He said it was his way of protecting himself, Bob, and the story." She shrugged. "Only somebody like Dave could get away with something like that, because he had such a damned good track record. He produced one controversy after another, and his facts were rock solid. Made a fortune for the paper."

I shrugged. "So what was special about this story?"

"Special?" She said it as though the word had some deeper meaning and gave me the once-over again. "That's the point. Nobody except him knew, but he did something he had never done before. He called Bob and told him this was the greatest story of his career, that he expected to get the Pulitzer for it, and that he feared his life was at risk."

"That wasn't in the police report."

"What can I tell you? I didn't edit the police report." She winked at me, and there was something infectious about her grin. "Bob asked him if he wanted to pull the plug. He said he didn't. The story was all but finished and he'd be bringing it in any day."

"How do you know this?"

"I wrote the story after he was killed, remember? Bob and I discussed it at length."

"What happened to his story and his laptop?"

"I have no idea."

"Could Bob have them?"

She looked doubtful. "And not publish the story? I don't think so."

I sighed. "We really need to see him. Can you . . . ?"

"Put you in touch with him? Sure I can. But what's in it for me?"

I felt Dehan stir and sigh noisily. Pearce ignored her and kept her smile focused on me. I blinked and said, "You don't get charged with obstructing a police investigation."

She raised an eyebrow and said with heavy meaning, "You're hard, I like that in a man. I'll tell you what, you take me out to dinner, give me an exclusive when the investigation is finished, and I'll put you in touch with Bob Shaw and dig up anything else I can on Dave and his investigation. How does that sound?"

I gave her my sweetest smile and said, "How could I possibly say no, Ms. Pearce?"

"Shelly."

I reached in my wallet and pulled out a card. As I handed it to her, she handed me one of hers. "Call me, John."

I stood. "I will, John." It was lame but she laughed. Dehan didn't. More seriously, I said, "When can I expect to hear from you, Shelly?"

"I'll call him in the next half hour and get back to you straightaway. But I am serious, John. I expect dinner." Again the once-over. "I am pretty sure I can help you."

I nodded once. "We'll be in touch."

Dehan was silent all the way to the elevators, all the way down, and across the lobby. When we got into the street, she jammed her hat on her head, pulled up her collar, and shouldered her way through the rain ahead of me. She waited by the passenger door for me to catch up, wrenched it open when I unlocked it, and slammed it hard after she'd climbed in. I got in, closed the door, and looked at her.

"What's the matter?" She made a face and shook her head. "Stop it, Dehan. What's got into you?"

She took her hat off, rammed it on her knee, and stared at me with blazing black eyes for a long count of four. Then she said, "Nothing!"

I sighed and fired up the engine. We pulled out onto 8th Avenue and started the long, slow, wet crawl north, toward the Bronx.

FIVE

THE CALL CAME AS I WAS PARKING. MY CELL WAS ON the dash. I glanced at Dehan, who was staring away from me, out at the rain, and said, "Can you get that?"

She picked it up and put it to her ear.

"Yeah." She waited a moment with one eyebrow raised, then said, "Just a minute."

She held out the phone without looking at me. I finished parking and took it.

"Yeah, Stone."

"I just knew you'd answer the phone like that. I would have laid money on it. It's Shelly."

I smiled. "Yeah? So I'm that predictable, huh?"

I heard Dehan sigh. I looked as she climbed out of the car and slammed the door behind her. Shelly was saying, "No, not at all. You're just butch. I like that. Listen, business before pleasure. I spoke to Bob. He says he's happy to meet you. I am WhatsApping you his number now."

"Thanks, Shelly. I appreciate it."

My cell bleeped and she said, "Is that it? Did it arrive?"

I checked. There was a message from her with his contact details. I put the phone back to my ear. "Yeah, I got it."

"Okay, now, speaking of pleasure. You owe me dinner, where are you taking me?"

I laughed. "You mean I get to choose?"

"That depends."

"On what?"

"On where you choose."

I let the smile show in my voice. "I'm not familiar with the restaurants in Manhattan. Don't you need to book six months in advance?"

"Unless you're happy with Californian wine and paper napkins, yeah. Besides, I was hoping you'd choose somewhere within staggering distance of your place."

I was surprised but didn't let it show. "Now there's a thought. I'll pick you up at seven thirty."

"I can't wait." Her voice was husky and appealing. It made me hesitate a moment.

"Shelly?"

"Yeah . . ."

"I'm a cop. If something comes up . . ."

"Don't worry, honey, I know all about cops. I'll see you at seven thirty."

I hung up and sat for a minute staring at the blank screen. Then I climbed out and walked through the rain into the station, wiping the water from my face with my sleeve. I went to the bathroom, dried myself off, and then went to get coffee. I thought about getting one for Dehan, but with the mood she was in, she might pour it over my head. I eventually found her at our desk. She was leaning back, reading something on her laptop.

I dropped into my chair opposite her and studied her for a moment. She shifted her position and moved her laptop so I couldn't see her face.

"What's going on, Dehan?"

"I'm reading articles by Dave Thorndike. It's Dave, not David, by the way."

"That's very commendable."

"Looks like you're going to be busy, so I have to find things to do."

"What's that supposed to mean?"

"Don't mean nothin', boss. You and Ms. Pearce, that's Shelly to you, are going to be conducting your own private, exclusive investigation. I figured meantime I could become acquainted with Dave Thorndike's work. His recent articles might give me a lead into what he was investigating."

"Dehan, that is ridiculous." She didn't answer. She just kept reading, like I hadn't spoken. I sighed. "I have Bob Shaw's number. That call was from Pearce . . ."

"You mean Shelly."

I sighed noisily. "She was calling to give me Bob Shaw's number."

"Cool."

We sat in silence for a bit, her reading and me watching the back of her laptop. Finally, I said, "So I thought we could call him and go and see him this afternoon."

"Cool. So when are you having your collaborative dinner?"

I counted slowly to five before answering. "This evening, at seven thirty."

She clicked her wireless mouse and sat up. "You got time to interview a witness before you go? Don't worry, if you're busy with your investigation, I can take it myself."

I frowned a frown that might have been a scowl. "What the hell are you talking about, Dehan? What witness?"

She fixed me with her big, dark eyes, stood, and walked to the printer, which had started to disgorge sheets of paper. She gathered them and brought them back to the desk, where she started sorting them into stacks. I gestured at them.

"What's this? Are you going to tell me what's going on?"

"These are Dave Thorndike's last three articles. I've printed two copies of each . . ." She paused while she stapled them into six documents and threw three of them across the desk at me. "These are for you. I've only glanced over them in the last ten minutes, but from what I've seen, they make interesting reading."

"Okay . . ."

"The witness who's on his way in is Bob Shaw."

"*What?*"

Her cheeks flushed and her eyes shone. She grabbed a piece of paper from beside the phone, scrunched it into a ball, and threw it at me. "He's in the book. I called him while you were arranging dinner. He'll be here in twenty minutes. Will you have time to attend the interview, Detective Stone?"

I stared at her. "Dehan, you are being ridiculous. What the hell is this about?"

"We've been here before, remember?"

I shook my head. "Where have we been before?"

"You see a hot piece of skirt and start sidelining me and cutting me out of the investigation. I don't need it, Stone."

"That is not what is happening."

She raised an eyebrow at me. "Really? Didn't I just sit and listen to you and Shelly Pearce arrange to go out to dinner to help each other in your mutual investigations?"

I sighed again. "Dehan, it just pays sometimes to be nice, rather than go storming in with the attitude . . ."

"Yeah? So how is your date tonight going to pay? By giving you Bob Shaw's number?"

"Okay, you made your point."

"Did I?" She sat forward and put her elbows on the desk. "I'm going to tell you something, then I'm going to ask you something."

"Okay . . ."

"First, I guarantee that if—and it's a big if, Stone—*if* you get any useful information from your date tonight, you will keep me *out* of the loop and act on it on your own, just like you did with Emma Girt in the Springfellow case[1], because . . . Ah! Forget it!

---

1. See *Let Us Pray.*

But let me ask you a question, Stone. How difficult would it be—how much of a stretch would it be—for Shelly Pearce to become a suspect in this case?"

I was surprised by the question and allowed it to show on my face. The best I could manage was, "Um . . ."

"Let me tell you. She is the one person, after Bob Shaw, who was most likely to have access to Thorndike's work. She was the person selected by the paper to investigate his death. Why? We don't know. Why? Oh, yeah, because we didn't ask her. Maybe you could ask her that on your date tonight. That is . . ." She held up both hands. "If it doesn't screw up your date. I'd hate the investigation to get in the way of your *date*!" She made a labored face like she had suddenly realized something. "Huh! Maybe that's why we are not supposed to date witnesses!"

We sat staring at each other for a long moment. "Are you done?"

She raised her eyebrow at me again. "I'm not sure I even got started yet, Stone."

"You want to finish?"

"No, I'd rather you explain to me what the hell you think you're doing dating a witness who is a potential suspect."

I nodded. "Okay, I get it. I take your point. Now let me answer."

"I can't wait."

"First, it is *not* a date. Okay? A date implies a sexual or romantic element. There is nothing like that here."

"Oh, come on, Stone! How stupid do you think I am?"

"Let me finish. Second, there is a chance that Shelly Pearce has information about Dave Thorndike that she is not sharing. If that is so, the easiest way of getting that information is for me to be friendly with her. Third, please have sufficient trust—and *respect*—to know that I would not have an affair with a witness, much less a potential suspect."

We stared at each other for a moment. She shook her head. "You were coming on to her, Stone."

"No. She was coming on to me. I was flirting."

"Great. Can you be objective about this woman?"

"Of course I can, Dehan!"

She pointed at me, and I was surprised to see real anger in her face. "The minute your feelings for this woman start to affect your judgment in this case, you come clean. And I will be watching. And if you try to cut me out again, I will apply for a transfer. You understand me?"

I watched her a moment before I answered. "Bring it down a notch or three, Carmen. I have no 'feelings' for this woman, one way or another. I don't plan to cut you out, and my judgment is clear. We're good, partner. There is no issue here. Trust me."

She grunted and studied my face a moment without humor. "You want to know what I read while you were arranging your date?"

"It's not a date."

"You want to know?"

"Sure, hit me."

"Don't tempt me. I got like ten or fifteen minutes to scan his last few features in the paper. Several of them mention Senator Carol Hennessy. And his last article was about her, and allegations that are going around the web of corruption and shady deals. It's not much to go on, but it seems he may have been developing an . . ." She hesitated. "An *interest* in her."

I pulled over the articles and looked at them. "No kidding." I started scanning the first page. "I vaguely remember something about her and her husband, back in the late eighties or nineties. A real-estate deal in California or something. Didn't somebody die?"

"I don't recall. I was a kid in the nineties. But there seems to be a lot of shady stuff in her past. It may not be related, but I figure there's a chance he decided to go into it in more depth. We should ask Shaw about it. Even if he didn't know the exact nature of the investigation, he must have known what it was about in general terms."

She went quiet and I looked up. She was staring at me fixedly. "What?"

"You should ask Pearce about it tonight."

"I will. Believe me, Dehan, she'll be so bored and disappointed by the time we've finished the meal she'll never want to see me again."

"Sure. Just ask her, will you?"

"I will. Now will you give it a rest?"

We spent the next fifteen minutes reading through the articles in silence. Dehan had been right. Dave Thorndike did seem to be developing not so much an interest as a near obsession with Senator Carol Hennessy. And it wasn't hard to see why. If half the allegations against her and her husband were true, they made the Mob look like a bunch of schoolgirls. And the curious thing was that, when I checked on Google, I could not find a single successful libel case brought by her, or her husband, against any of their accusers. In fact, I couldn't find any libel cases, period, successful or otherwise.

I frowned at Dehan, whose face was still hidden behind her laptop. "These allegations against her, they really damaged her career. She had a shot at the Oval Office."

"Uh-huh."

"But she never brought a libel suit against anybody."

"Uh-uh."

"I think this is important. It's damn good work, Dehan."

"Uh-huh."

I sighed noisily and went back to reading. Eventually, the desk sergeant buzzed to say that Bob Shaw had arrived. Dehan went to get him, and I went to get coffee, feeling vaguely uncomfortable.

SIX

Dehan was waiting outside interview room three as I approached. She had her hands in her back pockets and her hair tied in a knot behind her head. She smiled at me with her mouth, but frowned with her eyes. I handed her a coffee.

"Ready?"

She took it with her left hand and gently punched my shoulder with her right. "Yeah. Sorry."

I shook my head and opened the door for her.

Bob Shaw looked up and smiled uncertainly as we came in. He was in his late sixties, but still ruggedly handsome. Dehan sat, and I placed a coffee in front of him. "I'm not sure what it is. The machine says coffee, but who knows?"

He glanced at it and then at me. "Isn't this one of those rooms where you grill suspects?" he said. "Am I a suspect in some crime?" He was grinning, but the question was serious. "I spent the better part of forty years investigating the police. I know how you operate."

I smiled and sat. "The police have changed a lot in those forty years, Mr. Shaw. Today they watch us more closely than we watch you."

He barked, "Ha!," picked up the coffee, and peered inside.

"What is this? It looks like my piss after I drank too much agave beer down in Mexico."

"Maybe they found a way to synthesize it, because that is pretty much what it tastes like. Mr. Shaw, you are not a suspect in any crime. We just need to ask you some questions about David Thorndike."

He looked at me and chuckled. Then he gave Dehan an appraising once-over. "Okay, shoot."

"Do you know what happened to Dave's laptop and the article he was working on?"

He shook his head and looked slightly bored. "Really? After ten years? That's your question? They asked me that at the time. I told them I had no idea. He never showed it to me, and he sure as hell never gave it to me."

I nodded. "I figured, but you have to ask, right?"

He shrugged and pulled a face.

I ignored him and went on. "I know he told you nothing about the article, I know he never showed it to you, I know all that. But I want you to tell me what he *did* tell you."

"Nothing!" He spread his hands, raised his shoulder and his eyebrows.

Dehan smiled and snorted. "Bullshit."

He kept the same expression but turned it to face her.

I said, "It's bullshit, Mr. Shaw, and you know it. You would never have approved an investigation without knowing at least the basics. You knew *something*. And I know for a fact he called you at least once to tell you it was finished and he expected a Pulitzer. Now you know very well, as a reporter yourself, that there are little bits and pieces in what he *did* tell you that, when you put them together, add up to *something*!"

He sighed and started bouncing his head around. "Okay, okay, point taken. I'm just not all that comfortable sharing information with cops, know what I mean? You guys have a way of taking facts and distorting them for your own ends."

Dehan snorted again. "Unlike reporters."

"Hey!" He pointed at her. "Not on my papers, sugar! We were never yellow press. The *Times*, the *Tribune*, they might indulge in a bit of truth massaging and distortion of perspective to suit their political agendas. Not the NYT. We told it how it was and we took the consequences. And we always made sure our facts were solid."

I nodded. "Okay, so we operate the same way. Now, what *did* he tell you? What, in general terms, was the story about?"

He sighed, examined the coffee one last time, and finally started to talk.

"Dave had got a bee in his bonnet. And I think he was onto something. We had talked about it a few times over a drink. A couple of his articles had touched on it, and he was pretty psyched about the evidence he had got together so far. He was a damn good investigator. So he came to me and said he wanted to go undercover and start to dig deep."

Dehan said, "Into what, Bob?"

He looked surprised. "We on first-name terms now? Do I get to call you Carmen, Carmen?"

She smiled.

He snorted. "Sweetheart, I was shooting acid and challenging the establishment before your daddy had his bar mitzvah. Don't try and play me. Into what? Into Senator Carol Hennessy. Her name, and her husband's, were and are linked to a whole raft of dubious business deals: tax evasion, illegal exports, facilitating arms sales to oppressive regimes and governments that harbor terrorists. And as for suspicious deaths, you go online and you can download a PDF file with forty-eight names of people who died in suspicious circumstances after crossing her path."

He sat back, placed both hands palm down on the table, and studied them for a moment. "Now I guess it's forty-nine." He sighed. "I'm not saying that it's all true, but hell! I never saw anyone who attracted so much shit. Even Nixon didn't attract this much controversy. And Dave had a nose, you know what I'm saying? He had an instinct. He'd start digging and ferreting and scratching away, and if there was something hidden, he would find it. Man, it was like *dowsing*! He just *knew* when there was something hidden. And he became pretty much obsessed with the Hennessy story.

"So I told him. Go for it. I'll back you up. That was pretty much the last I ever heard from him. I had no idea where he was or what he was doing. That was the arrangement we had. I knew he would produce the goods. He was the best reporter I ever worked with, or ever knew for that matter. And believe me, I knew the best. But he was something special."

Dehan had been listening carefully. Now she asked, "What happened?"

Bob Shaw sucked his teeth for a moment, then said, "He went off the radar for a few weeks. Then he called me one evening. He said he was really excited about the story. It was his best work ever." He nodded several times. "And if he said that, believe me, it was good. He was talking about getting the Pulitzer, about rocking the establishment. He was even saying the shock waves from what he had would be so far-reaching it could lead to constitutional change regarding the accountability of congressmen. And Dave wasn't one to say that kind of thing without good cause. Whatever he had . . ." He shook his head. "It wasn't dynamite, it was an atom bomb."

I was frowning. "In less than two months? An investigation like that would take months."

He nodded. "I know. I would have expected six months at least. That kind of investigation is painstaking, and he was meticulous. More than most. But that was what he said. He was wrapping it up, and it would be cataclysmic in its impact."

"So what happened?"

"I told him to bring it in and let me see it. That was when he told me he was in fear for his life. He was afraid that somebody was on his trail and intended to kill him. Given the nature—and the subject—of his investigation, I was inclined to take him seriously.

"Next thing, I heard he'd been found murdered. Him, and forty-eight other people who had crossed Carol Hennessy's path."

Dehan gave her head a twitch. "That's quite a story."

"Yeah, that's what he thought. And I wish you or the Feds would dig into this woman's background, her and her goddamn smarmy husband. But that ain't ever going to happen because the establishment looks after its own."

Dehan shrugged. "You may be right, Mr. Shaw. I wouldn't know. But if she killed Dave Thorndike, we will take her down."

He made a face. "Yah, yadda yadda."

She ignored him and plowed on. "We have a witness who says that a couple of days before he was killed, his laptop and his papers had gone from their usual place on his dining table where he worked."

His eyebrows shot up. "Really?"

"Yes, now, if he didn't give them to you, who else would he trust enough . . ."

He was already shaking his head. He went to speak, hesitated, then creased his eyes and shook his head again.

I said, "Who, Mr. Shaw? You thought of somebody and dismissed them. Who was it?"

He hunched his shoulders and screwed up his face. "Nah . . . I thought maybe his lawyer. They were pretty close. I mean, as close as anybody ever got to Dave, you know what I'm saying? And in as much as he trusted anyone, he trusted him. But I can't see it. It doesn't make any sense, he would give him the story and not me . . . ?"

I nodded. It made perfect sense to me. "What was his lawyer's name, Mr. Shaw?"

"Oh, jeez . . . ! Uh . . . he was Chinese or Korean or something. Korean. What's that name—all Koreans have the same name, you know? Uh, Lee. Lee something. Or something Lee. They always have their names the wrong way 'round too. I don't know if he was Lee something or something Lee."

Dehan grunted. "Would you have this on file anywhere?"

He shook his head. "Nah. But Shelly will. Shelly will remember him. She knew him."

Dehan looked sour and asked, "Any idea what became of him? Who he worked for?"

"No idea. I just heard Dave talk about him sometimes. I never met the guy. Like I said, you're better off talking to Shelly. She moved in the same circle. It was a bit too rarified for me."

I frowned at him. A bell inside my head rang a quiet alarm. "Rarified?"

"Yah! You know, in my day it was different. You were an editor in my kind of paper, you unleashed your hounds and they did their worst. Today it's different. Editors have to rub shoulders with the mayor, senators, governors, ambassadors, princes, and oil barons. That was never my style, but Shelly excels at it."

"Are you telling me that Shelly knows Carol Hennessy?"

"Sure. They all know each other. Shelly, Hennessy, Lee, the mayor . . . They all move in the same circle. That's what I'm saying. It's the way it works."

Dehan drew breath and looked at me. Shaw barked a laugh and cut in before she could speak. "Draw your own conclusions, Detective. I drew mine a long time ago. I've always done the right thing. It's the way I was raised. You were probably raised the same way. But heroes are heroes because they do things decent people are too scared to do. I'm a decent man, but I ain't a hero. When Dave was murdered, it took the fight out of me. I hadn't the stomach for it anymore." He looked at me. "They're there, Stone. They're there, in their manor houses and their towers of glass and steel, and their palaces. They run the show. They buy and sell people, they send them off to war, to be exterminated in their thousands and millions. They experiment on them, they enslave them, they send them down mines to die, men, women, and children. And they don't give a damn." He flapped both hands at me. "I ain't big enough to go up against them. I'm old and they scare me. And Shelly . . ." He shrugged and shook his head. "Is there anything else?"

I sat and chewed my lip for a moment, then turned and looked at Dehan. She shook her head.

I said, "No, thank you, Mr. Shaw. You've given us plenty to be thinking about."

He went to stand, but paused and looked at Dehan. "You're a beautiful young lady, in the prime of your life. Be smart. Don't go up against this woman. She'll destroy you. She won't think twice. She probably won't even know your name."

She stared at him.

He stood and then grinned at me. "You? You're old and ugly like me. We get rubbed out, who cares, right?"

He laughed out loud. I smiled and stood. We shook hands and he left, leaving the door open behind him. I turned to face Dehan. She was sitting with her ass on the table and her arms crossed, watching me. We stared at each other for a long moment, thinking. It was a habit we both had which used to unsettle other people, but it helped us think.

Finally, she said, "Should be an interesting meal, Stone."

I nodded. "Yeah, I think so. I think Shelly Pearce might know more than we first thought."

"Keep your wits about you, Stone. Don't get suckered."

I smiled. "I've been around a bit, Dehan. I won't get suckered."

She sighed. "Guys . . . even smart ones like you, can be real stupid when it comes to women."

"Okay, I'll bear it in mind." I jerked my head at the door. "Come on, I have some reading to do before I go home and change. You want a lift?"

"Yeah . . . No . . . I don't know."

SEVEN

I TOOK HER TO A NICE ITALIAN RESTAURANT I KNEW ON Court Street in Brooklyn. The food and the wine were good, the tablecloths and the napkins were crisp linen, but you didn't have to book a month in advance to get a table.

She looked a little surprised when she saw we were crossing the Brooklyn Bridge, and when I pulled up outside Queen, she raised an eyebrow at me and said, "You live in staggering distance of Brooklyn Heights?"

I smiled, climbed out, and went around to open the door for her. It was warm and pleasantly busy inside. Vincenzo greeted me like an old friend and led us to a table for two. He handed us a couple of menus and I ordered two martinis while we had a look at them.

When he'd brought them and departed, I said, running my eyes over the daily specials, "Until this investigation is over, Shelly, I am afraid we won't be staggering anywhere together."

She raised her eyes to look at me and there was a flash of anger in them. "Boy, you really know how to woo a girl, don't you?"

I made a face like an apology. "I'm sorry. I shouldn't really even be having dinner with you."

She snapped, "You want to leave? You want me to get a cab home?"

I wondered briefly why women were so hard to talk to sometimes. "No, and no. I would like to stay and enjoy the meal and I would like you to stay and enjoy it with me." I sipped my martini, and as I put my glass down I said, "Your paper has a reputation for coming down hard on bent cops and abuse of power. I'm the same, and I tend to do things by the book. Otherwise, I am no better than the people I go after." I gave her my most charming, lopsided grin and added, "After all, you could be a suspect."

Her eyebrows shot up. "Me?"

"Not really, but technically you could be. If I got too close to you, I could not be involved in the case."

She raised an eyebrow and looked back at the menu. "How close is too close?"

"Anything under six inches."

She laughed.

I smiled at her. "Staggering home together would certainly be too close." I gave it a second and then added, "But I'll take a rain check."

She made a doubtful noise, but I could tell she was smiling. "We'll see how you behave for the rest of the evening."

I ordered clams *oreganata* and she had homemade mozzarella on grilled oyster mushrooms. For the main course, she ordered *saltimbocca alla Romana* and I had *vitello alla Marsala*, and we had a bottle of Barolo, which for my money is the only Italian wine worth drinking. But I'm controversial that way.

When the waiter had left with our orders, she drained her martini, and as she set the glass down she said, "So, you're a real do-it-by-the-book man, huh?"

"Is that a problem?"

"No, I just had you down as a bit of a rule breaker. Your own man."

"Well, I guess that all depends on what book you're using,

doesn't it? I do it by the book, but my book says that sometimes you have to break the rules."

"Really?"

"Yup."

"But you can't break the rule about getting close?"

"Nope."

She was grinning. It was a mischievous grin, and it was attractive. "And why not?"

"Because you might break my heart and turn out to be a diabolical, evil genius who murders dangerous reporters that know too much."

"Oh, sure."

"You know how dime thrillers always end. It was always the sexy femme fatale who did it."

She raised her eyebrow. "Is that what I am?"

I smiled. "A sexy femme fatale?" I signaled the waiter for two more drinks. "Sure. I think so."

She sat back in her chair and sighed, still smiling. "Okay, Stone, you're a charmer. Now tell me why you brought me here."

"To this restaurant?"

"No, not to this restaurant. Why did you take me out at all?"

"It was part of our deal, remember?"

She watched me, waiting.

"You are a very attractive, intelligent woman."

"And the real reason?"

I frowned. "Don't be too quick to judge, Shelly. Everything I said to you was true. I am investigating a murder, and you were close to the victim."

"So . . . ?"

I spread my hands. "Okay, what can you tell me about Carol Hennessy?"

"Ah . . ." She nodded several times. The waiter arrived with two more martinis. She took a sip and sighed. "Didn't take you long, did it?"

I thought about Dehan. "A little longer than it should have."

"She's a driven woman, very ambitious, and very firmly rooted in the ideals of the late sixties and seventies. She upsets a lot of men."

I frowned. It was a different angle to the one I'd read online. "A lot of men seem to have upset her too. And a lot of them wound up dead."

She gave a laugh that was not quite patronizing. "Listen, I specialize in credible conspiracy theories. I was raised on Kennedy and Watergate. There are two things you need to remember. Back in the sixties and seventies, this country was a very different place. The Feds, the CIA—even the cops . . ." She gestured at me with an open hand, like I represented all cops. "They had a free hand back then. They were practically unaccountable to anybody. They quite literally got away with murder, for a long time, and they thought it would go on forever. But it really isn't like that anymore."

"It isn't?"

"No. For a start, they are aware that the press is all over them all the time. Communication is global and instant. Trump sneezes and within thirty seconds the whole world has been alerted, via Twitter, Facebook, a billion blogs . . ." She made circular motions with her hand, indicating "on and on." "If Hennessy and her husband were involved in all the shady deals and murders that she is accused of, it would have come out by now."

I sipped my drink and set it down carefully on the table, frowning at it. I was trying to work out what Shelly Pearce was all about. I said, "And isn't that exactly what happened?"

She shook her head, with a mouthful of martini. "Mm-mm!" She swallowed. "No. What happened was that America was ready for a black president, but not for a female one. Do you know what proportion of the electorate is black or Latino?"

"No."

"Thirty percent. That's enough to carry an election. Do you know what proportion is female?"

"Half?"

"Slightly over. But where blacks and Latinos are politically aware, and will vote to protect their interests, the vast majority of women still have this conditioning that says we'll be better off with a man at the helm. Carol tried to fight that . . ." She paused, studying my face. "And you're right, there was a conspiracy. But the conspiracy was against her. It was a systematic character assassination, perpetrated by the right-wing media, to preserve the top office for that small, male elite."

Vincenzo came with our starters, and we ate for a while in silence. After a bit, I sat back and watched her for a moment. After a moment, she looked up, and I said, "There is a list of over forty-eight men who crossed swords with Carol Hennessy or her husband, and they are all dead, and from the looks of it, most of them died in unusual circumstances."

She sighed and took another mouthful of mushroom and mozzarella. She spoke around it. "Have you any idea how many people have crossed swords with the Bush family? With Obama, with Trump? Or in their day, the Kennedy clan, Nixon, or the Peanut King?"

"I don't know, but I can imagine."

"Hundreds, Stone. Many hundreds. And do you know how many are dead?"

"Obviously not."

"Well, I can tell you that if I looked into any one of their pasts, I could find twenty, thirty, or forty dead people who had at some time crossed them and were now dead, and with a bit of clever writing I could make it sound as though they died in 'suspicious circumstances.' Not a single one of those deaths was what you could call a 'hit.'"

I laid down my knife and fork and narrowed my eyes at her. "David Thorndike was exactly that."

Just for a moment she froze, then carried on eating. "There were other people who had good reason to want Dave dead."

"Of the forty people who died after crossing Hennessy, six

were mugged in the street and five were the victims of home invasions . . ."

"Burglaries where property was stolen."

"Ten were hit-and-runs, twelve were automobile accidents, three were climbing accidents, and six died of heart attacks, though they had perfectly healthy hearts."

"I see you do your homework."

"Is Carol Hennessy a friend of yours?"

"What's that supposed to mean?"

I ate my last clam slowly while watching her, then drained the last of my martini. "It isn't supposed to mean anything. Is she a friend of yours?"

She shrugged. "I wouldn't say a friend. More like an acquaintance." She ate her last mushroom and sat back, chewing. "Are we fighting?"

I smiled. "I hope not. I'm asking questions, you're giving me your opinion." I gave my head a little twitch. "I don't have to agree with everything you say, right? Even if it is the New Millennium."

She shook her head, still smiling. "It's men like you . . ."

"My last captain thought I was a dinosaur."

"He was right."

"She was also a bent cop."

"Was . . . ?"

"Who is Lee?"

"Boy! This is fun. Do you do all your interrogations in restaurants, or just the ones you hope to get laid by after the case is finished?"

She was still smiling, but the smile was looking strained. A waitress took our plates away; Vincenzo brought the main course and poured me a small amount of wine. I tasted it and gave him the nod. He poured and left. I raised an eyebrow at her.

"Are you going to hit me now or will you wait till after dessert? They do a *Coppa Antica* of homemade vanilla bean ice cream, pecan nougat, and Amareno cherries that you could kill for."

"Is that supposed to be a joke?"

"No. I'm just hoping you have enough of the sixties and seventies left in you to make room for a dinosaur in your busy schedule. I didn't have you down as the kind of woman who expects everybody to conform to a preordained standard. Or are we swapping the tyranny of the testicle for the tyranny of the ovary?"

She burst out laughing and a few people glanced at her. We ate in silence for a bit. Her smile looked a little less strained. After a bit, she said, "I confess you are kind of refreshing. Intolerable, but refreshingly so."

"Thanks."

"I'll wait till after the *Coppa Antica* to hit you with my handbag and walk out."

"Good to know. You never answered my question, by the way."

She chewed and studied my face for a moment. "What question was that?"

"Who is Lee?"

She concentrated on her food and gave a small shrug. "Lee? It's not a lot to go on."

"How many Lees did David know? This one was about as close to him as anybody ever got, he's an attorney and he is Korean."

"Oh, Jackson. Jackson Lee, his attorney. Why didn't you say so?"

I put a smile on the left side of my face, where it looks less humorous and more ironic. "I wanted to see if you would avoid answering."

Her smile faded. "You bastard."

I kept eating and smiling. She kept eating and looking hurt. I said, "I can play nice too."

She didn't look up. "Yeah?"

"Sure. Can you?"

Now she looked at me. "Again, Stone, what is that supposed to mean? Why are you giving me a hard time? When I suggested dinner, I didn't have this in mind, exactly."

I said softly, "Come on, Shelly. You've been keeping information from me from the start in order to protect Carol Hennessy. You suggested dinner so you could find out what direction my investigation was taking. The only question I have is, are you doing this to protect a woman you admire or because she has you on her payroll? And you can drop the injured girl act. You don't get to be the senior editor of the *New York Telegraph* by being sensitive and easily offended."

She drained her glass and refilled it. "Boy, Stone, you know how to make a girl feel special. You're some piece of work."

"You hadn't picked that up when we came to see you earlier today?"

She sighed and started eating again. "Fair enough, you got me. It's true." She chewed, sipped, watched me. "But I also liked you. Is that permissible? And I'm not on anybody's *payroll*, except the paper's."

"I'm glad to hear it. I like you too. You know where I can reach Lee?"

She rolled her eyes. "Hold me. I'm going to blush. I can't handle this dinosaur flattery. No, I see him in passing sometimes, but we haven't spoken for years."

"You think he has the laptop?"

She thought about it for a moment, then shook her head. "No. I don't think so. That doesn't make sense. Because the only person he would give it to would be Bob. Bob hasn't got it, so it was stolen by whoever killed him."

I frowned like she was contradicting herself. "If you're right, that points to Hennessy."

"No. You're assuming the article implicated Hennessy. But what if it exonerated her? What if it pointed at somebody else?"

"Like who?"

"I don't know. I just know that Carol Hennessy is not a killer or a criminal. She is a woman driven by her ideals."

I grunted, and we finished our main course and the wine. The conversation drifted to more general subjects. She was good to talk to. She was intelligent and well informed. Most of the time we disagreed, but she was good to disagree with. Over the *Coppa Antica* she went quiet for a bit. As she was finishing, she said, "So how long have you and Detective Dehan been partners?"

I was surprised by the question. "Better part of a year, why?"

She shrugged. "She's a looker."

I thought about it and smiled. "She is that. Fortunately, she doesn't seem to know it."

"And she's smart too."

"Yeah, what are you getting at?"

She laughed and called over the waiter. "Bring me a Courvoisier, and a black coffee." He went away with her order. "You're driving. No spirits for you, Mr. Dinosaur." She stopped, watching me, a little sad. "You really don't know, do you?"

"Know what?"

"I'm not sure whether to tell you or leave you in your primeval darkness of blissful dinosaur ignorance."

"Cut it out. Stop playing games. What are you talking about?"

"John, that girl is hopelessly in love with you!"

I laughed out loud. "Don't be absurd! *Dehan?* That's ridiculous!"

She smiled. "Is it?"

"We're partners, pals, we've been through a lot together. We're solid. She's the best partner I've had. We have a good rapport . . ."

I was vaguely aware of talking too much and let the words trail away. She was watching me with one eyebrow raised high.

"Ridiculous. About as ridiculous as you being in love with her."

I made a face that said she was being stupid. "Come on, Shelly. That's crazy. Cut it out."

"You already said that."

"Like Batman and Robin, we are just good friends."

After that, the conversation kind of petered out and I called for the check and drove her home to her apartment in Manhattanville. By the time I pulled up outside her block, the rain had stopped and the blacktop had a silver sheen to it. I went to get out, but she put her hand on my arm to stop me.

"You want to come up for that cognac?"

"You know I can't, Shelly."

"I know. I thought I'd ask anyhow." She kissed me on the cheek. "See you around, Stone."

I watched her cross the sidewalk and let herself into the lobby. She didn't look back.

On the way home, I drove past Dehan's block on Simpson Street. My watch said it was twelve midnight. She'd probably still be awake, and I could tell her about Jackson Lee, and Shelly's view of Hennessy. I slowed for a moment, then for some reason I couldn't define, I dismissed the idea and headed home.

EIGHT

THE RAIN RETURNED OVERNIGHT, HEAVY AND STEADY. I picked Dehan up outside her apartment at eight. She had her absurd Australian hat and long coat on again, and I tried not to think about what Shelly had said the night before as I watched her dodge through the cars to get to the passenger side and climb in the car. As she pulled the door closed, I said, "G'day, Sheila."

She took off her hat, set it on her knees, and tied her hair up behind her head. "Yeah? What's good about it?"

"It could be worse. That's good."

"How was your date?"

"It wasn't a date, Dehan."

"How was your whatever-it-was?"

"Odd. We have much to discuss."

"Like?"

"Like Jackson Lee, David Thorndike's attorney. Like Shelly Pearce's admiration for Carol Hennessy."

"Seriously?"

I nodded. "I detected a pretty strong political affiliation there. So much so, Dehan, that I think the whole reason for getting me to take her out was to see if Hennessy was a suspect."

"Wow. So she wasn't after your body? That's hard to believe."

"Flattery will get you nowhere. But yes, that is the way it looks."

"Tough break."

"Not really, Dehan." Then I added, without really knowing why, "She's not my type."

"Oh."

Then, as we moved through the hiss and the spray of the sodden city, under the bellying lead skies, I told her about our conversation over dinner. Though I left out her final observations, which I knew, in any case, were absurd. She was very quiet throughout, and as I pulled into Fteley Avenue and parked outside the station house, she said, "We're getting into some pretty deep water here, Sensei."

"We need to run this by the captain—sorry, inspector! If we go after Hennessy there will be consequences."

She pursed her lips and nodded. "We also need to find this Jackson Lee. My gut tells me he knows where the laptop is."

"I think your gut is right."

We climbed out and crossed the road, me hunched into my collar and her striding like a scarecrow turned galactic bounty hunter. We found Captain John Newman, now promoted to inspector, peeling off his hat and coat in his office. He smiled his urbane smile, like he really was pleased to see us at eight twenty a.m., and said, "Stone! Dehan! Come in, come in, please, sit. You're mighty early. What can I do for you?"

He went behind his desk, and we all sat at the same time.

"Sir, do you recall the David Thorndike case, 2008?"

He shook his head. "Not by the name. Give me a clue." He smiled like he'd said something funny.

I said, "Investigative reporter, *New York Telegraph*. He was shot in the head. It went cold through lack of evidence."

"Oooh, yes. I do recall something. He was married and having an affair. Both came under suspicion but, as you say, there was a lack of evidence. Is that what you're on?"

It was Dehan who answered. "Yes, sir. But there are . . ." She hesitated. "Interesting features about the case."

"Interesting features, Detective?"

"Well, for a start, the nature of the killing is not typical of a crime of passion. It's more like an execution. But then, it was carried out with his own weapon, a 9mm Glock, and I never heard of a professional hit man borrowing the victim's gun before. But then, on the other hand, the article he was working on, and his laptop, vanished without a trace . . ."

The inspector nodded. "Those are interesting features, I agree. Any thoughts?"

I sighed. "Well, you are not going to like this, sir, but the latest evidence we've uncovered points pretty forcefully in one direction. It suggests that Thorndike was investigating allegations of corruption and murder that were being leveled against Senator Carol Hennessy, who was at the time a presidential candidate. Just a few days before he died, he told his editor that his article was not going to be dynamite, it was an atom bomb, it could impact the very Constitution and would win him a Pulitzer. A couple of days later he showed up dead, and his article and all his research were gone."

He rubbed his face with his hands. "You are going after Carol Hennessy now? Former Secretary of State Carol Hennessy? With the greatest respect to you both, have you gone completely insane? You want the Forty-Third Precinct to take on the White House?"

Before I could answer, Dehan opened her mouth. "With the greatest respect to you, sir, the U.S.A. is governed by the rule of law. That means the secretary of state does not get to commit murder. She is subject to the same laws as the rest of us. And I am pretty sure that the White House does not condone murder."

He looked at her frigidly. "You are damn close to impertinence there, Detective, but I take your point. All I am saying to you is, before you go after somebody like that, be damned sure of your facts."

Dehan opened her mouth, but I looked at her and she closed

it again. I knew what she was going to say, that being sure of your facts was no more important with the ex-secretary of state than it was with a trash collector or a bum on the street. Inspector Newman must have known it too, because he held up both hands in a placatory gesture.

"Always," he said. "We *always* need to be damn sure of our facts. But if you screw up in an investigation against Bob Brown at the grocery store, the most he is likely to do is file a complaint and get Internal Affairs to drag you over the coals for a while. But the minute Carol Hennessy realizes you are investigating her, she is going to bring some very heavy guns to bear. Let's not be naïve about this. You are laying your jobs on the line, and mine with them."

I nodded. "We are aware of that, sir, which is why we are here. And, more to the point, if what our investigation so far suggests turns out to be true, we'll be lucky to lose just our jobs."

He grunted. "What do you want to do?"

"We have one lead to follow up first, one Jackson Lee. Back in the day, he was Thorndike's friend and his attorney. We want to see where that leads us. It may lead us away from Hennessy, in which case, all well and good. But in all likelihood, sir, I think in a day or so, we will be seeking an interview with Senator Hennessy."

"And then there are going to be fireworks."

"She doesn't have a reputation for being cooperative, sir."

He shook his head again. "Other detectives find a body and it was the wife or the husband, or the lover. You investigate a murder and the captain of the precinct has to resign, the local bishop turns out to be in bed with the Mafia, and now you're going after a senator. I don't want to even imagine what your next case might dredge up!"

Dehan answered with a deadpan face. "Actually, sir, we were thinking of having a look at the Kennedy shooting."

He stared at her, then managed a smile.

"All right, Detectives, I trust you to act with the utmost

discretion and tact. I have seven years before I retire, and I would like to keep it that way." We stood and moved to the door. There he stopped us. "And, Detectives, if you decide to go after Hennessy, I want you to keep me posted every step of the way."

"Yes, sir."

Back at our desk, I picked up the phone and called Bismarck, Jones and Epstein, the firm of attorneys Shelly had told me Lee worked for. They eventually put me through to personnel. Personnel asked me to hold the line, and after fifteen minutes an agreeable young man said to me, "Detective Stone? I'm afraid Mr. Lee left our firm about nine years ago."

"What department was he in?"

"Um . . . intellectual property. That's copyright and . . ."

"I know what it is, thanks. Is there anyone in IP who would remember him?"

"Oh, just one moment . . ." He put me on hold again, but only for ten minutes this time. "Detective Stone? Cynthia Adamopolous is most likely to have known him. Would you like me to put you through?"

"Please."

It rang four times.

"Cynthia Adamopolous' office. How may I help you?"

I explained who I was and how she could help me. She put me on hold for another ten minutes. Then a voice like a Valkyrie with a parking ticket said, "Adamopolous speaking."

"Ms. Adamopolous, my name is Detective John Stone, with the NYPD. I am trying to get hold of Jackson Lee. I believe he used to work at your firm in your department."

"Yeah, nine years ago. What do you want him for?"

"We don't want him for anything. We just want to ask him a few questions."

"Is he a suspect in a crime?"

"No, would that make a difference?"

"It could."

"Is he your client?"

"... No."

"Then it couldn't. Do you know where I can contact him?"

"I know he had an apartment in Manhattan. I'll see if I can find out. I'll call you back ..."

"No. I'll hold."

I heard her sigh. "Sure ..."

I heard her get up from her desk, and after a moment there was a quiet, muttered conversation. After a couple of minutes, she came back. "Detective Stone?"

"Did he say he wasn't in?"

She was quiet for a moment. "I didn't speak to him. I can give you his Manhattan number, but I believe he is at his house in Oyster Bay. I'm afraid I haven't got the address or the number."

"Thank you for your help, Ms. Adamopolous."

I phoned his Manhattan number and got a Latin-American woman who pretended not to understand me. When I finally persuaded her I was not going to arrest Señor Lee, she told me she thought he was at Oyster Bay and didn't know when he would be back. After a little more persuasion, she finally gave me the address and the number at Oyster Bay. I dialed and it rang five times. Then a pleasant voice said, "This is the Lee residence."

"Is that Mr. Jackson Lee?"

"No, sir, Mr. Lee is not available at the moment. Who is this?"

"This is Detective John Stone of the New York Police Department. I need to speak to Mr. Lee."

"As I say, I am afraid he is not available."

"Well, when will he be available?"

"I am afraid I don't know."

"How can I get hold of him?"

"I don't know that either."

"Where is he?"

"He is away, traveling, Detective. And I am not sure when he will return. If you like, when he next contacts me, I can pass on your message and ask him to contact you."

"That would be very kind. Who are you?"

"I am Peter Hollis, Mr. Lee's personal secretary."

I squeezed a cheerfulness into my voice that I did not feel and said, "Well, thanks for your help, Mr. Hollis. I'll hope to hear from him soon."

"That's my pleasure, Detective. Good day."

I flopped back in my chair and stretched noisily. Then I stared at Dehan for a while. She was staring at the screen of her laptop. She spoke without looking at me. "Did you find him?"

"Yup. He's at Oyster Bay."

"We've been there before."

"Don't remind me.[1]"

"You talk to him? Is he willing to see us?"

"Not exactly. He thinks I think that he's traveling around the world in eighty days and he'll call us when he gets my message."

"Oh." She heaved a big sigh, rubbed her eyes, and stretched. I heard her spine crunch and clunk. She switched off her laptop and closed the lid as she spoke. "So are we going to surprise him? What's the plan?"

I studied her for a long moment. "You are. You are going to surprise him. You want to drive?"

She grinned. "This sounds like fun. Sure."

"Great. We'll get some lunch on the way back."

She stood. "Can we get some lunch now?"

I grabbed my coat. "Now? It's eleven thirty."

She shoved her hat on her head and stepped into the relentless rain.

"Not in Bermuda, it's not."

---

1. See *Garden of the Damned.*

NINE

It was a long, tedious drive south over the Throgs Neck Bridge to Long Island, and then east on the Long Island Expressway. Even the most beautiful landscape on Earth can look ugly if you throw enough gray rain and slow-moving traffic at it. And there was plenty of both that day on Long Island. A drive that should have taken forty-five minutes took us an hour.

All the way across the bridge, Dehan sat and stared at the massive, slow sheet of dark water beneath us. At one point, she said, "My dad used to bring us this way, in the summer, sometimes."

I smiled and asked, "Yeah? You spent summer vacations out here?"

She nodded but kept staring at the water.

At Alley Park, we turned east onto the Expressway, over the marshy woodland beneath. There she heaved a big sigh and turned to smile at me. It wasn't a happy smile, but it was a smile.

"So, you going to be seeing Shelly again?"

I was a little surprised by the question. "You pointed out yesterday that she was a potential suspect, and you were right. It looks as though she might be in Hennessy's pocket."

She gave a noncommittal shrug. "Or she might be a feminist sticking up for a politician she believes in."

I frowned at her and grunted.

"If she's on the level, after the investigation, will you see her again?"

I smiled. "This again? What is it with you and trying to get me fixed up?"

She shrugged and returned to staring at the traffic. About five minutes later, she said, "I wasn't trying to fix you up. I was just wondering if you liked her."

I suddenly had the weird feeling that I had stepped through a door into a totally alien landscape, and the person sitting next to me was no longer my partner but a complete stranger. I wanted to ask her what the hell had been eating her for the last couple of days, but for the first time since we'd been partners, I found myself holding back. Instead, I glanced at her and said, "You okay, Dehan?"

She turned and gave me a once-over. "Sure, why?"

"I don't know. You don't seem yourself for the last couple of days."

She shrugged and shook her head. "I'm myself. Who else would I be? Don't worry about it."

Only I did worry about it. I tried to ignore it and focus on Jackson Lee and David Thorndike's article, but instead all I could see and hear in my head was Shelly staring at me and saying, "That girl is hopelessly in love with you!"

We drove on in vaguely uncomfortable silence until we came to Jericho. There we turned left and north and I said, "Okay, we make this real simple. You break down outside his house, blocking his drive. You go in and ask for help. Can you please make a call and wait inside out of the rain."

"What if Lee doesn't show? What if his secretary tells me to take a hike?"

"Trust me, Lee will show, and Hollis won't send you packing."

"How can you be so sure?"

I was sure because even in a ridiculous Australian hat and drenched to her skin, she looked like a million bucks wrapped for Christmas, and no red-blooded man would turn her away from his door. I was about to say that, but instead I said, "Just look helpless, lay it on thick, I guarantee Lee will show."

"If you say so. So what do I do when he shows?"

"Make sure it's him and call me. Then we confront him."

"And he tells us to get the hell off his property."

"Okay, here is where we have to be smart. Don't lie to him. We are here legitimately looking for Jackson Lee. We got lost and broke down, and through pure luck, happened to break down outside his house."

"Luck . . ."

"And you don't identify yourself as a cop straightaway, because you don't realize it's his house."

She grunted. I turned off Sandy Hill Road onto Blair Road and for a couple of minutes wound through leafy lanes among secluded mansions. After a moment, she said, "I still don't get why you think he's going to show and talk to me . . ."

I felt a sudden stab of impatience and snapped, "Because you're hot, Dehan! You're not the kind of woman a man turns away!"

I scowled at her and saw she was grinning. She slid down in her seat and pulled her hat over her eyes. "Jeez, boss. I thought you'd never say it."

"Good grief!" We turned into Cove Road and I slowed. "Okay, it's that one up ahead." I pulled over to the side of the road and stopped. "I'll wait in the shelter of the trees by the gate. You pull up in front of his gate, kill the engine, and lift the hood. Then go in."

"Okay, you got it." She took off her hat and handed it to me. "Here, keep your head dry. I'm going for the 'sexy, fresh-out-of-the-shower' look."

I smiled. "Thanks."

I climbed out, planted the hat on my head, and took shelter under the trees by the gate. Dehan slid across into the driver's seat, drove the twenty yards to the gate, killed the engine, and rolled into his drive, blocking the entrance. I watched her get out, and within a few seconds she was drenched through—and she was right, soaked to the skin she looked both helpless and very sexy.

She lifted the hood and peered into the engine. She made a few helpless gestures for the benefit of anyone who might be watching, then turned and ran toward the house. I smiled to myself. She was one in a million.

I approached the gate and settled against the fence to wait, with the rain spattering on the blacktop a few feet away and tapping coldly on the canopy of leaves above my head. Vaguely, over the sounds of the water, I heard a door open, a man's voice, an exchange of words, and some laughter. Then the door closed again.

I waited ten cold, uncomfortable, wet minutes with my feet getting numb, and then my cell rang. It was Dehan.

"Hey, where are you?"

"What the hell are you talking about?"

"Oh, good. Listen, your car broke down, you should really consider getting something that isn't sixty years old. But as luck would have it, it broke down right in Jackson Lee's driveway. Can you beat that? Just keep walking down the road till you see your car. He's a real nice guy. He made me coffee and everything."

"You're funny. Did you know that?"

"No, nobody ever told me that. See you in a minute."

I hung up and walked around the fence into the driveway feeling cold, wet, and sour. I hammered on the door, and after a moment a pretty Filipino girl in a French maid's uniform opened the door.

I smiled without much humor. "I'm Detective Stone . . ."

"Yuh, they are expecting you." She reached out. "Let me take your coat and your hat."

She hung them up and led me across a broad hall with

parquet floors to a large set of doors. She pushed them open and said, "Detective Stone here, Mr. Lee."

I stepped into a long room with two sets of French windows overlooking a waterlogged lawn framed by pines, oaks, and tall cypress trees. The room was elaborately elegant, with a large, marble fireplace set between the French windows, a heavy, beige Wilton carpet, ornate sofas and armchairs with exposed, tooled wood, and English foxhunting prints on the walls in thin, black frames. Lee was standing by the fire, and Dehan was sitting in an armchair, holding a cup of coffee. She looked freshly toweled. They were both watching me. Lee was tall, maybe six two, and like his room, he was elaborately elegant.

"Detective Stone, may I offer you a hot drink? Please come and sit in front of the fire. Or perhaps you would like to go and dry off in the restroom?"

I approached the fire. "Thank you, Mr. Lee. We won't keep you."

"That was quite a coincidence, your breaking down right in my driveway."

I sat and gave him my most blank stare. "About as much of a coincidence as your returning from your travels on the very day we come looking for you."

"Touché. I understand you want to ask me about Dave."

"Yeah, just a couple of questions. When did he give you his article and his laptop?"

He stared at me for a long moment, then frowned and swallowed. "Excuse me?"

I repeated very deliberately, "When did he give you his article and his laptop, Mr. Lee?"

"I'm afraid I don't know what you're talking about, Detective. Dave never gave me any article or any laptop. What makes you think he did?"

I frowned. "You were his attorney."

"So?"

"He was a very cautious, suspicious, security-conscious man.

He didn't give it to Bob Shaw . . ." I shrugged and shook my head. "So I assumed he gave it to you."

He gave a small laugh. "That's a pretty big assumption, Detective. And a mistaken one. In fact, I had started to distance myself from Dave some time before he died."

Dehan put down her cup on the coffee table. "Oh, why's that?"

He sighed. "To be perfectly honest, he was starting to grate on me."

She scrunched up her brow. "Grate on you? What does that mean?"

"He was a class A narcissist. He thought the entire universe revolved around him, and treated people accordingly. I had known Dave and Samantha for a few years. I liked her. She was a good person and frankly deserved a damn sight better than Dave. I got tired of the way he treated her."

I asked bluntly, "Were you in love with her."

He laughed. "Oh no, you don't! No, I was not in love with her. I just liked her. And he was an ass. And when I heard that he had shacked up with that girl . . ."

"Katie O'Connor?"

"Yeah, Katie O'Connor."

"Who told you he'd shacked up with her?"

He blinked at me a few times. "Well, um, he did."

"How come? I thought he'd gone off the radar."

His eyes flitted around the room for a moment, then he gave a small laugh. "It's a long time ago. I don't remember the details, but as I recall it, he had just had this girl move in with him. He called me and we met for coffee . . ."

Dehan interrupted him. "What for?"

"Excuse me?"

"What did he call you for?"

"To have coffee."

I sighed. "What my partner means, Mr. Lee, is that David had gone undercover. He was immersed in his investigation and typically, when he was doing that, he would not contact anybody at all. So what made him contact you at that time, aside from having coffee?"

He thought for a moment, then shook his head. "I honestly don't recall."

"And that was the last time you saw him alive."

"Yes, I suppose it was."

"You suppose it was?"

"It's a figure of speech, Detective. It was in fact the last time I saw him, alive or otherwise."

"Did he at any time give you any indication of what his article was about?"

He shook his head again. "No, he never discussed his articles with me. That was between him and Bob."

I nodded. "I just have a couple more questions, Mr. Lee, and then we'll leave you in peace. Back then you specialized in intellectual property rights, is that correct?"

"Sure."

"That must be a very lucrative area of law."

He smiled. "Very much so. When you think about the kind of properties you're dealing with." He spread his hands. "*Star Wars, Star Trek, The Lord of the Rings, The Da Vinci Code, Harry Potter* . . . You are talking about hundreds of millions, perhaps billions of dollars' worth of property every year. And the property is all ideas! Whom do those ideas belong to? Well, that's where I come in, to help the judge decide."

"I see, yes. Well, that kind of answers my second question. Why does a reporter need a lawyer?"

"Oh, sure! With a journalist, not only are you dealing with intellectual property rights, but also libel. You have to be very careful as a journalist. You are treading a very fine line."

Dehan was smiling at the fire. She knew what was coming next. I made appreciative noises and said, "Wow, yeah. On a paper like the *Telegraph* that's pretty important. You must have saved his bacon a couple of times."

He gave a self-deprecating smile. "More than twice."

"And here's the thing that confuses me, Mr. Lee. How could you help him, if he never discussed his cases with you?"

He froze. Then after a moment, he laughed. "Kudos, Detective Stone. Well played. Naturally he discussed his cases with me. And as his attorney those discussions were, and are, covered by client confidentiality. I did not discuss his last article with him because, as I have explained to you, by then I had started to distance myself from him."

Dehan spoke up suddenly. "How well do you know Shelly Pearce?"

He pushed out his bottom lip and shrugged. "Our paths cross occasionally, socially."

I added, "How about Carol Hennessy?"

He looked surprised. "Senator Hennessy? Hardly at all. Again, our paths cross from time to time . . ."

I stood. "Thank you for your time, Mr. Lee. As you see, it really wasn't worth hiding from us."

"I assure you, that was *not* my . . ."

Dehan stood and cut across him, "But next time, you might be wise to!" He looked at her in alarm, and she laughed and slapped his shoulder. "Just kidding, Jackson. Thanks for the coffee. See you around."

He managed to force a laugh and walked us to the door. I put the hat on Dehan's head, raised my collar, and we made a run for the Jag. I slammed the hood closed and we climbed in and closed the doors. I could see Lee watching us from the door, warped through the water on the windshield. I turned the key and gunned the engine, then watched him step into the house and close the door.

I reversed onto the wet road and we headed off on our long, wet journey back toward the Bronx.

TEN

As we emerged from the upper-middle-class, leafy perfection of Oyster Bay, the rain was like a funeral procession of giant, wet shrouds marching in across the sodden landscape from the immensity of the Atlantic. We followed Cove Road south as far as the North Hempstead Turnpike, then turned west, following the empty highway through tall pines and the naked skeletons of other trees I could not identify. We drove in silence until I said, "Questions."

"I have a couple: Why did he lie about Dave not discussing his work with him? And why did he want to avoid seeing us . . . ?"

I made a face and sighed. "Those questions sound unanswerable, Dehan. But what happens if we change the interrogative particle?"

She laughed. "The what now? The interrogative . . . ?"

"Interrogative particle. The 'W' word: what, why, where . . ."

"And whom?"

"Yes, and also whom."

"Okay, I know you don't like 'why.' It's too open, I agree. Let me try. What made him lie about Dave not discussing his work with him? Okay, you're right . . ."

"Two things immediately become clear, don't they?"

"Yeah, either he *did* discuss the article with him, and he didn't want us to know . . ."

"Or they fell out over something. Something serious enough for Dave to break his rule of not meeting people while he was on a story."

"And something, maybe, serious enough for Lee to kill Dave and take the story and the laptop."

"So what is our next question, avoiding the very open particle 'why'?"

She thought for a moment. "What did they fall out over, that could be that serious?"

I nodded. "Yes, that, and also, if he did take the laptop and the article, what stopped him from publishing it?"

She frowned at me and nodded. "It has to be worth a lot of money to the paper. The way Dave described it to Bob Shaw, it could be worth millions."

We lapsed into silence again, hypnotized by the rhythm of the windshield wipers and the steady hum of the Jaguar moving ever forward through the long tunnel of winter trees, stark shapes twisted against the low ceiling of ash-gray clouds.

Eventually Dehan sighed. "You know how it is, Stone. It always comes back to one thing."

"Sex?"

She looked at me a moment, then shrugged. "I was going to say love, but I guess they're not so different in the end."

"If we believe William James and Donald Symons, love is a powerful cocktail of neurotransmitters and hormones, primarily oxytocin, dopamine, estrogen, and testosterone, that drive the most powerful elements of love." I glanced at her. "Attachment, partner preference, and sex drive. Dopamine can make a person very goal-driven, and testosterone can give a person the aggression and the focus to do almost anything to achieve that goal."

She looked away into the gray light. "That has to be the ugliest view of love I ever heard."

I smiled. "I'd have to agree with you. Unfortunately it's a view that is backed up by a lot of hard science."

"Doesn't it miss something? Isn't there a little more to it than that?"

"I think so . . ." I hesitated for a second. "But that's another discussion, to be had over a steak and a bottle of wine or two. The point is, sex and love are part and parcel, at least where murder is concerned." I paused a moment to think about what I was saying. "Mothers, siblings, even children, might kill to protect their family. But murder, that dark drive to kill, that is usually fueled by the darker side of love, isn't it? The desire to possess, to own, to dominate, they are all appetites that are woven into the sex drive."

She was frowning at me, like she was four and I had told her that Santa Claus had just shot Bugs Bunny down a dark alley and stolen his money so he could get drunk at the local clip joint.

"What about nurturing, care, respect, honor, tenderness . . . ?"

I smiled at her. "Hey, don't get me wrong, Dehan. I'm not saying that's all there is. I'm not even saying that's what I believe. All I am saying is, as you know yourself, ninety percent of murders are committed for love. Love has a dark side, and that dark side is all about possession, ownership, and domination."

"I guess."

I was silent for a bit. Outside, the rain had eased. The wipers had slowed to a steady sixty beats per minute. A voice in my head was telling me to change the subject, but somebody else seemed to be operating my mouth.

"Those other elements, respect, tenderness, I guess those are what we are capable of distilling from those darker drives." I glanced at her and gave a small shrug. "There are things the mighty god of science has not yet explained, Dehan. Consciousness and love are two of those things."

She studied my face for a while as we approached Little Neck Bay and crossed over the bridge.

"I guess we got a bit sidetracked, huh?"

"I guess murder is not mechanical. Murder is a huge step for any person. It's the product of deep, powerful passions. There is no harm in having some understanding of those passions. Ronald Laing said that life was a sexually transmitted disease, and that the mortality rate was one hundred percent. He might have added that murder was too."

She nodded and looked away again. "You're deep, Stone. You're deep." I snorted quietly, but she ignored me. "So it always comes back to love, and more specifically, sex. Are we saying that Lee and Samantha might have started having an affair?"

"It's one possible motive, isn't it?"

"Uh-huh, but it raises two questions." She lifted her left hand with two fingers raised. "One, why'd she go . . . sorry, what made her go and marry somebody else, not Lee, after Dave was killed? And two, once again, what happened to the article and his laptop?"

"In answer to your first point, maybe it wasn't mutual. She was feeling abandoned and frustrated because of Dave's neglect. Lee was there. They had sex. For her it was an escape, for him it was more."

"Okay, and the article?"

I thought for a moment, as we approached the Throgs Neck Bridge. "He realized that publication of the article posed a threat not just to Dave, but to Samantha as well."

"Huh . . . So if this is right, they meet to discuss the article and the risks involved in publishing it. Lee is already having an affair with Samantha, and it's getting serious for him. Dave reveals the nature of the article and Lee sees the risks involved—forty-plus people have died already as a result of crossing this dame. He tells him not to do it, that he is putting Samantha in danger as well as himself."

"How is that exactly? Spell it out for me."

"Okay, we are assuming that Hennessy has a long track record of eliminating people who threaten to expose her or cross her in some way. Lee sees a risk that if Dave goes ahead with the article, Hennessy could threaten him, but she could also go after his wife." She spread her hands. "If they take *him* out, the article could go ahead anyway, and worse still, give more credence to the story. Let's face it, the *Telegraph* has a reputation for not giving in to intimidation. The murder of a journalist could just boost sales. But if she threatens Dave's wife, he may not publish at all. All I am saying is that Lee might have seen this possibility."

I nodded. "Okay, it's possible."

"But Dave doesn't give a damn. He's going ahead anyway. So Lee goes to see him, kills him, and takes the article and the laptop and drops them in the Hudson."

"Hmmm . . ."

"Hmmm?"

"It's almost a perfect fit. How would we prove it?"

"That's tricky. We would need a confession from Samantha that she had an affair with Lee, just to get started. We could get them both in for questioning and play them against each other."

I shook my head. "Lee would plead the fifth, hire a team of lawyers, and long before we got to trial he'd see we had squat. And we'd never get to trial because the DA would also see we had squat. And before *that* happened, we wouldn't even be able to charge him."

"So what do you suggest?"

"For the moment I think the Lee–Samantha avenue is blocked, but if there is anything in it, it might open up if we approach from another angle."

"What angle?"

"Hennessy. I think I'd like to poke Hennessy and see if she jumps."

"Seriously?" She frowned at me. "What will you poke her with? You just said we had squat."

I grinned. "Squat can hurt if you sharpen it enough. At the very least it can look scary."

We joined the Cross Bronx Expressway and the traffic started to get heavier. Dehan said, "You want to put that into plain language?"

"You ever heard of Milton Erickson?"

"No. Should I have?"

"He was a surgeon, a psychiatrist, and a hypnotist. He came up with this idea of being 'artfully vague.'"

"Artfully vague?"

"Yeah. If I say to you, 'You are feeling all those feelings you get when you start to feel sleepy,' even though I haven't mentioned any of those feelings, your mind will automatically supply them. You might even start to feel sleepy."

"Huh. Okay, so . . . ?"

"I say to you, 'In his study, he had all the things you'd expect from an old-fashioned gentleman.' I haven't mentioned a single stick of furniture, but your mind has produced all the images of what *you* would expect in an old-fashioned gentleman's study. Right?"

"Yup."

"So if I suggest something to you, but I am artfully vague about the details, your brain will unconsciously supply what's missing. What I am curious to find out is, if I suggest, in an artfully vague way, to Carol Hennessy, that we have new information about David Thorndike and his article, what details will her brain supply? And how will she respond? If I poke her, how will she jump?"

"I agree that would be interesting, but, Stone, what precisely are we trying to find out?"

I took a deep breath. It was a good question. "I think what I would really like to know right now is, did Carol Hennessy know that David Thorndike was investigating her? And, if so, did she know that he was ready to publish his article? The answer to those two questions would focus our investigation."

We had pulled onto the Boulevard and were approaching the turnoff for the 43rd. Dehan grunted. "You're a devious son of a bitch, Stone. You promised me lunch on the way. You got me soaked, made me lie to an attorney, filled my head with suggestive ambiguity, and never even bought me lunch."

I spoke without thinking and an ugly gnome in my head started beating an alarm bell with an iron hammer. I tried hard to ignore it.

"You're right. Tell you what, I'll get some sandwiches and coffee from the deli. You find a number for Carol Hennessy, and tonight we'll grab a couple of steaks and a bottle of wine to make up for lunch. Whadd'ya say?"

I thought she hesitated a moment. "Yeah, sounds good."

"You got other plans?"

She shook her head. "Nope. No other plans."

"Good."

I pulled into the parking lot at the station house and we climbed out into the heavy drizzle. I watched her run across the road in her long coat with her hat squashed on her head and run up the two steps into the porch. Then I made my way down to the deli on the corner to get lunch.

All the way there and all the way back, I kept turning over a single fact. It didn't tell me anything, it didn't lead me anywhere that I could see, but I knew it was important; not just important, it was central. Yet I couldn't see what it meant.

Jackson Lee had not stolen the article and the laptop. Because the article and the laptop had disappeared from the apartment before David had been killed. That meant that David—and by the looks of it, *only* David—knew where his laptop and the article were.

Whoever killed him did not kill him to get the article. And that fact was crucial, but I couldn't see how.

ELEVEN

WHEN I GOT BACK TO OUR DESK, DEHAN WAS ON THE phone. I put her sandwich and her coffee down in front of her and she put the phone on speaker.

"Mr. D'Angelo, my partner, Detective Stone, has just joined me and I have put the phone on speaker so that he can hear us."

"Indeed, good afternoon, Detective Stone. I was just explaining to Detective Dehan that Senator Hennessy has a very busy schedule and it will not be possible for her to speak with you at the moment."

I dropped into my seat and said, "I am sure Detective Dehan made it clear that this was a murder inquiry."

"Indeed she did, and I can assure you that Senator Hennessy is very concerned about the issue of law and order in our city. However, Senator Hennessy has no knowledge of any specific cases where crimes have been committed . . ."

"How do you know?"

"Excuse me?"

"How do you know that she has no knowledge concerning any specific cases?"

"Senator Hennessy does not have any personal knowledge relating to any particular cases where a crime has been . . ."

"Mr. D'Angelo."

". . . committed, because Senator Hennessy . . ."

"Mr. D'Angelo!"

". . . does not have and never has had any connection with . . ."

"Mr. D'Angelo!"

A few of the detectives at the other desks turned to look. Several of them were smiling. D'Angelo finished. ". . . any criminal activities. Yes, Detective Stone?"

"Quit quoting copy at me."

"Excuse me?"

I sighed. "Stop reciting at me. We are conducting a murder investigation, not writing an article for a college magazine. We believe Senator Hennessy may have information relevant to our investigation. We need to talk to her."

"I am quite certain Senator Hennessy has no information relevant to your inquiry, Detective."

"Really?"

"Indeed."

"Well, this might come as a surprise to you, D'Angelo, but I don't actually give a rat's ass about your opinion. I need to talk to Hennessy. Now, give me a date and a time or I am going to come down to your office with a dozen journalists in tow and we're going to make the headlines on the six o'clock news."

"Detective, are you threatening the senator?"

"I don't know, why don't you give me your opinion on that? And while you're thinking about it, tell me when we can come and talk to her."

"Please hold."

I looked at Dehan. She was holding her sandwich in both hands and chewing while she watched me.

I said, "I want somebody who can interface between me and the world, and tell everybody what I know, what I don't know, what I think, what I have and haven't seen and done. And I don't want anybody anywhere ever to question what my mouthpiece says. This is what we call democratic accountability."

She listened without expression throughout my little speech. When I'd finished, she swallowed and said, "Indeed."

I unwrapped my sandwich and bit into it. I was halfway through eating it when D'Angelo came back on the line.

"Detective Stone?"

I said something that sounded like a mouthful of "Yumph!"

"Senator Hennessy is not available to comment at this time . . ."

I sat forward, switched the phone off speaker, and picked it up. I spoke very quietly. "Now you listen very carefully to what I am about to say, D'Angelo. I am going to be at Hennessy's office this afternoon at three o'clock. I expect her to be there to answer my questions. If she is not, I am going to turn up the day after with six patrol cars, sirens wailing and lights flashing, and I am going to send six more to her house, and believe me, pal, hard as I try to keep it quiet, somehow the press will find out about it. So you had better think this through, and give your boss the right advice."

I hung up.

We sat and chewed and stared at each other. She drained her coffee and sighed. "She won't be there."

"I know. D'Angelo will be there, and he'll be instructed to find out what we know and what we are after."

"What will you tell him?"

"I'll be artfully vague."

She raised an eyebrow at me. "Can you do that? Can you be artfully vague to somebody through a third party?"

"No, not really. But I will give him a message to carry to her."

"Let me guess."

"I'd be glad if you did."

"That we know where the article is."

"Too on the nose; after all, she might already have it, and the laptop." I scratched my chin. "Though it's unlikely."

"That we know the contents, that there was a copy . . ."

"Better. Let's play it by ear." I stood. "We'd better tell Newman. He wanted to be kept in the loop."

I put my coat on one-handed as we stepped out and pressed the inspector's speed dial.

"Inspector Newman."

"Inspector, it's Stone here. Just to let you know, we've made an appointment with Senator Hennessy and we are on our way now. I'll let you know how it goes."

"Splendid. Good work, Stone."

"Thank you, sir."

Dehan looked at me and gave her head a small shake. "That's keeping him in the loop?"

I shrugged. "What can I tell you? The man's busy. I don't want to waste his time."

———

THE HENNESSY FOUNDATION was on the thirty-second floor of the Rockford Building on 6th Avenue. The reception area was functional, with a deep blue carpet and a white desk set by large, glass double doors emblazoned with a spray of twenty-three stars. The girl behind it was regulation pretty with blond hair and blue eyes and a smile that was friendly but tinted with arrogance—Hennessy was the People's Woman, and anybody on her team was a cut above the common man. Orwell would have known exactly what they were about.

I showed the girl my badge and she tried not to wince. Ugly truth had no place in the Hennessy Foundation. "I'm Detective Stone, this is Detective Dehan. We're here to see Senator Hennessy."

She narrowed her eyes so that her smile stopped looking like a smile. "Have you got an appointment?"

"I don't know."

"See, you're going to need an appointment."

I looked at her with no expression until she blinked and

started to look nervous, then I said, "Call D'Angelo and tell him we're here."

She picked up her phone and pressed a button.

"Mr. D'Angelo, there are two detectives here to see the senator . . . Yes, sir." She hung up and looked at me with unhappy eyes. "He'll be here in just a moment if you would like to wait over there." She pointed at some blue chairs up against the wall. I didn't look at them. I kept watching her without expression.

"What happens if I don't want to wait there? What happens if I want to wait somewhere else?"

"You can wait wherever you like, sir."

"I know. I'm a cop."

I turned to face Dehan. She had her coat open and her hands thrust in the back pockets of her jeans. She was eyeing me with a small frown on her brow. I shrugged. "In the bad old days, they used to tell you what you couldn't do. Today they tell you what you have to do. It gets on my nerves."

The doors opened and a man in an Italian suit, who looked as if he'd been shrink-wrapped after grooming, stepped out and approached us.

"Detectives Stone and Dehan." He held out his hand and as we shook it he said, "The Hennessy Foundation welcomes you."

I smiled. "How about you?"

"Excuse me?"

"You're excused. Where is Senator Hennessy?"

"As I told you on the telephone, she is not available to answer your questions."

"Okay, D'Angelo, let's go somewhere where we can talk privately, because there are some things I need to explain to you so that you understand them."

He gave a small intake of breath that was not quite a gasp and said, "Please follow me."

He led us through the double glass doors across a large, open-plan room carpeted in blue and into a small conference room, about thirty feet by twenty. There was a large, high-gloss oval table in the middle with twelve chairs around it. There were no windows. I pulled out a chair and sat. Dehan sat next to me, and D'Angelo hesitated a moment. I nodded at a chair and said, "Sit."

He sat.

"These bullying tactics will not get you anywhere, Detective Stone."

I raised a hand. "Let's quit the posturing and cut to the chase. I need to talk to Hennessy. More to the point, she needs to talk to me. Now, I don't know what kind of access you have to her . . ."

"I am her personal secretary." There was no expression on his face when he said it, but you could smell the pride. Maybe it was his pheromones.

"Good, so you need to make her understand that we are investigating the David Thorndike murder. I want you to make a note of that name . . ."

He nodded once. "I have."

"And we need to know what happened to the *original* manuscript of his article, and his original notes on his laptop. Have you understood that clearly, D'Angelo?"

He blinked three times before he answered.

"Yes, I have understood."

I studied his face closely. He looked about forty-one or -two, but he might have been as much as forty-seven. I asked him, "How long have you worked for Hennessy?"

"I have worked for the Hennessy Foundation for twenty years."

"So you must remember the Thorndike case."

He gave his head a small shake. "Not really."

"But you must understand how important it could be to Senator Hennessy . . ."

"I am not qualified to comment on that point."

I nodded and smiled. "Sure. But I am. I am going to expect a call tomorrow, arranging a meeting with the senator. Now, one way or another I am going to see her and talk to her. It can either be in a discreet, private interview here, in her offices, or it can be in a very public display, down at the station in the Bronx."

He shook his head and narrowed his eyes. "You can't force her to go down to the station."

I leered at him. "Are you sure about that, D'Angelo? According to New York state law, under what circumstances can I take her downtown?"

He hesitated for a second. "Only under arrest."

I leaned forward. "Talk to your boss, D'Angelo. Let's get this resolved quietly and without embarrassing anybody. I think Carol Hennessy has had more than enough embarrassment in her career already, don't you, Dehan?"

She nodded. "I reckon so, Stone. Sometimes a simple conversation can save somebody a lot of trouble and upset."

I went to stand, but stopped. "One last question, D'Angelo. Were you Hennessy's private secretary back when Shelly Pearce interviewed her about the Thorndike murder?"

He frowned. "Yes. I have been with the senator for twelve years."

"Right." I smiled wolfishly at him. "But I bet you get to see Pearce often now, huh? Tell me something, is she as good-looking in person as she is in her pictures?"

He looked at me in mild disgust. "I am really not qualified to answer that question, Detective Stone. Now if there is nothing else . . ."

"C'mon! We're guys. Don't be so uptight! Is she a looker? Huh? I heard she likes to drink! Did she ever come on to you?"

"Ms. Pearce is a perfect lady, Detective Stone, and her behavior has always been exemplary. Now I am really going to have to ask you to leave."

"Fine! We're going!" I stood and pointed my finger at him like a gun. "But I'll be waiting for that call. Don't make me do anything your boss will regret. You got me?"

"I understand! Good day, Detectives!"

We rode the elevator down to the lobby. All the way I was

smiling. When we got to the big doors it was already getting dark and the headlamps and the traffic lights were spilling over the wet blacktop like broken Jell-O.

"Come on, Dehan, let's beat the rush hour. We'll check in at the station, then do some shopping and head to my place. Whadd'ya say?"

She nodded, and we ran through the rain to the car and clambered in. As she closed the door, she said, "You want to tell me what all that sexist misogynist crap was about?"

I smiled. "Sure, I thought you'd get it. I wanted to know if Shelly Pearce was a regular visitor to Hennessy's place. She said she only knew her in passing because they moved in the same social circle. Seems, according to D'Angelo, that it's a little more than that."

I turned the key and listened to the comfortable rumble of the big old engine. "Ritoo Glasshopper must learn to trust ancient Sensei."

"You're deep, Sensei. I have to hand it to you. You are one deep son of a bitch."

I chuckled and pulled out into the dark, wet flow of cars. "Well, gee, Dehan! Thanks!"

Her face suddenly lit up. "Say! You want I should make moussaka? We have time today!"

"Sounds good to me!"

"Yeah! We'll make moussaka!"

And we moved off, toward the Bronx.

TWELVE

Back at the station, I was half expecting Inspector Newman to call us up to his office and chew my nuts off for giving the senator a hard time. The chances were pretty good that Hennessy's attorneys would make an official complaint. I had rattled her cage and I had to expect her to spit at me a bit. But when we went up to report to him, Newman listened quietly to our slightly edited story and nodded when we'd finished. By the looks of it, the mighty Hennessy war machine had not rolled into action after all. That was interesting in itself. He shrugged and said, "Well, as long as you are doing it by the book and there is no serious comeback for the precinct, that is fine by me. What is your take on it?"

I thrust out my bottom lip and stared at Dehan, who raised her eyebrows. I let her answer. "It's hard to say at this stage, sir. Until we get a better idea of what happened to the article and the laptop, it is all conjecture. We are hoping that Senator Hennessy can cast some light on that for us."

"Yes, admirably sensible approach. I applaud you both. Keep me posted."

We thanked him and made our way down the stairs. At our desks, as we were closing down our computers and collecting up our stuff, Sergeant Maria Lopez came in carrying a manila envelope.

"Detective Stone. A letter came for you while you were out."

I took it, thanked her, and stuck it in my pocket. Dehan glanced at me as she stuffed her laptop in her bag. "Aren't you going to open it?"

I shook my head. "I'll look at it at home, while you're cooking, darling."

She spluttered. I grinned at her and wondered what the hell I was doing. A couple of the guys glanced up as we left, and I heard laughter behind us as we stepped back out into the evening.

We stopped at Kmart on Bruckner Boulevard to get some wine and some ingredients, then drove on to my house on Haight Avenue.

I lit a fire and poured two martinis while Dehan went upstairs to dry her hair and change into dry clothes. Over the last year we had slipped into a routine. Once or twice a week, sometimes it was a bit more than that, she would come over and stay. We'd make a meal and have a few drinks and discuss whatever case we were on. At least, it started out with cases, but lately she'd been coming over to see the fight too, and we'd spent Christmas together. It had only been about a year, but in that time she'd kind of taken possession of my spare room, and always had a change of clothes there. In fact, I had come to think of it, unconsciously, as her room.

It was a comfortable feeling that I enjoyed. It was the closest thing I had to family now, which was why Shelly's comments had unsettled me. If she was right, it would change everything. I knew she wasn't right, the idea was absurd, but it's like when somebody tells you not to think about cockroaches. After that, it's all you can think about.

I heard her coming down the stairs, talking, and smiled.

"I was going to have a shower, then I thought I'd better get the moussaka on, cause it's going to take at least an hour, and we want to make an early start tomorrow, right? So we don't want to be eating too late . . ." She stopped, tying her hair up in a knot behind her neck. "What?"

I realized I was staring and shook my head. "Nothing. You're right. Here's your drink."

She took the glass and smiled. "Nice fire, Sensei."

She sipped and went into the kitchen, pushing up the sleeves of her sweatshirt. I followed, and while she began getting the things from the fridge, I rested my ass against the sink, took a knife, and opened the envelope Maria had given me at the station.

It was two sheets of paper, printed and stapled together. I flipped to the end of the second page. There was no signature. I started to read. Dehan, holding two eggplants, bumped me with her shoulder and said, "Move, Big Guy."

I shifted over and she started washing the vegetables. She glanced at me and then at the letter. After that, she dried her hands and started cutting the vegetables into rounds. "What is it?"

"It's anonymous. Mainly it's an itemized list of Hennessy's victims between the years 2000 and 2008, but it claims she used one particular hit man during that period. Give me a couple of freezer bags, will you?"

She handed me two transparent plastic bags from the cupboard, and I slipped the notes into them.

"We'll send them for prints tomorrow. Listen." I started to read. "'The importance of Thorndike's investigation, and the reason it proceeded so swiftly, was that he made contact with that hit man, I do not know his name, so we will call him K.

"'K agreed, for reasons which are not clear to me, to tell Thorndike everything in exchange for his own anonymity. He gave times, dates, and locations regarding his meetings with Anthony D'Angelo, acting on behalf of Carol Hennessy, and later meetings with Hennessy herself. He gave details of payments made, both in cash and transfers to a numbered account in Belize, each coinciding with one of the hits.

"'It was K's policy to keep photographic, video, and audio

records of his meetings as insurance against being shopped by his employers. He made electronic copies of all of these available to Thorndike. What Thorndike had in his article was damning, conclusive proof that Carol Hennessy had ordered the assassination of at least ten people who had threatened one way or another to expose her corrupt deals.

"'These deals ranged from real estate scams in the nineteen eighties and nineties and illegal arms deals with oppressive regimes, to illegal deals with states that supported Islamic terrorism in the first decade of the new millennium. Most of the latter deals were conducted through the Hennessy Foundation in the guise of aid to third-world and developing countries.

"'There were also allegations of mental and emotional instability against Carol Hennessy, ranging from sadomasochistic orgies, hysterical rages against her staff, in which she threatened them with violence, to inappropriate lesbian advances on members of her election campaign team.

"'The victims listed were all either involved in investigations against her or were witnesses who had volunteered to testify in those investigations. There follows a list of the ten victims that K confessed to having eliminated, along with the date of the execution, the price he was paid, method of payment, and the reason for the execution.'"

I turned the page. The names were listed by date. I scanned quickly through them without really paying attention.

Harold Little
Albert Brightman
Jack O'Connor
Carl Beeman
Emmanuel Odembe
Kathleen Henson
Danniele Frostrup
Philip Olsen
Ralph Denby
Gustave Boucher

I looked up at Dehan. She had just dumped a pile of diced lamb into a blue cast-iron pot and the smell of herbs, frying onions, and olive oil was strong on the air. She said, "We need to work through those names systematically and check for any discrepancies." She listed on her fingers. "Are they in fact dead, did they die as and where our informant says, did they have the connection to Hennessy that he or she claims . . ."

"If they check out, we need to find this informer." I waved the letter. "And, above all, we need to find K."

"Question: Why hasn't—sorry, what stopped our informant from giving us K's name, and how does our informant have this information? The pool of people who could know all this is very small."

I looked back at the letter. "It says he doesn't know K's name."

"Okay, so we are looking at somebody who is close to Dave, but not so close that he confides everything. That narrows it to two people."

"Lee and Katie."

She made a face like brain strain. "But that doesn't make any sense at all! Why tell us one thing face-to-face and then send an anonymous letter?"

I nodded. "What would make a person do that? Well . . . either they have a reason for concealing the fact that they know, because it puts them at risk somehow . . ."

She shrugged. "That's possible."

"Or there is a third person he was close to, who is remaining hidden."

She puffed out her cheeks and blew noisily. "That's a lot of hiding people, Stone. Dave, K, and now our anonymous informer."

I grunted and sipped my drink while she cooked. I watched her put layers of meat, potato, and eggplant into the iron dish and then stand stirring a béchamel sauce. Eventually, she said, "Open the wine, will you? It'll need to breathe. You want a salad?"

Absently, I said, "Do I look like a wabbit?" and grabbed the bottle.

She shrugged, put the moussaka in the oven, and reached for the salad bowl. "Yeah, a bit you do. We'll have a salad."

I moved her aside and took the corkscrew from the drawer and started pulling the cork. "Let me ask you something. If you were a world-class assassin, and you had decided for some reason to turn on a client of the caliber of Carol Hennessy, would you hang around in New York?"

She turned and looked at me with a half-bisected avocado in her hand.

"No. No, I wouldn't."

"Where would you go?"

"I'd go somewhere remote. I'd probably go to an island in the Indian Ocean, or Brazil. If for some reason I stayed in the country, I'd go to Wyoming, or Colorado, one of the Dakotas."

I pulled the cork and it popped loudly. I smelled it, and she stepped over to smell too.

"That's the 'nose,' right?"

I nodded.

"The bouquet is different. It comes later."

I smiled. "That's right."

"I've been reading about it." She returned to the salad. "You don't know how long you've got in this life, Stone. The end can come suddenly, out of nowhere. You have to appreciate every moment." She waved her knife at me. "And you know something else I realized?"

"What's that, Dehan?"

"People have to *learn* to appreciate. Appreciating, enjoying, they don't just come naturally. You have to learn. It's a way of thinking. It's like thinking with your body instead of just your brain."

"Wow."

"So anyway, keep talking. K is not in New York. Where is he? Set the table."

I grabbed a handful of knives and forks from the drawer. "The only person who knew is dead. But he can still tell us."

I went and started setting two places at the table.

She was cutting tomatoes into the salad bowl. "He can? How?"

"Because at some point between his last article, where he was laying into Hennessy, and his taking the apartment in Manor Avenue and starting his investigation, he made contact with K. That was what triggered his sudden obsession. That's why he was so excited. Because here was an opportunity to go after a really big prize. Now, if K wasn't living in New York, that means either K traveled here to see David, or David traveled there, wherever he was, to see him. And that has to be the more likely scenario. So somewhere on David's bank or credit card records, there are going to be trips to some location where he met K. It's a place to start."

She nodded. "Yeah, that makes sense." She thought about it a moment. "Plus, any visitors he received at his apartment on Manor Avenue, Mr. Gupta would have noticed. And he didn't mention anyone . . . unless . . ."

"The woman he thought was Katie, on Friday night?"

"Could it be? K changes his mind and takes out David?"

"K is a woman . . . ?"

She sipped and smiled. "Man . . . I am no expert, but I always thought female assassins were just in Hollywood. Usually they are ex-military, or CIA."

"I am inclined to agree, but the fact is we don't know." I sighed and shook my head. "Let's face it, Dehan, we still know practically nothing. It is all allegations, hints, theories . . . but we have zip in the way of facts."

She sucked her teeth for a moment and pointed at the letter. "But that, that baby might change everything. If we can track K, that *will* change everything."

We stared at each other for a long moment. Finally, I said, "Dehan, we are looking at political conspiracy. These people are very powerful and very dangerous. I know what you are going to say, but I have to ask. Do you want out?"

"Really? Come here so I can smack you in the mouth. No, Stone, we take these bastards down and we make them pay. That's our job. So let's do it."

I nodded and went to check the table and finished setting it. I stared at it unseeing for a few seconds. Then, without really knowing why, I said, "Dehan?"

"What?"

"I never had a partner like you."

She turned to look at me. Her face showed surprise, and something else: a smile.

I gave a stupid grin. "You're the best partner I ever had. You should know that."

She waved a salad fork at me and turned away. "Stop it. You're going to embarrass me. You want the salad as a starter? We could start with the salad. Did you put salad plates out . . . ?"

I watched her, sipped my martini, and smiled.

THIRTEEN

Morning brought patches of cold blue sky and frothy mountains of very white cloud tinged with watery turquoise. It was a relief to have a break from the relentless gray and the steady downpour. There was a hint of spring in the morning light, but the wind still bit with icy teeth.

Our first stop that day was to have the note and the list copied before sending them to the lab for fingerprinting. After that we went up to update the inspector and ask about contacting David's bank and credit card agency to have them release his records to us for 2007 and 2008.

When we asked him, he nodded with interest and frowned.

"What is it exactly you are looking for? Have you got a copy of the letter with you?"

I handed him the copy we'd made. He took it over by the window and put on his reading glasses. He read it with care, twice, and sighed heavily before handing it back to me.

"You'll review all of these deaths, obviously."

"That is Dehan's task for this morning, sir."

"And you want the financial records why?"

"If this alleged hit man exists, sir, we think he would have lived somewhere fairly remote. He would logically want to stay away from Hennessy and her operation. He would want to be somewhere where he left the smallest traceable footprint possible. So David would presumably have had to travel to meet with him, wherever he was, and record his interviews. We are hoping to find a record either of a long trip somewhere, or several repeated trips, that might give us some indication of where K is. It's a first step in tracking him down."

The inspector looked depressed.

"This is going to be one unholy mess."

Dehan coughed. Newman raised an eyebrow at her. "With all due respect, sir, it's not going to be a mess, it already is a mess. What we are going to do is clean it up."

"Thank you, Detective, for that enlightening perspective. Sadly, I don't think our political masters share your view." He sighed again. "But there is no way of avoiding it, is there?"

I shook my head.

"Very well, Detectives, I'll see to the records. Proceed with great care and be very, very sure of each step you take. If even half of this is true, we are up against a very formidable opponent."

We promised him we would be very careful and left. On the way down the stairs my cell phone rang.

"Stone."

"Detective, this is Jackson Lee."

"Hello, Mr. Lee, how can I help you?"

Dehan turned and watched me. Lee was saying, "Look, I wonder if I could come in and see you today? I've been troubled since you left, about our conversation yesterday. Thing is, I wasn't totally transparent with you, and I'd like to have a fuller discussion. The situation is not simple or straightforward."

"Of course. I appreciate that. When are you likely to be here?"

"I'm on my way now. Say in about half an hour?"

"That will be fine. Just tell the sergeant at the desk and one of us will come and get you."

I hung up, and we stood frowning at each other on the stairs.

Dehan said, "We rattled her cage, and next thing everybody is volunteering information."

"How about that?"

"You think it's connected?"

I raised an eyebrow. "I don't know. Let's see what he has to say."

He arrived about forty minutes later in a sharp Italian suit that was as vulgar as it was expensive. I had a uniform lead him up to interview room three and left him waiting for ten minutes while I sat with my ass against the desk and spoke to Dehan.

"The anonymous letter incriminates Hennessy, so I don't see that that can be a direct result of our rattling her cage. But now, less than twenty-four hours after talking to D'Angelo, Lee turns up wanting to change his story. What I'm interested to see is if he also incriminates her, or if he is going to try to shift suspicion away from her in another direction."

"If he does, you're thinking maybe he's on Hennessy's payroll?"

I thought for a long moment, then shook my head. "To be honest, I don't know, Dehan. I haven't got a handle on this yet. Let's go see what Lee has to say. We're going to play our cards real close, okay?"

She nodded and we went upstairs.

When we stepped into the room, Lee was studiously unruffled and stood to greet us. "Detectives, how are you? I must apologize. This whole thing has taken me a little by surprise."

I gestured at his chair as I pulled out my own and said, "Please, sit down, Mr. Lee. I am grateful to you for coming in. You want to add something to your statement from yesterday?"

He frowned. "Yeah. It's a little complicated." He ran his fingers through his hair and smiled at Dehan. "See, David was a very talented journalist. I mean, really good. And we had a good rapport. Frankly, I saw in him not just a friend but a damn good client for the future. A guy like David on a paper like the *Telegraph* . . ." He laughed. "That's the goose that just keeps on laying! But, you know, it was always the policy on the paper that they would publish the most controversial articles, they didn't care who they went up against or who they upset, *as long as the facts were solid*. And that was one area where David had always been really meticulous."

Dehan raised an eyebrow. "But?"

"Well, here's the thing. What I told you yesterday was true, so far as it went. I was fond of Samantha, and it did piss me off to see Dave screwing around with another woman. But there was more to it than that."

"What, exactly?"

He shrugged and made a face. "It was like he was becoming obsessed. He had lost all objectivity. It seemed like to him all the hearsay and stories and accusations had become facts and evidence. You were right, of course: he always discussed his stories with me so we could consider the legal implications. And I kept telling him that all he had regarding the Hennessy story was what you could find on the 'net. It was unsubstantiated rumor."

I frowned. "That was all he had?"

"Pretty much, Detective. And, well, I couldn't help feeling it was Katie who was getting to him. The two of them seemed to be . . ." He shrugged, shook his head, appeared to search for a word, and then repeated with more emphasis, ". . . *obsessed!* It's the only word that really describes their behavior. When he asked to meet me, I was expecting something sensational. If you have spoken to Bob Shaw, then you know he was talking in terms of Watergate and shaking the foundations of the Constitution." He shook his head again. "But there was nothing like that in what he showed me. If I say that the evidence was circumstantial, I am being generous. It was more like innuendo. If he had published that article, as he showed it to me, Hennessy's lawyers would have dragged him over the coals, bankrupted him, and he would never have worked again." He gave a small laugh. "Except that Bob would never have published it in the first place."

I took a deep breath and drummed my fingers on the table.

"Forgive me, Mr. Lee, but I am finding it difficult to believe that a professional with David's reputation and experience could delude himself to that degree."

He answered quickly. "And I would have to agree with you. If I hadn't seen it with my own eyes, I would not have believed it myself. But there he was . . ." He spread his hands and looked apologetically at Dehan. "I don't mean to sound sexist, but the fact is that when people fall in love they can become . . ."

Dehan supplied the word, "Stupid."

He laughed. "Well, yes. Stupid is as good a word as any. And the impression I had was that he was besotted with Katie, and she was driving him on this, frankly, pointless crusade."

She smiled and gave her head a little twitch to the side. "Wouldn't be the first time a woman drove a guy crazy, that's for sure." Then she became more serious. "So you think she had some kind of axe to grind?"

"It's possible, but I don't honestly know. I never met her in person. But when I spoke to Dave, he just wouldn't shut up about her. I know this, he involved her in his investigation a damned sight more than anybody before—including myself. She was privy to stuff he wouldn't share with me."

"Like what?"

He made a "really?" face. "I don't know, because he didn't make me privy to it. But he repeated several times that 'he and Katie' had unearthed information that was dynamite. More than dynamite. But when I asked him what it was, he refused to tell me and made excuses. In the end, I came to the conclusion there was no actual information. It was all the product of late-night drinking, smoking dope, and getting paranoid."

I said, "You think he was paranoid? Actually paranoid?"

He made a face. "I don't know. I'm not a psychologist. But from what I know as an informed layman, he certainly had started to display a lot of the behavior patterns associated with paranoia."

I studied his face for a few moments.

"How close are you to the Hennessys, Mr. Lee?"

"You asked me that yesterday, Detective, and the answer is the same today as it was then. I am not close to them. We have barely a passing acquaintance." He sighed. "I am not trying to protect Senator Hennessy, if that is what you are implying. I have no love for her or her politics."

"Here is what I don't understand, Mr. Lee . . ." I frowned and scratched my head. "What is there in what you have told me today, that you could not have told me yesterday?"

He nodded several times like he understood my question perfectly, but the answer was plain to see.

"You must remember, Detective Stone, that David and I were friends for a long time. As I told you yesterday, I was also very fond of his wife, Samantha. We moved, and to some extent still move, in a fairly small social circle. In a small circle like that, reputation counts for a lot. David had, and still has, a very good reputation, and believe it or not, Samantha still benefits from that reputation. She is an editor; her late husband was a well-respected journalist. They are both part of, if you like, the 'clan.' If it gets out that he was not only being unfaithful to her, but also that he had lost it and become delusional, that would be humiliating and even damaging to Samantha. I am sure you can see that."

"So why the change of heart?"

He took a deep breath. "This is a murder investigation. I believe that David's state of mind, *and* Katie's, at the time of his death, could be significant factors. I don't pretend to know who killed him, Detective, but I do believe it's important that, at least from my point of view as a lawyer, he was not at any time a significant threat to Carol Hennessy." He gave a sudden laugh. "My God! The internet is rife with wild and outrageous allegations against her, and frankly, what David was presenting as earth-shattering proof was no better than what is on the 'net."

I nodded. "I see." I paused a moment to think. "Mr. Lee, did David ever mention a source? A particular source that could provide him with conclusive evidence, proof, of the allegations he planned to make in his article?"

He narrowed his eyes and stared at my face, as though he was trying to read what was behind it.

"A source, like who?"

I smiled. "Well, that's what I am asking you, Mr. Lee. Did he ever mention such a source?"

He shook his head. "Not in so many words, no. Nothing specific. He rambled about having sources, in the plural, but he never mentioned a particular person. I mean, who . . . ?"

I waited for him to finish his question, but he didn't. Finally, I said, "So if I said to you that David had made contact with the hit man who had carried out Carol Hennessy's last ten contracts, you could not relate that to anything that David had told you in your last meetings with him?"

He stared at me fixedly. After a bit, he gave his head a few short, quick shakes. "No, no, that doesn't sound like anything he said to me. I wouldn't give any credence to that."

"You wouldn't?"

"No." He laughed without much humor. "No, I wouldn't."

"Based on what, Mr. Lee?"

He licked his lips and swallowed. "Based . . ." He laughed again. "Based on the fact that he never said anything of the sort to me. I mean, God! Don't get me wrong! Like I said, I am no fan of hers, and there is no question that the people who cross her *do* tend to drop like flies! But that does not by any stretch of the imagination constitute evidence!"

Dehan sat forward and placed her elbows on the table. Her expression was more curious than challenging. "Let me see if I understand you, Mr. Lee. If what you are saying is right, and Dave posed no threat to Carol Hennessy . . ." She spread her hands. "No more threat than a thousand cranks on the web, then it follows that she and her team were probably not even aware of him."

He nodded. His expression was one of relief. "I am pretty convinced of that, Detective. I would lay money on it. They didn't even know he existed."

"So, if that is correct, this apparent execution-style killing was no such thing."

"That's going a little beyond where I am qualified to go, Detective, but if I were her defense attorney, I'd be asking, what makes it an execution? The fact that he was shot once in the head? That doesn't make it an execution, right? That just means the killer was a cold-blooded son—or daughter—of a bitch! In fact, correct me if I'm wrong"—another small laugh—"but isn't the classic execution in the back of the head? You make the guy kneel down and shoot him at the base of the skull. I'd say a shot in the face, or the forehead, is not an execution. I'd say it was pretty personal. You're looking right into the victim's eyes, right?"

"So, really, cutting right to the chase, Mr. Lee, what you are saying is that your money is on Katie. Your personal opinion is that Katie killed Dave."

He raised both his hands palm out as though he was backing away from her. "Woah! I never said that!"

She pressed him. "But it is what you are implying, isn't it? If it was not an execution motivated by his proposed article, then who else would have reason to kill him?" He hesitated, but she supplied the words. "Samantha or Katie? Who else?"

He shook his head. "Not Samantha."

"She didn't even know about Katie or the apartment at that time. She didn't find out until after he was killed."

He nodded. "That's right."

Dehan glanced at me. "So who does that leave us?"

He ran his fingers through his hair again. "Well, I mean, when you put it like that, I guess . . . But really, Detectives, it is not my place. I just thought I should tell you about the content of my meetings with Dave at that time."

I nodded and smiled at him. "And I am very glad you did, Mr. Lee. It has been very helpful. Was there anything else?"

He shook his head. "No. That was it." He glanced at his watch and smiled at us apologetically. "I should really be getting on."

"Sure."

We all stood, and he shook hands with us. "I hope I haven't confused things even more than they were already!"

I put my hand on his shoulder and guided him toward the door. "Not at all, Mr. Lee. You have been a great help."

I watched him go down the stairs and turned to look at Dehan, who was leaning on the doorjamb of the interrogation room. She said, "So he was pretty subtle about it, but he made a real play to shift the suspicion onto Katie."

I nodded. "He did. He did do that." I walked back and stood looking down at her. "And I am still trying to decide whether there was a veiled threat in among all that bullshit."

She nodded. "Yeah, I got that too. 'People who go up against her drop like flies. But that's not evidence.' Subtle."

"You know what my gut is telling me, Dehan?"

"It's too early for lunch, Stone."

I shook my head. "No, my gut is telling me that Lee is in bed with Hennessy."

She raised an eyebrow. "Literally or figuratively?"

"Certainly figuratively, possibly literally too. But be that as it may, two gets you twenty that he is her boy. The question is, to what extent?"

She became serious. "Shit, that works. Dave tells Lee about his investigation. Lee tells Hennessy they have a problem. Hennessy tells him to solve the problem, and Lee goes 'round to Dave's apartment, pops a cap in him with his own gun, and disposes of the article and the laptop. He certainly had enough knowledge of Dave's habits to know where the gun would be. Plus, Dave knew him well enough to let him in without having to force the lock."

I nodded. "I think we need to look a little closer at Lee and Hennessy. Let's dig a little deeper into their pasts, business activities, boards they sit on, directorships, clubs, favorite restaurants . . . the works. I want to find what connections there are between these two, going back ten or eleven years. They won't be obvious, but there is something here, Dehan. I can smell it."

She narrowed her eyes. "I'm going to start with him. I'll write his biography since 2007, what he's done, where he's been, who he's screwed—see if any red flags pop up. Then I'll do hers and see how they cross-reference."

"Good. I'll make a start on her. I'll look at the activity of the Hennessy Foundation too, look at their major projects and investments. We can compare notes and see if they overlap anywhere."

She punched me gently on the shoulder and we made our way downstairs. There was a spring to her step. We paused in the lobby to look out at the day. The sky was clearing and a brisk, cold breeze was scattering the clouds. She grinned at me. "We done good, Sensei. You want a coffee and a donut?"

"You know I do."

FOURTEEN

We worked in silence for the next couple of hours, drinking lots of quasi-coffee and eating too many donuts. Research of this sort is the slowest and most tedious form of investigation, because all you can do is read, make notes, and try to assimilate and remember what you have read, and where you have read it.

Dehan worked with close focus and an air of determination. I stopped often to stretch, to stand and walk around, to get more coffee and more donuts. But every time I looked at her, with her dark, intense eyes and her black hair knotted behind her head, the expression on her face was one of total concentration. I am certain that in the hours that she spent there, she hardly moved a muscle. Yet her body seemed perfectly relaxed and at ease.

At one thirty I looked into my empty coffee cup, checked my watch, and said, "I'm going to get some lunch. You want to take a break?"

She stared at me for a moment, as though only her eyes were seeing me, but her brain was still looking at her computer screen.

"What?"

"Lunch. One thirty. Rest. You. Take."

She frowned, then her face cleared. "Oh, right. No. Get me two beef and salad, will you?"

"Drink?"

"Water."

I stepped into the bright, icy afternoon, thrust my hands into my pockets, and made my way toward the deli on the corner. Everything I had read over the last two and a half hours tended to consolidate the reputation the Hennessys had acquired for being corrupt and believing themselves above the law. But it also consolidated my personal view that they were as clever and skilled as they were corrupt. It's a thing you get used to when you're a cop. There are certain people you just know are guilty. You know it, they know you know it—everybody knows it. But there isn't a damn thing you can do about it because they consistently cover their tracks just enough so that there is no actual proof.

From the Clearwater real estate scandal back in the early '80s to the establishment of the Hennessy Foundation and its links to Islamic fundamentalist groups and the arms trade, every step along the way where their associates had been indicted, tried, and even jailed, the Hennessys had managed to walk away unscathed. One journalist dubbed them the Teflon Two, because nothing would stick to them.

I had made a pretty comprehensive chart of the major deals they had done from 1979 to the present. Now it seemed all their business interests were concentrated under the umbrella of the Hennessy Foundation, shielded behind their status as an NGO, which enabled them to receive very handsome donations tax free from very questionable international figures.

I had then focused on the last eleven years and started to list all the enterprises, initiatives, and companies that were owned or partially owned by the Hennessy Foundation, or in which the Foundation had invested substantial sums of money. It had proved to be a massive undertaking. There were more than two thousand enterprises and initiatives that had received some kind of investment from them over the last eleven years. By the same token, the Hennessys themselves had not personally invested a dime in anything over that same period.

And to complicate matters more, there was the associated Hennessy Investment Fund, whose job it was to take all the capital held by the Foundation and invest it so as to maximize the Foundation's resources in order to fund their work "helping others to live the best life they can."

Along the way they had also provided a number of Islamic terrorist groups with the best arsenals they could, and placed themselves among the one hundred richest and most powerful people in the country. Carol Hennessy came in around number sixty in the Forbes 100.

I climbed the steps and made my way back into the detectives' room. There I stopped for a moment and observed Dehan. She had not moved. She was still sitting, reading from the screen of her laptop. Suddenly I knew, beyond any possibility of a doubt, that this unrelenting, unflinching, totally focused hunter would find her prey. She would not move until she had found that link between Lee and Hennessy. I also knew beyond a doubt that the link existed. It was there. It was skillfully hidden. But Dehan would find it.

And I knew one more thing: somehow I had to look Hennessy in the eye and let her know that we were after her, and we were going to get her. When I did that, when she saw that in my eyes, she would falter and she would make her mistake. And then we would get her and her triggerman.

I put Dehan's sandwich down in front of her along with her bottle of water. Then I dropped into my chair and picked up my phone.

It rang twice and Shelly answered.

"Hey, tough guy. Realized the error of your ways? Can't stay away?"

"Something like that. I need you to introduce me to Carol Hennessy."

"No can do. I don't have that kind of access."

"I don't believe you, but let's pretend. What *can* you do?"

"The next best thing. There is a fundraiser tonight at the Rockford Center, Schools for Tropical Guinea, something like that. You want to come as my plus one?"

"Yes. When?"

"Tonight. Seven thirty. I'll pick you up."

"Is it black tie?" I saw Dehan look up, stare at me for a moment, and then continue reading.

"Yup."

I sighed. "Okay, but you'll have to pick me up from my house."

"You have a deal. I hope this gets me brownie points."

"It will. See you at seven."

"My pleasure!"

"Yeah, and thanks."

I hung up.

Dehan swiveled her eyes at me as though she would want to slap me if she didn't feel such an overpowering sense of contempt. She said, "Shelly Pearce?"

"Mm-hm. Don't be jealous, darling. I have to see Hennessy, and I mean to see her tonight."

She raised an eyebrow and turned back to the screen.

I threw her my keys across the desk. "Pick me up tomorrow morning."

She eyed the keys, then my face, and I swear green venom dropped from her lips when she said, "Are you sure you'll be there?"

"Yes, Dehan, I am sure I will be there. Don't be an ass."

She swiveled her eyes back to the screen, and after a couple of minutes she picked up the keys and put them in her pocket.

———

THE ROCKFORD CENTER was a permanent exhibition located in a large dome, set in its own garden and surrounded by fountains. Opposite was the Rockford Building on the Avenue of the Americas in Manhattan. The exhibition it hosted was described as "an ongoing tribute to those philanthropists committed to elevating humanity to its highest potential." It consisted of an ever-changing display of photographs, films, and installations that illustrated variously how wonderful these philanthropists were, how limited the potential of those they helped was in comparison to the potential of the philanthropists, and how starkly impoverished were the lives of those who were poor—truly poor—in the poorest countries of the world. Put more briefly, it seemed to say, "Look at us, aren't we wonderful!"

Shelly had picked me up in a limo. She looked aggressively attractive in a crimson dress with a gash up to her right hip, and a diamond necklace that looked real and did nice things for her cleavage.

The chauffeur deposited us at the end of a red carpet that led to the glistening plate glass entrance of the exhibition center. There was a handful of photographers and a small crowd of celebrity spotters, but they ignored us because Mark Zuckerberg and his wife were just ahead of us. Shelly took my arm and leaned in to me.

"Have you read the guest list?"

I tried not to sigh. "No."

"It reads like the Forbes 400. Bill Gates is here, George Soros . . . all of them."

I wondered for a moment how it felt for Carol Hennessy to know that there were almost sixty people in America who were richer and more powerful than she was. I put the question to Shelly as we stepped through the door and she handed over her invitation. I took two glasses of champagne from a passing tray and gave one to her. She took it and studied my face as she sipped.

"You're gunning for her, but have you any actual, concrete evidence?"

"You know I can't answer that question."

She thought for a moment, then said, "You know, John, we

are both investigators, and we both know that evidence is a very subjective thing."

I shook my head. "No, it isn't. Evidence should be objective."

"Okay, if you are talking about DNA or fingerprints. But you know as well as I do that if one person states firmly enough on TV that they saw smoke beyond the trees, by the end of the day there will be a hundred people who believe they saw smoke beyond the trees, even though there was no smoke to be seen. And within a week there will have been a raging forest fire, where there was none."

I sighed. "Shelly, I am not in the business of framing innocent people. I am not here to take somebody down just because they look guilty. I'm with William Blackstone when he says that it's better that ten guilty men go free than that one innocent one should suffer . . ."

She smiled. "It's a hundred guilty men, and it was Benjamin Franklin."

I smiled back. "In a letter to Benjamin Vaughn in 1785, paraphrasing William Blackstone in his Commentaries on the Laws of England in 1765. You see, you are not the only one, Shelly, who likes to be sure of her facts."

"Touché. But be careful, John Stone, nobody likes a know-it-all."

"That would explain a few things."

She laid her hand on my chest. "Come on, let's mix."

For the next hour, we sipped and mixed and chatted, mainly with other members of the press and very few billionaires. Eventually, I found Hennessy. She was talking to a small crowd of people who had the look of foreign dignitaries from developing countries. D'Angelo was there, in the background. He caught sight of me and Shelly and looked away. But after a moment, he muttered something in his mistress' ear. She seemed to ignore him, but after a while she looked over to us. I glanced at Shelly and saw that their eyes met. But Shelly looked away, and so did Hennessy.

I raised an eyebrow. "I guess you're not going to introduce me, then."

She shook her head. "No. I believe she is a good person, John. I don't believe any of the stories about her, and I don't believe she is capable of murder." She shrugged. "She has devoted her life to helping the dispossessed and the underprivileged. I admire her."

"But you won't obstruct me."

"If you can prove—with hard facts—what you believe to be true, then you should do your job. But don't expect me to help you in persecuting her."

"You're close, aren't you?"

She hesitated. "We were once. But that's another story. I admire her."

That was when I saw him. He was about twenty yards away, beyond an ice sculpture, in an evening suit that probably cost as much as my car.

I turned to Shelly. "Will you excuse me for a moment, Shelly? I'll be right back."

She looked a little sad. "Of course. Go do your job, Detective Stone."

I crossed the room and strolled up to Jackson Lee. He was chatting urbanely to a cluster of attractive women in sparkling dresses. They seemed to think that what he was saying was funny. I wondered if he would think that I was funny.

"Good evening, Lee. What a surprise to find you here."

The women all turned to stare at me. Lee blinked at least half a dozen times. "Detective Stone. What are you doing here?"

I smiled as though his question surprised me. "The same as you. I was invited. Didn't you know, Lee? I am a great benefactor of the underprivileged, of society's marginalized minorities, of those who have no voice and are the victims of abuse. Those are my people, and I look out for them."

He didn't answer, and I looked at the sparkling girls with which he had surrounded himself. "Mr. Lee and I have a little business to discuss in private. He'll catch up with you in just a little while, won't you, Lee?"

"Um . . ." He looked at them and nodded. "Yes, indeed. I'll catch up with you in just a moment."

They looked put out, muttered something about "Yeah, sure," and drifted away.

I leered at Lee. "Introduce me to Hennessy."

"*What?*"

"Do it now."

"I can't just go over and . . ."

"I'm not giving you an option, Lee. I know you're connected. This is your chance to start backing the right horse."

He frowned and shook his head. "No! Leave me alone. How the hell did you get in here, anyway?"

"You'd be surprised at the friends I have, Lee. Now I am going to give you one more chance to do the right thing. Introduce me to Hennessy, now."

"No!"

"Do you know what I have in my pocket?"

He sighed. "Stone. Leave me alone or I'll call security."

I grinned. "I really wouldn't do that, Lee, because by the time they get here, the two ounces of crack cocaine I have in my pocket will be in your pocket, and you'll be facedown on the floor and cuffed and facing prosecution for possession in the third degree. That's a class B felony, Lee, punishable by one to nine years in prison. And you can be sure I will make it a show trial."

"You wouldn't . . ."

I laughed. "Why not? Because you're connected? Screw you. Did you see who my date is, tonight? The editor in chief of the *New York Telegraph*. You know what she'd pay me for that exclusive?"

He had gone very pale. "You're out of your mind."

"Very probably. Now we are going to stroll over, like old pals, and you are going to introduce me to Carol Hennessy."

"Jesus Christ!"

"Somehow, I don't think he's on your team."

He placed his empty glass on a passing tray and picked up a full one. He drained off half of it, took a deep breath, and led me across the crowded room to where Hennessy was talking to D'Angelo. They were moving slowly away from the group she'd been talking to.

She looked up at us as we approached, and I noticed that her eyes were a very pale blue, and very hard, like diamonds that managed somehow to be ugly. I also noticed that D'Angelo was shaking his head at Lee. Lee's voice croaked as he spoke.

"Senator Hennessy, what an honor. I have been required, in the strongest possible terms . . ." He laughed as he gestured toward me. "I have literally been given no option but to introduce you to . . . to my acquaintance, Detective John Stone, of the NYPD."

She looked at me with cryogenic eyes and a face that was devoid of any expression at all.

"Detective Stone, aren't you a little out of your element?"

I shook my head. "Not at all. I feel right at home here. It's just like Hunts Point, only with less diamonds and more coke."

"Is that a joke?"

"No."

"What do you want, Detective Stone?"

"I want to talk to you, Senator Hennessy. And let me tell you something before you answer. I will talk to you. I am not a Rottweiler. Rottweilers piss themselves and whimper when they see me coming. I am not relentless or obstinate either. Relentless and obstinate adopt the fetal position and sob when they see me coming. You need to know that I am here, Senator Hennessy, and you need either to kill me, or talk to me. Which is it going to be?"

There was a very embarrassed silence. D'Angelo had gone ashen, and Lee was staring at me with his mouth slightly open. But Hennessy was giving me all the confirmation I had been looking for in my little speech. I have seen people decide to kill me several times in my career. Looking into the eyes of somebody who has decided to kill you is a unique experience. They transmit some kind of subliminal message which tells you that that part of the brain that deals in empathy and compassion has shut down, and they have made a commitment that goes beyond what normal human beings are capable of. They are going to do a terrible thing to you. That was what I saw in Senator Carol Hennessy's eyes. And I also saw something else. She had arrived at that decision without difficulty. It was a place she was used to.

She gave a small sigh.

"Very well, Detective Stone. Come to my office tomorrow, at the Foundation. We'll talk there and we'll reach some kind of understanding."

"Good. What time?"

She turned to D'Angelo. "What time?"

He blinked several times and drew breath. "Um, three. Three tomorrow afternoon."

She looked at me with her ice-blue eyes, calibrating me, calculating, trying to read me. "Satisfied?"

I shook my head. "No. I'll see you tomorrow, Hennessy."

I walked away, toward where I had left Shelly. She was talking to a couple of guys with expensive hair perms but excused herself as she saw me approaching and came to meet me.

"You are either going to make my career or destroy me. Which is it?"

I shrugged with my eyebrows. "That's up to you. You have to make a choice about whom you are going to back. But I'll give you a tip, Shelly, because I like you and I believe you are a good person."

"So much bewildering stuff in one short speech. A cop who says whom? You like me? I'm a good person? A tip?"

"All of those things. Within the next forty-eight hours, Senator Carol Hennessy will make an attempt on my life. When you see that happen, make a choice about where you stand."

She stared at me. "You're crazy."

I nodded. "Very probably."

She stared at me for a long moment. Then shook her head. "You are too intense for me, John. You are just all, totally, all or nothing. There is no gray area for you, is there? You're just full on, all the time."

I wasn't sure what to answer. For a moment I had a flash of my wife saying something similar to me, a long time ago. And at the same time I saw Dehan, lounging in her chair, staring at the screen of her laptop, totally focused, full on, no gray areas. Then my cell rang. I pulled it from my pocket and looked at the screen. It was Dehan.

I glanced at Shelly. "I have to take this."

She sighed. "Detective Dehan?"

"Yeah, Stone."

"Hey, Sensei. Hope I didn't get you out of bed."

"Funny."

"Soon as you can, Stone. You need to see what I've got."

I looked Shelly straight in the eyes and said to Dehan, "I'm on my way." I hung up. "I'm sorry."

She gave a cute, lopsided smile and said, "I misread you, Stone. I misread you both. It's not that she's in love with you, though she clearly is. It's that you're both in love with each other, but you won't admit it." She stepped forward and kissed me on the cheek. "Be happy, John, but just remember, under all that attitude and cocky self-confidence, she is just a vulnerable, lonely girl."

I smiled and shook my head. "I have no idea what you are talking about, Shelly. But thanks, and you know you have the exclusive on this."

She patted my arm and I left, with a hot pellet of excitement in my belly. The game had shifted; now we were moving in for the kill.

FIFTEEN

IT WAS AFTER NINE P.M. WHEN I CLIMBED OUT OF THE taxi under the frozen stars and walked into the station and made my way to the detectives' room. Most of the desks were empty, but Dehan was still there, sitting in a pool of lamplight. She looked up as I approached and grinned at me.

"Whoa! Look at you! James Bond, eat your heart out. How come you never dress like that for me, Stone?"

I dropped into my chair and studied her grinning face for a moment, smiling at her. "I'll tell you what, if you wear a long, red satin dress with a split from ankle to hip, a pearl choker, and those little high-heeled shoes with a strap across the ankle? You know the ones? You wear that, and I'll take you to dinner in my tux. Deal?"

"In your dreams, Sensei. Get your head out of the gutter and focus on this." She threw a sheet of paper across the desk at me. "Pre-2008 Lee was an attorney working for Bismarck, Jones and Epstein, a reputable firm in Manhattan. In February 2008, he ditches David Thorndike, a good client, and two weeks later Thorndike is murdered. Now, buckle up. Three months after that, Lee resigns from Bismarck, Jones and Epstein to take up two directorships, one on the board of Consolidated Imports, the other on the board of PC Derivatives. Both New York–based import-export companies. His position in those companies is non-executive. In other words, he gets paid for doing nothing."

"Holy cow."

"The cow gets holier. Over the next nine years, he accumulates four more directorships, all non-executive: Allied Petrochemicals, Gulf Shipping, United Investment, and Petro-Plastics. I guess he must be really good at doing nothing, because he keeps getting headhunted by multinationals that want him to do nothing for them—and are ready to pay big bucks for it. He is on the board of directors of six corporations, making an average of six hundred grand from each one every year. His total annual income is three million, six hundred and forty-five thousand bucks. For doing zip."

"Do we know anything about these companies . . . ?"

"Did I tell you you could unfasten your seat belt? Siddown, lover boy. Each and every one of these companies belongs, directly or indirectly, to the Hennessy Investment Fund, in that they own controlling shares in them, or they own a company that owns them." She grabbed another sheet of paper and slid it across the desk to me. "Consolidated Imports and PC Derivatives both belong directly to the Hennessy Investment Fund. Allied Petrochemicals belongs to the Global Corporation, in which the Hennessy Fund has a forty-five percent stake. Gulf Shipping belongs to Consolidated Imports, and Petro-Plastics belongs to United Investment, which in turn belongs to PC Derivatives. All, ultimately, are controlled by the Hennessy Investment Fund, and of course Carol Hennessy is the CEO of the Fund."

"So the directorships were a payoff."

She shrugged and spread her hands. "It's not proof, yet, but it is very, very suggestive. He was in Hennessy's pocket. When Dave told him about the article, he passed it on to Hennessy, with the added warning that he knew how good and how thorough Dave would be in his investigation. Plus, if we are to believe the anonymous letter—and it's a big 'if'—there was the added risk that

Dave was in touch with her hit man. That's something even Mrs. Teflon couldn't slide out of. So she makes a deal with Lee. He kills Dave, and she takes care of him for life."

I thought about it for a long moment, turning it around and examining it from every angle.

"That is good work, Dehan. Exceptional. I have a meeting with Hennessy tomorrow at three. We should get Lee in, at midday, and confront him with this, see if we can make him crack. Then go for Hennessy."

She made a "yeah, but" face and said, "Nnnyeah, maybe. Just hear me out a bit."

"Talk."

"Okay, we both said how weird it was that as soon as you rattled Hennessy's cage by talking to D'Angelo, we got an anonymous tip-off *and* Lee suddenly came clean."

"Right, that's true, and it's still weird."

"Well, what if the mysterious hit man who was operating for eight years as her exclusive executioner is just a red herring? I mean, she used Lee for Dave, right?"

"Probably. We haven't proved that yet. And besides, he was presumably retired by then and spilling the beans."

"Okay, but even just from a common-sense point of view, who has an assassin on a retainer? Who *expects* to have that many people iced?"

I scratched my chin. "Yeah, I take your point. But if anybody did, I would expect it to be Carol Hennessy."

She looked unhappy. "I'm not comfortable with it."

I shrugged. "Okay, I agree. We keep it in reserve until we can confirm it. You happy with that?"

"Yeah. Like the *Telegraph*, we confirm every fact before we commit to it."

We sat staring at each other for a while. It was something we did sometimes when we were thinking. It freaked other people out, but it helped us to focus and concentrate. But this time, she frowned at me and said, "What?"

I gave my head a little jerk. "You are a very exceptional investigator, Dehan. And an exceptional person."

She made no expression with her face but kept watching me while she picked up an eraser and threw it at me.

"Cut it out, Stone. Stop getting intense on me. That's *my* job. I'm Jewish, remember? You're the cool Anglo-Saxon WASP. Especially dressed like that. Jeez! Lock up your daughters!"

I laughed. "Well, as long as I am dressed like this, what do you say? You want to grab a meal?"

She gave a mischievous smile. "Yeah, why not? Even if you didn't dress for me."

"I told you, red satin."

She stood and grabbed her jacket. "Maybe I'll surprise you one day."

I grinned. "But don't forget the little strappy shoes and the pearls."

"Looks like you won't."

We stepped into the cold night. A biting wind was coming off the Sound, and I paused a moment and shivered. I glanced up at the sky, but the glare from the city had obliterated all but the brightest stars. She stopped a couple yards ahead of me on the sidewalk and turned back, dangling my keys from her fingers, watching me and smiling. The amber light from the streetlamps touched her skin. It was an odd moment, as though my brain had decided to take a photograph of that instant, to preserve it for all time. I smiled back.

"Do you remember the town of Shamrock, in Texas[1]?"

"How could I forget?"

"We came out of . . . What was that place?"

"Big Vern's Steak House. I had never seen so many stars." She had known what I was going to say without my having to tell her. I stepped down, and she went on, "Good steaks too." She linked her arm through mine, and we walked toward the Jag. "I've never

---

1. See *An Ace and a Pair.*

been on the arm of a man in a tuxedo before, and I probably never will again. You going to drive or shall I?"

I didn't answer for a moment. My mind was elsewhere. Finally, I said, "How about you drive there, and I drive home?"

She hesitated a second, and I saw her brows contract. "Okay . . ." I went around to the passenger side and leaned on the roof watching her. She said suddenly, "What's up with you today, Stone? There's something *odd* about you."

I sighed. "I don't know. Something Shelly said. It's stupid. It's nothing."

Her frown deepened. "What? What did she say?" Then her frown turned to a scowl. "You're not getting feelings for her, are you?"

I laughed. "No, far from it. It was something about you. Well, about both of us."

Now she was intrigued, and she leaned on the roof across from me. I was beginning to shiver, and I could hear her teeth chattering. Big clouds of condensation were billowing from our mouths.

"What? What did she say?"

"Nah! It was stupid, and it would probably make you mad anyway . . ."

"Stone! Tell me! What did she say . . . ?"

I smiled, then grinned. The light from the lamp over her head made her eyes shine, and she grinned back. For just a second I had the strange feeling that we had already said everything that we needed to say, that we both knew everything that was in the other's mind, and no more speaking was necessary. We stood like that for a moment that was timeless, in silence, smiling at each other.

Then the high whine of an accelerating engine ripped the night in half. I saw her blink in slow motion and turn to look. Tires screamed on the wet blacktop, and I saw the dark Audi skid around the corner. I was already shouting at Dehan to duck. Moving impossibly slow, she turned to look at me. I was running, as though I were wading waist-deep in water, scrambling around the trunk of the Jag as the Audi accelerated. I saw the back window roll down. I saw the flash of fire, once, twice, three, four, five times. Then the noise like firecrackers going off. But by then I was throwing myself at Dehan, dragging her to the ground.

The sound of the engine receded. The tires squealed around the corner at the end of Fteley Avenue, and I lay for a moment, staring down into her face. She was motionless. Her eyes were wide, staring up into mine. Then I saw the blood on her blouse, and the blood on my hands. I said, "Dehan, no . . ." I felt the searing, burning pain in my chest, and black oblivion enfolded me.

SIXTEEN

I OPENED MY EYES BRIEFLY. I FELT STRANGELY AT PEACE. There was intense, burning pain, but I was somehow detached from it. A dark sky stretched to infinity overhead, pierced by one or two silver stars; and there was lamplight. A cold breeze touched my face. There were voices, shouting but indistinct. They sounded worried.

I closed my eyes and returned to the peace and the stillness.

———

SOMETHING DISTURBED THE STILLNESS. My eyes opened of their own accord. There was a lot of glare, and the whole world seemed to be churning about me like the waters of a vast river thundering through rapids. In the midst of it, a man peered into my face and shone a light in my eyes. I wanted to ask about Dehan, but I didn't know how to speak. My mind tried to reach out to him, to seize hold of him and scream at him. What about Dehan?

What about Dehan?

In my mind I saw her staring eyes, the dense blood on her

blouse and on my hands. I tried to talk, but no sounds emerged from my mouth.

What about Dehan?

A voice said, "What about his partner?"

Dehan!

"Gone . . ."

There was a hollowness, a bottomless emptiness. A hurt that was beyond words. I closed my eyes and sank down into it.

———

A LIGHT that was too bright. Beings in ugly green shrouds with masks over their faces. Cold steel instruments cutting into me. But above all a deep pain, an intolerable pain that wanted to drain away my will to live.

Somebody said, "Jesus! He's awake!"

But I closed my eyes and embraced the darkness, because only the darkness could take away the appalling ache.

———

BLACK GLASS.

Black glass, frosted at the corners by the cold night, stained with amber light by the streetlamps outside. Silence. The drapes open, which seemed odd. The sound of a single car, far away in the night. The lights are out. The room is dark. There is an empty chair by my bed.

I close my eyes and sink back into the emptiness.

———

THE GRAY LIGHT of dawn has washed the amber from the windowpane. The heavy clouds have returned, as though painted in watercolors, bellying low and raining on New York. Drops of rain, trickling in sporadic runs down the glass. Beneath the glass, the radiator. In front of the radiator, the chair that last night had been empty. And in it, deeply asleep, pale and exhausted, Dehan, uninjured, unhurt.

I smiled. I may have wept a little. Deep gratitude seeped through my heart and my aching body, warming my soul like a fine Irish whiskey. I lay watching her for what might have been half an hour or more, as the day stirred and stretched and yawned.

I closed my eyes, not to sleep, but to assimilate the fact that the blood on her blouse had been mine. That the look on her face had been shock. That she was not gone, she was here, alive, beside me. Eventually I heard her stir, sit up, and yawn. I opened my eyes, and she offered me a tired smile.

"Hey, Sensei. How'ya feeling?"

I offered her a blink and a small sideways twitch of my head. "I'm okay. I've had worse hangovers from cheap whiskey. How long have you been here?"

She shrugged. "A while."

"They said you'd . . ." I paused, enjoying the sight of her. "They said, when we arrived at the hospital, they said you'd gone. I thought they meant . . ."

She stared at me a long time, then smiled. "I'd gone for a checkup. They made me. When they said you were out of danger, I went to get a change of clothes." She paused and looked at the floor. "Stone, they weren't gunning for me. They were gunning for you. If you'd just ducked instead of . . ."

She clenched her jaw and looked away. I saw a tear spill from her eye, and she wiped it away with the back of her hand.

I managed a small laugh, which caused more pain than you'd think possible. "Hey! Did you think I was trying to protect you?"

She glared at me with wet eyes.

I laughed again and winced. "Nah! I was just trying to draw their fire away from my Jag! Was it damaged, by the way?"

She laughed wetly and blew her nose. "No. It came off better than you and me. I got a bruised ass."

"That's a relief." I paused a moment, then said, "So I'm guessing I took a slug. Did they catch the shooter?"

She shook her head. "You were lucky, Stone. Very lucky. You shouldn't be here. You took two slugs. One hit your left shoulder. It was through and through and managed to miss anything important. Four inches farther south and it would have gone right through your heart. The other . . ." She heaved a big sigh and stared at me. "It must have been as you were dragging me down, the way you were moving, it was a miracle . . ."

I smiled at her. "Did the earth move for you?"

"Stop it, you big dummkopf. The slug caught you at an angle and lodged between your ribs. A fraction of a second earlier, it would have punctured your heart."

I shrugged. "Lucky me. How bad is the damage?"

"There was no major, invasive surgery. Doc said you'll probably be home in a couple of days."

I grunted. I thought about it for a moment. "It's pretty cool."

She made a long-suffering face. "What is?"

"Getting shot in a tux while saving a beautiful woman just before climbing into your classic Jaguar. How many kids dream about doing that?"

She didn't smile. "John, I think you need to take this seriously."

"Okay, I'll take it seriously, but I need you to do something for me, Dehan."

"Of course, anything. Just name it."

"Find me some coffee and a couple of croissants, will you?"

She left, and while she was gone I practiced moving my shoulder. The damage the slugs had caused was minimal, but the pain was intense. Fortunately it was my left shoulder. Using my right arm, I eased myself up into a sitting position and thought about getting out of bed. However, the thought of Dehan coming back and seeing my bare ass stopped me. I figured I'd give it a try after breakfast.

She returned fifteen minutes later with a bag of croissants and a large paper cup of black coffee. She also brought Newman with her and a woman in a white coat who smiled at me and said, "I'm Dr. Stadler. I operated on you last night. My advice to you is do the lottery today. If your luck holds, you'll hit the jackpot."

"That's a nice thought. That close, huh?"

She nodded. "We are talking microseconds and millimeters. That was a lethal shot. As it is, the damage it did was minimal."

"How about the other one, in my shoulder?"

"Ironically, that one did more damage, but neither of them has caused any kind of serious harm. We'll keep you in overnight to monitor you. Then I recommend a couple of weeks of dolce far niente, preferably in bed." She pointed at my shoulder. "It's going to hurt, so I'll prescribe some powerful painkillers. It'll be a few weeks before you are back to normal."

I nodded. "Okay, thanks, Doc."

"I'll drop in and check on you later."

Newman opened the door for her, and when she'd gone, he came and sat next to the bed in Dehan's chair.

"We're checking CCTV footage in the area, John. Detective Dehan gave us a fair description of the vehicle. With a bit of luck, we may be able to trace the car."

I shook my head. "It will be stolen."

He nodded. "In all probability. Now, listen to me, I want you to consider taking a couple of weeks off, John. More if you need it. Dehan can take care of things . . ."

"Not going to happen, sir."

"Now, John, be reasonable and think this through."

"I don't need to think it through. I rattled her cage and she tried to kill me. Now is not the time to take a couple of weeks off. Now is the time for me to go in for the kill. What does it say about the NYPD, about the Forty-Third, about you, if we let this woman send killers after our officers, and our only response is to back down? What message do we send to these parasites who believe themselves above the law? No, sir. You can order me off the case if you want, and that is your call. But I am telling you

right here and now, sir, with or without the blessing of the department, I am going after that woman, and I am going to take her
down."

"John . . ."

"Her and her goddamn empire!"

"John . . ."

"What?"

"I want you to take a few days at least, and I want you to do
some thinking."

I scowled at him. "What about?"

"You're too old to be running around getting shot."

I felt a hot pellet of anger well up in my gut. "What are you
saying?"

"I want you to think about early retirement, John, or at the
very least taking a desk job."

"You have got to be kidding!" I looked at Dehan. She was
leaning against the wall with her arms crossed and a sullen look on
her face. "Dehan? Are you a part of this?"

She shook her head.

Newman had both hands raised. "Now take it easy, John. I
don't want you to get upset."

I sat forward and scowled at him, pointing my finger at him
like a pistol. "No! You listen to me, Newman, and you listen
good! If you want me off this investigation, then you are going to
have to fire me. And then you will achieve three things." I held up
three fingers. "One, you will send a clear message to Hennessy and
all her associates that the Forty-Third will roll over and spread its
legs anytime somebody waves a gun at us. Two, I will continue my
investigation unofficially and I will tear down the Hennessy
empire with my bare hands if I have to—and I will bring her and
all her goddamn associates to justice! Three!" I was almost shouting. "You will embarrass the whole damned department, because
where the Forty-Third rolled over, the cop who got shot manned
up and took on corporate and political crime and corruption,
where the Forty-Third was too damned *chicken*!"

Dehan spoke quietly. "And you'll have to fire me too, and I'll back him every step of the way. What Hennessy has done flies in the face of everything we stand for. We cannot show weakness and we cannot back down. Stone is right, sir. She has as much as admitted her guilt. Now we go in for the kill. When the job is done, then we rest and heal."

He sighed and flopped back in his chair.

"I am not rolling over, John. But we need to put this in the hands of a younger . . ."

"Less experienced cop? So he can get shot too? I have her running scared and panicking. I have her making rash mistakes. I have the experience. *Goddamn it, John! This is our case!*"

He nodded and raised his hands again. "All right, all right. Tell me at least you'll take a couple of days to heal."

"I will if you stop upsetting me!"

He smiled reluctantly. "Fine. Just, be careful; you're both fine officers, and, well, I have come to consider you both friends. I don't want to lose you. Now, if you feel strong enough, put me up to speed. Where are you in the investigation, and how the hell did this happen?"

I gave them both a detailed account of my evening at the fundraiser, and then between us Dehan and I filled him in on what she had discovered about Lee's directorships. He listened with a deep frown furrowing his brow. When we had finished, he grunted.

"I see why you feel so strongly. I don't mind telling you I have received a couple of telephone calls from the highest levels over the last couple of days asking me what you are playing at. I don't have to tell you that we are facing a very formidable opponent, and a political conspiracy that has very far-reaching tendrils."

I nodded. "David was not exaggerating when he said that it was not dynamite, it was a nuclear bomb."

Dehan spoke suddenly, and there was bitterness in her voice.

"It's a cancer. If we leave it, it will spread, and it will end up corrupting everything. It has to be cut out and destroyed before it goes any further."

He studied her a moment, then nodded. "Whatever it costs, Detectives. You have my full support." He smiled at me. "I agree with you. Time to show what we are made of."

He stood and left, and Dehan took his chair. "So what now?"

I took the lid off my coffee, tore a chunk off one of the croissants and dunked it in the hot black brew, then stuffed it in my mouth.

"What now?" I said with my mouth full. "Now we have an appointment at three p.m. with Carol Hennessy, and I mean to be there and scare the living bejaysus out of her."

"You are going to the meeting? *Today?*"

I nodded as I dunked again. "Yup."

She shook her head. "You are one hard motherfucker, Stone!"

I grinned, wolfishly. "I know. And soon Carol Hennessy will know it too."

SEVENTEEN

DEHAN DROVE BECAUSE MY LEFT ARM WAS IN A SLING. In a right-hand-drive manual like my Jag, you need your left hand to shift the gears, and between the two of us we only had one functioning left hand. While she drove, I called my friend Bernie at the Bureau Field HQ on Broadway.

"Stone, how's it hanging, pal?"

"At the moment it's hanging in a sling."

He roared laughter down the phone. "I'm sorry to hear that, my friend. That's a great loss to womankind, hahaha!"

"Yeah, if only *they* knew that. But it's my left arm that's in a sling, Bernie, so no great loss to anybody. Listen, we need to talk."

"Oh, sure, anytime. Nothing serious, I hope."

"I was shot last night. And that's kind of what I want to talk to you about. I'd like to meet somewhere private. I'll pick you up on Broadway in an hour and a half. And Bernie, don't mention this call to anybody. I really mean that. Nobody. And don't tell anybody where you're going."

"Sounds serious."

"It is. I am particularly interested, Bernie, in assassins. World-class assassins. Operating between 1999 and 2008."

"Holy smoke . . ."

"Is right. Okay. I'm going to get off the line. Catch you later." I hung up. "Have we picked up a tail?"

She shook her head. "It's hard to tell with all this traffic, but I don't think so."

I grunted and flinched as I put my phone in my pocket. "So far, the two times that Hennessy has jumped, it has been after we made direct contact, either with her, or with D'Angelo and Lee. So far we haven't been in touch with any of them, and there is no reason to believe she has ears or eyes inside the Forty-Third. So, chances are she doesn't know yet that we are still alive. Why would she? So, it's going to be interesting to see if she's cancelled the meeting."

Dehan nodded. "Right. If she thinks we're dead, she won't bother to show." She was silent for a moment. "If she's not there, how do you want to play it?"

I thought about it. "I'll tell you what I'd *like* to do. I'd like to arrest D'Angelo and haul his ass in for questioning, and do the same to Lee. And play the bastards against each other."

She glanced at me, and her eyes were sparkling. "You want to do that?"

"I'd love to. But it's premature. Let's build up the tension a little more before we drag anyone in."

She parked just outside the main entrance to the Rockford Building on 6th Avenue and we rode the elevator to the thirty-second floor. The same prefab-pretty receptionist was at the desk and looked at me unhappily. I leaned close to her and said, "Yes, I have an appointment with Senator Carol Hennessy at three p.m. Let her know I'm here, will you?"

She took a deep breath. "Senator Hennessy is not here. She is out for lunch."

"How about D'Angelo? Is he here?"

She shook her head slowly. "No . . ."

"Is that true? You can get into a lot of trouble for lying to the cops. You know that, right?"

She nodded. "He is with her. He goes just about everywhere with her."

"Okay, so you are going to deliver a message for me. You are going to deliver it personally to Senator Hennessy, understood?" She nodded. "Tell her that the next time I see her, she is going to be in cuffs at the Forty-Third Precinct, and I am going to put her away for the rest of her sorry life. You got that?"

She nodded. "Yes, sir."

We rode the elevator down in silence, climbed back in the Jag, and took West 52nd east to Park Avenue, then followed that south to Union Square and Broadway. I called Bernie and told him we were on our way. He said he'd meet us outside the pet crematorium on Worth Street.

He was there in the doorway when we arrived. Dehan pulled up with her hazards on and Bernie ran and climbed in the back. We pulled away and headed north up Church Street. Then Dehan took a roundabout route, turning back on herself several times, till we came to Central Park South. There, we left the Jag in a parking garage and took a walk by the pond as far as the Gapstow Bridge. There, Bernie squinted at me and said, "Are you going to tell me what this is all about?"

I scanned the path around the water, then glanced at Dehan. "Did you see anything?"

She shook her head. "I think we're okay."

He frowned uneasily. "You're getting a little paranoid in your old age. What the hell is going on?"

"Somebody tried to kill me last night, Bernie. They very nearly succeeded. It was a hit, and we have solid reasons to believe that it was ordered by Senator Hennessy."

"Holy shit." He sighed. "You've always been smart, Stone, but you've never been wise, have you?"

"I don't want to get you involved, not yet anyway. The fewer people involved the better. But there is one thing you can help me with."

"Of course, anything."

Dusk was already turning the air grainy, and the cold blue sky was touched with burnished light from the dying sun. The ducks on the pond squawked and made wet flapping sounds, and the birds in the trees fluttered sporadically, like they were closing up for the evening. While Dehan kept a watch over the quiet scene, I explained to Bernie everything that had happened, and everything we had learned so far. Dehan clapped her hands and stamped her feet, moving this way and that, and Bernie listened with a deepening frown.

When I'd finished, he puffed out his cheeks and blew a big cloud of condensation that drifted away like cigar smoke.

"We've been after her, and her husband, for a long time. But they have their operation stitched up tighter than a nun's chastity belt. If what you say is true . . ."

"We may yet free the nun. What I need is a lead on this hired gun, Bernie, whoever he is. I need to know if he actually exists, and if he does, is there anyone on your wanted lists who might fit the profile."

He pulled a sheet of paper from his inside pocket. "I brought this." He opened it and handed it to me. "These were the hired killers that we were aware of in the period you mentioned. Since the nineties, hired assassins have been increasingly affiliated with terrorist groups. During the Cold War and the eighties, you had a number of pros out there who were ex-military, or trained by one of the secret services, and they were strictly mercenaries, guns for hire."

Dehan said, "Like the famous Jackal who tried to take out de Gaulle."

He nodded. "Yeah, exactly. But these days you really don't get that so much. The market for that kind of hit man is much smaller than it was, and not so lucrative. What you have now is jihadists, or in-house operatives working for the Russian Mafia or the Mob."

I shrugged with my right shoulder. "So that means our list of possibles is small."

"Yeah, pretty small. Active between the turn of the century and 2008, that we were aware of, and that the CIA shared with us, were Sean Hagan, trained by the IRA back in the day. When the IRA called the cease-fire, he put himself on the market as a hired gun. He worked for the Russians, did a few jobs for the Mob, retired about 2008.

"Then there was Saul David. We're not sure if that's his real name. He was trained by Mossad, though they later disowned him. Like Hagan, he worked for the Russians and organized crime generally. As far as we know, he is still active. Our intel is that he was operating mainly in Europe from 2000 to 2010.

"Then there is Adrian Philips, British subject, trained by the SAS but dishonorably discharged for torturing a prisoner. Known to have right-wing political views. Believed to be responsible for taking out several Mullahs and terrorist cells, not clear on whose orders, possibly CIA black ops. He was active in the States during the period you're interested in."

Dehan said, "Sounds like he could be our man."

Bernie smiled. "Only problem is he could not have been talking to David Thorndike."

I asked, "Why?"

"Because he was killed in a bomb blast in Pakistan in late October 2007." He pointed at the last name on the list. "And finally you have Hector Hernandez. No formal training, just a love of his work. Freelances for the Cartels when they need a quiet job done, and has been employed by the Mob for some jobs."

I sighed. "None of them leaps out at me. Did any of them have a special MO, a preferred method . . . ?"

He shrugged and pushed out his bottom lip. "Hernandez liked the knife. Most of his kills were stabbings. Hagan tended to shoot his victims. He was a good marksman. Saul David and Philips were the real pros. They would use whatever method was to hand, and most times they would make it look like an accident."

I nodded and looked at Dehan. She said, "That's our man. Saul David."

I scratched my head. "Only David is still active, which doesn't make a lot of sense, and Philips is dead."

Bernie studied my face a moment. "Why doesn't it make sense that he's still active?"

I gazed at the pond. "In the anonymous letter, it said that he had decided to tell Thorndike about the killing for reasons that were not clear to the person writing the letter. I always assumed that he had retired and was trying to clear his conscience in some way."

Bernie didn't look convinced. "If that was true, Stone, wouldn't he just come forward and inform the Bureau?"

"What other reason could he have?"

Dehan said, "Money? Maybe Dave offered him a cut of the proceeds."

I nodded. "Yeah, it could be that. Or it could be political. If he was radical right-wing, and his employer was left-wing, he might want to cause her damage."

Bernie spread his hands. "But then you're back to square one. Why not go directly to the Feds?"

I sighed and shook my head. "We keep going in circles. If it was money he was after, when David was killed, why didn't he approach Bob Shaw, or Shelly Pearce? Why did he go quiet?"

Dehan stared at me. "Maybe he's dead."

I looked down at the sheet of paper. "Philips died October 2007. David died the sixth of March 2008. Just four or five months later."

The sun had dropped behind the trees and the air had turned suddenly icy. Bernie shuddered and said, "I ought to be getting back. Look, you know that the minute you get something solid, this becomes a federal case, right?"

I nodded. "And we'll hand it over to you the minute I know it'll be prosecuted."

He laughed. "That is a cagey reply, Stone, but I hear you, and that is good enough for me."

I thanked him for the list, and he shook our hands warmly. "I'll make my own way back. The less we are seen together at the moment, the better. Be safe."

Dehan leaned her elbows on the bridge next to where I was standing and we watched him walk quickly away on his short, energetic legs. His camel coat flapped around his knees as he pulled it tight across his chest and turned up the collar. I sighed and shook my head again. "The information keeps building, and the more it builds, the more it incriminates Hennessy and D'Angelo—and Lee, but we still haven't a shred of anything that we can call actual, real evidence. Every bit of it is circumstantial."

She nodded. "We need David's contact. We need that hit man."

I smacked her arm with the paper and said, "Come on. You must be exhausted, and I know I am. Let's get back to the precinct."

She stared into my face.

"What did you leave at the precinct?"

I frowned. "What?"

"You're not going to any precinct, Mr. Stone. You are going home, where I am going to cook you a chicken stew, and you are going to rest!"

I smiled, perhaps a little smugly, and allowed myself to be pushed toward Park Avenue South. As we walked, my phone rang.

"Stone? This is Inspector Newman here. We have Thorndike's records. What do you want me to do with them?"

"I'm on my way home, sir. Doctor's orders . . ."

"Really? So soon? I thought they were keeping you in."

"Yeah. The Stone constitution. Can you email them to me?"

"Sure thing, John. You make sure you get your rest, you hear?"

"I hear you, sir."

I hung up, and Dehan glanced at me. "Dave's financials?"

I nodded. "Yup. Maybe this will give us what we're looking for, Dehan. It's either *cherchez la femme* or *cherchez* the filthy buck."

And as dusk turned to evening, and the lights started to wink on around Central Park, she took my good arm and we headed back toward the car, and home.

EIGHTEEN

She sat me on the sofa with my laptop and went upstairs. I'd been putting on a brave show, but the fact is, if somebody drives a half inch of lead through you, twice, no matter how nonlethal the wound, it's a deep shock to your system. Our organisms just don't like having things on the inside that are supposed to be kept on the outside, like half-inch lumps of lead. So the truth was I felt pretty wrecked and grateful for the chance to rest. I lay back on the sofa and closed my eyes, aware that my hands had started to tremble. I heard her go into my bedroom, and a few moments later she came back down with four cushions and a blanket.

"You're not stubborn," she said. "You're obstinate. It's different, you know."

She lifted my feet onto the couch and took off my shoes. I frowned at her. "What are you doing? I might have had holes in my socks. A man's socks are a very personal, intimate thing."

"Listen to you! You're rambling. You're probably feverish." She packed the cushions behind my back and laid the blanket over me. "You know what the difference is, between stubborn and obstinate? Stubborn is determined and committed; obstinate is just plain stupid."

"Hey! You backed me up in the hospital."

"Yeah? That's 'cause I'm obstinate." She put my laptop on my lap. "Are you in pain?"

"Only a lot."

"Listen to me! Of course you're in pain. I'll get you some painkillers and a whiskey."

"That should do the trick." As she walked away, I said, "I am never sure with you, Dehan, if you put it on for fun, or if this just happens to you when you are in the proximity of a kitchen."

She didn't answer. I opened up my computer and switched it on. My shoulder was beginning to throb badly, making it hard to think and focus. I could hear Dehan banging around in the kitchen. After a bit, she came back and put an occasional table beside me and handed me a glass of water and two painkillers. She had a weird look on her face which I was in too much pain to read. When she'd seen that I'd swallowed the pills, she turned on her heel and marched away to pour me the largest whiskey I had ever been given in my life. I squinted at her and saw that something weird was happening to her face. Her mouth seemed to be twitching.

"I'm going to have a shower. I may be a while. Then I'll make you a chicken stew. You'll eat a chicken stew, right? Don't be obstinate. You need to eat."

I nodded and smiled. "I'll eat a chicken stew. It sounds good." I deepened my smile. "Thanks, Dehan."

"Oh, shut up!"

She turned and went very quickly up the stairs. I took a long pull on the whiskey and closed my eyes while it did its work. *Uisce beatha*, the water of life. After a bit, I opened my eyes again and accessed my email. There were two from Inspector John Newman. Each had a PDF attachment. One was David Thorndike's bank statements for 2007 and 2008; the other was his credit card statements. I saved them to my David Thorndike folder and took another slug of whiskey. It began to mix with the painkillers, and life began to seem tolerable.

Upstairs I heard the shower start to hiss.

The statements I needed were from October 2007 to February 2008, five months. I began to go through them, item by item. Dimly, I was aware that Dehan's shower was in fact quite a long one, but I paid no real attention. At some point the water stopped hissing, and there was a long silence. But what little concentration I had was focused on the long list of expenses before me: mortgage, electricity, telephone, Wi-Fi, repayments on his car, ATM cash withdrawals.

As I came to the end of February, without having found anything significant, but having acquired a feeling of pleasurable "otherness" from the whiskey and the painkillers, I heard Dehan's feet, brisk on the stairs. She reached the bottom and looked at me.

"How you doing there, Sensei?" She sounded nasal and puffy.

I gave her a Cheshire grin. "I'm good. But you sound like you have a cold coming on. Maybe you should have some whiskey too."

"Not a bad idea, Stone. I think I'll do that."

She poured herself a drink and went into the kitchen to start cooking. I moved to his credit card. I closed my eyes for a bit and drifted among the comfortable sounds: the refrigerator opening and closing, a pot extracted from a cupboard and placed on the cooker, vegetables being chopped on a wooden board, the squeak and pop of a cork from a bottle of wine. After a bit, she started to sing softly.

I may have drifted off, because when I opened my eyes again the stew was on, there was a wonderful smell on the air, and she was washing up.

I looked at the screen in front of me and saw that in December of 2007, David had used his credit card to buy two tickets to Sri Lanka. A Christmas gift to themselves, perhaps.

I made a note and kept scrolling. Then, in the last two weeks of January, I found a series of credit card payments at gas stations in New York, Pennsylvania, Ohio, Indiana, Illinois, Missouri, Oklahoma, Texas, New Mexico, and Arizona. Neat. Then, three days later, the same thing but in reverse order. There were also a couple of motels.

I scrolled down a little further and found in the third week of February the same thing. A three-day gap and a repeat of the same states, then once again in reverse order. I sipped my whiskey and looked up. Dehan was leaning on the breakfast counter looking at me.

"You want to eat on your lap, or at the table?"

"At the table. He made three long trips in the period October to March, 2007, 2008. One, which we can probably eliminate: a two-week trip to Sri Lanka at the end of December. He bought two tickets, so I am guessing it was a Christmas holiday with Samantha. However, mid-January he takes a very long drive to Arizona and back. By the looks of it, he stayed about three days. Then, in the third week of February, he repeated the trip. So we can say conclusively that during his investigation into Senator Hennessy, he made two long trips to Arizona, where he stayed a total of six days, three and three."

She smiled. "Bingo."

"We can also say then, with some degree of certainty, that this putative hit man . . ."

"Putative hit man?"

"Supposed hit man, was in Arizona at that time. We can zero in up to a point with his motel. And a couple of the gas stops in Arizona were probably made on his way to see K, or his way back."

"That's good work, Stone."

I closed my eyes. "Tomorrow we'll call Samantha in, ask her about Arizona. Do they have some connection with the place? What reason would he have for going there? We'll ask her about Sri Lanka too. There's probably nothing in it, but it's close enough to Pakistan to warrant looking into it."

She came around, switched off the laptop, and took it away.

"Okay, Sensei. That's enough for today. The stew will be

another half hour. Now you sleep for a bit. I'll call you when it's ready."

At least, I'm guessing that's what she said, because by then I was already asleep.

———

SAMANTHA ARRIVED at ten thirty the next morning. She didn't look happy to be there. I wasn't happy to be there either. Most people don't realize it, but often as not, healing hurts more than getting injured in the first place. I was doped up, and I knew I was going to have to rely on Dehan to make sense of the interview.

I had asked Samantha when I phoned her whether she still had any of David's papers and notes from previous investigations. She told me she had, and I'd asked her to bring with her anything from the end of 2007 and January 2008. She'd said there wasn't much, but she'd bring it.

As we sat across from her, she pushed a small stack of note-books across the table toward me.

"These are his notes and ramblings from the end of 2007 and early 2008, just before he left. You're welcome to them. I'm sick of the sight of them. I tried to give them to Bob and Shelly, but they didn't want them. I just couldn't quite bring myself to throw them away."

I took them and thanked her.

"Samantha, I have only a few questions for you, but your answers could be extremely important, so I want you to think very carefully and try to be as accurate as you can. You need to be aware that this investigation could go well beyond you and David and your relationship. Do you understand that?"

She looked at me a moment before answering. Then she nodded and said, "Yes. Of course."

"First of all, in 2007 you spent Christmas in Sri Lanka. Can you tell me about that? Why Sri Lanka of all places?"

She sighed and made a long-suffering face.

"That was Dave all over. He suddenly developed this interest in Buddhism. All he could talk about was Buddhism. Buddhism this and Buddhism that and Buddhism was the answer to everything. And we had to go to Sri Lanka because Sri Lanka was the home of some special type of original Buddhism."

"Theravada."

She nodded at me. "Yeah, I think that was it. So as Christmas was coming up, I agreed to spend the vacation in Sri Lanka. It was nice, but I missed the snow and the lights." She smiled and shrugged.

Dehan asked, "Where did this interest in Buddhism come from?"

She shook her head. "I have no idea. He was like that. Ideas would just pop into his head. He'd become obsessed for six months and then forget all about them. Buddhism only lasted about a month or so . . ." She trailed off. "We got back, he went off to investigate his article, and that was the last I ever saw of him alive."

Dehan gave her a moment, then pursued her point. "So, your trip was two weeks over the Christmas period. His interest in Buddhism would have started around the beginning of December?"

"I guess so, yeah." She frowned. "Is his interest in Buddhism important?"

I was wondering the same thing. Dehan shrugged, then smiled. "You never know."

"Samantha."

She turned to face me.

"Can you think of anything unusual or in any way peculiar that might have happened during your visit?"

She heaved a big sigh. "I don't mean to be difficult, Detective Stone, but with Dave, everything was peculiar and unusual. His behavior was never normal." She ran her fingers through her hair and sighed again. "What stands out most for me is the fact that that trip was supposed to be an opportunity for us to start mending our relationship, to start healing. We had been through a difficult patch, and I was getting frankly sick of him. I had hoped, rather naïvely I guess, that we could turn it around."

"What happened?"

She shrugged. "Buddhism happened. There was a temple . . ." She paused, thinking, and gave a small laugh. "They have so many syllables in Pali! Jetavanaramaya? Something like that, in the city of Anuradhapura. He used to go there every day to talk with the monks, read, study. The fact is I hardly saw him during the whole holiday."

I glanced at Dehan. She was frowning. She asked the question I should have asked, only my brain was wading through sludge.

"Was there any one, particular monk that he befriended?"

Samantha looked a little surprised. "Yes, there was. And if you give me a moment I'll remember his name. Ananda. Ananda Sri Pannasiha. I remember because I used to tease him that he thought this guy was the panacea to all ills. And he wasn't. Indirectly he was putting the last nails in the coffin of our marriage."

"Really? It was that serious?"

She looked sad and nodded down at her hands on the table. "I think so, Detective Dehan. I was aware that he had lost all interest in me. He shared more with Jackson and Bob than he ever did with me. To be honest, when I found out he'd been shacked up with that bimbo . . ." She looked Dehan square in the face. "I was mad. I was *really* mad. But I can't say I was surprised."

I asked, "Did he stay in touch with this monk, Ananda?"

"I have no idea."

Dehan bit her lip for a moment. "How about before? When did he first make contact with him?"

Samantha nodded. "Yeah, I think they may have exchanged a couple of emails before the trip. I'm pretty sure they did, because he chose Anuradhapura deliberately."

I made a note on my pad, and as I was writing, I asked her, "What connection, if any, did David have with Arizona?"

"Arizona?"

I looked up. She was staring at me.

She shook her head. "None whatever, as far as I am aware. Why?"

"During January and February 2008, he made two trips by car to Arizona. I am wondering if you would know what took him there."

"That was during the time he had gone 'dark,' as he used to call it. He was investigating his article, so anything he did during that time would have been directly related to his article. If he went to Arizona, then you can be sure that Arizona had something to do with what he was writing about."

I flopped back in my chair. A sudden, blinding realization had exploded through my numbed brain, and I was kicking myself for not having seen it sooner. Dehan was saying, "So, as far as you are aware, Arizona had no special significance for Dave."

"No, not at all. I had never heard him mention Arizona. As I said, it must have had something to do with his article."

We talked a little longer, then Dehan walked her out and I returned to my desk and sat thinking about what Samantha had said. I could see it with perfect clarity, but in that moment it made absolutely no sense whatsoever.

A minute later, Dehan came back and dropped into her chair.

"I think we have it, Stone. I think we are closing in."

I nodded. "Yeah. Looks that way."

"We going to Arizona?"

"I think so, but not yet."

"What's wrong?"

I shook my head and chewed my lip. "I don't know. Something doesn't fit. Something is all wrong."

NINETEEN

"WHAT? WHAT IS WRONG?"

"Call the Jetavanaramaya temple, Dehan. Contact them, talk to this Ananda Sri Pannasiha. I want to know what he and David discussed for two weeks that seemed to galvanize him into this investigation of Senator Hennessy. I'm going to go through these notes of his and see if I can get some idea of what made him suddenly decide to go to Sri Lanka and explore Buddhism."

"Got it!"

While she searched for the number, I started working my way through his notes. They were mainly in a diary and two A4 notebooks, plus any number of loose sheets and paper napkins that had been stuffed in at various points.

I opened the diary. There were a lot of quotes about Buddhism. Several times he had written down the question whether Buddhism was a religion or a philosophy. One entry, dated the 31st of December, 2007, asked, "If Buddhism does not acknowledge the existence of an absolute God, an absolute, ultimate judge, then how can there be good and evil? How do we decide what is right and what is wrong?"

He must have been a howl at the New Year's party. Another entry, scrawled on an undated paper napkin, said, "Kama is conditioned not only by our actions, but above all by our intentions. So our dying thoughts acquire a huge importance as it is they that will condition the nature of our next birth."

There followed several pages of brief, almost illegible notes, names, dates, phone numbers. If all else failed, they would all have to be followed up.

The last entry in the diary was, "'Why, then, 'tis none to you, for there is nothing either good or bad, but thinking makes it so. To me it is a prison.' *Hamlet to Rosencrantz, scene two act two*."

I looked up at Dehan. She had the phone to her ear and was bouncing a pencil up and down on its eraser. She jerked her head at me like, "What?"

"He was having some kind of existential crisis."

"I thought you had to be either Jewish, French, or Russian to do that."

"You're being facetious."

"I am? They won't answer the phone. It makes me mad when people don't answer the . . . Oh, yes, hello, is that . . . Yes, good evening. Is it very late . . . ?" She looked at me. "What time is it in Sri Lanka? I didn't think." Then back to the phone, "Hello? Hello? I'm calling from New York, in the U.S.A. . . . Excuse me?" She gave a nervous laugh and looked at me again. "He's laughing. Hello? My name is . . . Yes, hello. My name is . . . Excuse me? No . . . no . . . I am looking for . . ." She sighed. "Thank you, you too. I am looking for Ananda Sri Pannasiha . . ." She smiled. "Yes! You know him! That's great! Can I speak to him . . . ? Hello? Hello? . . . What? No, wait!" She slammed down the phone. "Son of a bitch!"

I smiled. "I guess it's about ten or eleven at night over there. What happened?"

"I have no idea. The guy was real sweet. I am pretty sure he was speaking English, at least most of the time. He was delighted to hear me mention Ananda. For all I know he may have been Ananda! Then he blessed me, said something I didn't catch, and hung up."

"Maybe try again when it's not almost midnight. You probably got the poor guy out of bed."

"Yeah, but I tell you what. I'll start with an email, then follow up with a call tomorrow."

"Makes sense."

She started typing. "What's eating you? Why does it matter that he was having an existential crisis?"

"I'm not sure. There's something else. Something that has been right in front of our noses from the start and we have been ignoring it."

She glanced at me and carried on writing. "What?"

"Something Samantha said. She said that if he went to Arizona while he was . . ."

"Dark."

"Yeah, dark, it meant it was directly related to his investigation —to the article."

She shrugged and made a face. "Yeah, we pretty much knew that."

"Yeah, but then she stressed that when he was working on an article, nothing else mattered. *Everything he did while he was working on an article was related to that investigation.*" I flipped back to my notebook. "Here it is, '. . . anything he did during that time would have been directly related to his article.'"

She paused and frowned at me. "Yeah, so?"

I shrugged. "So he chooses that time, when he was supposed to be obsessively focused on an article, to start a live-in relationship? And not just any article. *The* article of his career."

She flopped back in her chair. "Son of a gun."

"And these notes." I flicked them with the back of my fingers. "Practically everything I have seen so far is quotes from Shakespeare and Buddha about the nature of morality."

"Katie." She scratched her head. "*Cherchez la femme* . . . There is always a damn woman involved."

"Shit!" I slammed my hand into my forehead. "I am so goddamn stupid!"

Mo at the desk across the aisle looked up and smiled blandly at me. "No argument from over here."

Dehan scowled at him. "Butt out and get a life, asshole!"

He wheezed a laugh and withdrew into his file.

She turned back to me. "What?"

I pulled the list of K's supposed victims from the file and tossed it across the desk at her. "You said we should go through them. You were right."

She glanced at it. "Jack O'Connor."

I pulled my laptop over one-handed and started typing five-fingered. Dehan said, "I got it." She rattled at the keyboard and sat back. After a moment, she started reading.

"Johnathan Joseph O'Connor, accountant for the Clearwater Real Estate Development Company. Blew the whistle on his employer and was going to testify against them, and also the Hennessys. Word was he was going to reveal large-scale tax evasion and also had information regarding the alleged suicide of Victor Fosberg, which some conspiracy theorists were calling a murder, and attributing to Hennessy, claiming she had had an affair with him.

"O'Connor, his wife, Kathleen, and youngest daughter, Penny, aged eight, were found shot to death in a presumed house invasion. His wallet was taken along with her purse and jewelry, and their safe had been busted open . . ." She took a deep breath, made a "Pffff" noise, and looked at me. "Eldest daughter, named after her mother, Kathleen, managed to escape and was later adopted by her mother's sister. She was aged twelve at the time, and that was in the year 2000. Which would make her about twenty-eight now."

"It's her, isn't it? It has to be; and that was why David hooked up with her. And she's our anonymous informant."

"Shall we bring her in?"

I nodded. "Yeah. I want to know how much she really knows about his article. But above all, I want to know why she concealed the fact that she was Jack O'Connor's daughter."

I reached for the phone and started to dial one-handed. She grabbed it and pulled it away from me. "I got it."

She dialed and I scowled. She shrugged and gave me a fake smile. "It's quicker . . . Hi, Katie? It's Detective Dehan. Hi, good, not bad, listen, we have a couple of questions which we need to clear up . . . Nah! Just routine really, but it has to be done. Could you come in and see us? I know it's a pain, but it would be a real help. This lunchtime? That would be great. Thanks, Katie." She hung up. "I'm such a nice person."

Mo snorted across the aisle. "In what universe?"

"Go screw yourself, Mo! Nobody else is going to!"

I looked at my watch. It was almost twelve. "Okay, Dehan, walk me down to the deli and we'll grab an early lunch. Help me think this through."

She pulled on her jacket and hung my coat over my shoulders. I heard Mo snigger but ignored him, and we stepped into the bright, cold morning. As we started to walk down Fteley Avenue toward Banyer Place, she began to talk.

"Okay, back in 2007 Dave Thorndike makes contact with a Buddhist monk in Sri Lanka. This monk somehow, for some reason we cannot fathom at the moment, puts Dave onto K."

I nodded. "All right. And with any luck, tomorrow we will have a slightly better idea of how that happened, when Ananda answers your email."

"We hope. Okay, now, whatever Ananda told Dave, it must have been pretty hot, because almost as soon as he got back to New York he was off. He got his apartment, hooked up with Katie, and within a couple of weeks took his first trip to Arizona. That is a very busy two weeks."

"It sure is. We then have a period of . . . let's see. Say he gets back to New York on the twentieth or the twenty-first, there is a period of about a month where he is presumably working on his article. He then takes a second trip to Arizona . . ."

Dehan took over. "And when he gets back, he's real excited. He contacts Bob Shaw and he contacts Lee. He tells them this is the biggest thing since Watergate, he's going to get the Pulitzer, and they're going to have to change the Constitution. He is high. He's euphoric."

"Good, now let's take the next steps one at a time. What happens next?"

"He tells Katie that he is married and she dumps him. She goes to stay with . . . wait a minute . . . !"

"The landlord assumed it was her sister. Clearly it was a friend, because her sister was killed along with her parents."

We stopped walking and stared at each other for a moment. Then she shrugged and we carried on. "I guess. Okay, so then she comes back to collect her CDs and books, yadda yadda, and he meets up with Lee, who claims A, he's pissed that Dave is cheating on Samantha and B, there is no merit to his story, and he decides to distance himself from him."

"Okay, but in a minute I want to go back to that yadda yadda."

"I miss something?"

"Maybe, but carry on, you're doing good."

She grinned at me. "Uh-uh, Sensei, Superman is doing good. I am doing well."

"Smart-ass."

"So, Friday night, Katie goes to dinner with some guy at a restaurant. That night we know from the landlord that somebody arrived. Dave let them in, and next morning the landlord found him dead."

"Okay. Now, meantime, when we started investigating—that is, after we questioned Katie, Samantha, Shelly, and Lee—two things happened. First, we received an anonymous letter introducing K, Hennessy's hired killer, and second, Lee turned up less than twenty-four hours after we'd spoken to him . . ."

"Having avoided seeing us from the start."

"Correct. And wanted to change his story. The change is to shift suspicion onto Katie, and stress that Dave's article had no merit and contained no real evidence." We had reached the deli and we stopped outside the door. I looked down into her face. "Can we, from what we know so far, from the facts that we have, can we begin to construct a workable theory?"

She turned away from me and stepped into the shop. The mechanical bell clanged over the door and I followed her in. There was a smell of smoked meats and cheese and freshly baked bread on the air. Dehan asked for two beef on rye, and the Italian guy behind the counter asked why I always came in instead of her. To me, he said that if I sent her for the sandwiches we'd get bigger, better sandwiches. Everybody laughed except Dehan, who told him to take a hike.

After a noisy five minutes while he made up our order, we stepped into the street and started walking slowly back toward the station.

"The answer to your question, Sensei, is that we can make a theory, but not an hypothesis."

"Christ! I created a monster!"

"Hear me out. We still have to make a lot of assumptions. We don't know what the connection is yet between Ananda and K. I might be able to guess, but the fact is we don't even know if there *is* a connection. We can guess that Dave was going to Arizona to interview somebody, and we can guess that it might be K. But the closest we can get to a theory, in my opinion, is that Dave connected with K somehow and Hennessy had him killed."

I grunted. She had told me no more than I could have worked out for myself, if my brain had not been fogged by painkillers and pain.

"What's your theory about Ananda?"

"It's a reach, Stone, but you know that all the traditional martial arts grew out of Buddhism, right?"

I nodded.

"In Japan they are still very closely associated with Zen Buddhism. It wasn't uncommon for warriors, especially the samurai, after a life of killing, to withdraw and become Buddhist monks. Now, it is just possible that K, after he retired, sought guidance and teaching from a Buddhist monk in Sri Lanka."

"That might explain those notes of David's about morality and right and wrong. It wasn't his existential crisis, it was K's."

"Right. And like you said, Pakistan is not a million miles from Sri Lanka. If K was in fact Adrian Philips, he may have been there seeking some kind of spiritual redemption, and that same need for redemption may have driven him to contact the *New York Telegraph* and Dave in the first place. In which case, Ananda may have been a kind of go-between."

"That makes a lot of sense, Dehan. That is very good. Thank God you're thinking. Okay, let's see what Katie has to say. And maybe we'll get a useful reply to your email tomorrow."

"And then, Arizona! Road trip! You think the inspector will go for it?"

"With this arm? This time we fly. Yeah. I think he hasn't much choice."

"Even better. So what's the problem with my yadda yadda?"

"When Katie went back for her CDs and books, the article and his laptop were already gone."

She stopped dead and stared at me. Then she sighed, shook her head, and started walking again. "So what's special in Arizona, in the way of food?"

"A lot of corn and black beans, and chimichangas."

She looked at me in mild disgust. "Corn and black beans? Seriously?"

"And chimichangas."

"Great. No bison steaks?"

And we pushed our way back into the station.

TWENTY

KATIE ARRIVED AS WE WERE FINISHING OUR LUNCH, and we had the sergeant show her up to interview room three, where we joined her five minutes later. We offered her coffee, but she declined and said, "I would really like to get this over and done with, Detectives. I have a great deal to do."

I nodded, said, "Sure," and we sat opposite her. I had a slim manila file with me and I opened it. I pulled out the list of names and slid it across the table to her. She studied it a moment, shrugged, and looked me square in the eye.

"So what?"

"Why did you lie to us? You told us you had no idea what Dave was working on."

She buried her face in her hands and sighed. After a moment she ran both hands through her hair and flopped back in her chair. "I didn't lie to you. Not exactly."

Dehan snapped. "Not exactly? Not exactly doesn't cut the ice! We are not playing games here, Katie. This is a murder investigation. Not exactly telling the truth is lying!"

Katie flashed her an angry glance. "No, Detective Dehan, it's not!"

Dehan stabbed at Jack O'Connor's name on the list with her

finger. "Are you Kathleen O'Connor? Are you this man's daughter?"

"Yes."

"And you want us to believe that you didn't know Dave was investigating his murder?"

She shook her head. "Of course I knew."

I spoke quietly. "Level with us, Katie. Keeping information from us is not going to help anybody."

She sat for a long moment, staring down at the tabletop, just giving her head little shakes. Finally, she looked up at me with weary eyes. "Can't you understand that all I want is to have this man out of my life? He lied to me, he used me, and then he thought he could just have me. I turned and I walked away. Why is he still in my life?"

I sighed. "Katie, I am sorry. I really am. What can I say? Life isn't fair. It never was. The fact is that you can get it right a million times, and life goes on. You get it wrong once and you spend the rest of your life living with the consequences."

She gave a small smile you could describe as rueful. "He contacted me because he had tracked down Jack O'Connor's only surviving daughter. At first I told him to leave me alone, but he was nothing if not persistent. Relentless might be a better word. In the end I agreed to talk to him."

Dehan was frowning. "Things must have happened pretty fast."

Katie turned to her and seemed to study her face for a moment, then nodded. "Yeah. They did. Dave was a pain in the ass, but he was a fascinating pain in the ass. He was intense, *really* intense. When he focused his mind on something it was . . ." She stared at the wall, shrugged, shook her head. "It was like his mind was *eating* that subject or that person, *devouring* it. Where other people are inhibited by things like good manners, social conventions, danger . . ." She shook her head again. "David was not fazed by anything. He didn't even consider things like that. If X was the objective, then nothing, and I mean *nothing*, would stand in his way." She paused, looking down at her hands on the table. "There is something very compelling, very attractive, about that quality in a man."

She raised her eyes to look at Dehan again.

Dehan said, "I get that."

"Before I knew it I was staying at his place every other night, moving my clothes and my music in . . . It wasn't so much a whirl-wind as a tornado."

I repeated the question, "So why did you lie to us?"

"I told you I didn't lie. Yes, I knew that he was investigating my father's death. I also knew that he believed Carol Hennessy was responsible." She stopped talking, looking at each of her fingers in turn, as though she might find the answer to life's injus-tices on one of them. "At first I wanted to help him. I thought he wanted me to. I had always believed that my father was assassi-nated, and that the robbery, the murder of my mother and my sister, they were merely to make it look like a home invasion. I have always believed that. And when Dave came along saying that he believed it too, and that he thought he might be able to prove it . . ."

She trailed off. Dehan waited a moment, then asked, "Did he tell you *how* he was going to prove it?"

Katie seemed not to hear her. "At first I didn't want to get involved. I was terrified of the brutality of that man. The ruthless-ness, the efficiency with which he did it. Do you know what it's like to be a child, to witness something like that and feel completely powerless and helpless in the face of such . . ." Her face creased with disgust. ". . . *Power*, such strength and violence? I still have nightmares about it. But he persuaded me that if I helped him it would be a way of achieving closure. And I believed him."

Dehan started to repeat her question. "Did he tell you . . ."

"No. He got me to talk. I went over the murder a hundred different ways, until I had become numb to it. But he never told me anything about his article or his investigation, or his other sources."

I thought for a moment and asked, "What can you tell me about K?"

She frowned at me. "Who's Kay?"

I slid the anonymous note across the table to her. "Are you going to deny that you sent this?"

She read through it carefully. When she'd finished, she raised her eyebrows and pushed it back across the table to me.

"I have no idea who wrote that, Detective Stone, but what you're suggesting doesn't make a lot of sense to me. I'm right here." She gave a small laugh, like I was being absurd. "Why would I send you an anonymous letter when I can talk to you face-to-face?"

I nodded and sighed. "I was hoping you would explain that, Katie."

"I'm sorry, Detective, you are way off base. When Dave revealed to me that he was married, I saw what a stupid bitch I had been. He shared *nothing* with me. Do you get that? *Nothing.* I gave him." She paused, watching my face to see if I understood. "He kept everything from me, his article, his investigation, his life, the truth!"

I pulled back the letter and the list and slipped them into the folder again.

"What can you tell me about his two trips to Arizona?"

She gave an exasperated half laugh half sigh. "Again? He was away for about a week in January and a week in February. Did he go to Arizona? If you say so. He didn't tell me. All I knew was that he was away."

I took a deep breath and spread my hands. "If you won't cooperate with us, Katie, then there is no point in my talking to you any longer."

She hesitated a moment without looking at either one of us. Then, she said quietly, "I'm sorry," and she got up and left.

Dehan and I stared at each other for a minute, but neither of us had anything to say, so we stood and made our way downstairs. I found Sergeant Garcia and gave her the manila folder with instructions. When I'd finished telling her what I wanted, she said, "Listen, the car was identified. I didn't want to interrupt your interrogation, but they got it on CCTV at a gas station. They got the number." She handed me a slip of paper. "Patrolman Junkers traced it. It was reported stolen the same night of the shooting."

I made a face that was rueful. "To be expected."

"No, but a neighbor got it on her cell. She filmed the whole thing! The inspector wants you up in his office to look at the video."

I bellowed across the detectives' room, "*Dehan! Upstairs!*"

Everybody looked, and as Dehan crossed the room there was much laughter, applause, and wolf-whistling.

I was knocking on Inspector Newman's door as she came up behind me. "What the hell is it, Stone?"

Newman's voice called, "Come!"

I pushed in as I said to Dehan, "They got footage of the car." "Shit!"

To Newman I said, "Is it any good?"

"You tell me."

He had his laptop open on the desk. He pressed Play and turned it so we could all watch. I sat, and Dehan crouched beside me with her hand on my shoulder.

The quality was grainy but good enough to see the dark Audi parked on a leafy street. It was between two plane trees, under a streetlamp. There was a group of three men under the tree by the trunk. The nearest was wearing blue jeans and a brown leather jacket. The two others were in dark clothes and were hard to make out.

The guy in the jeans looked up and down the street, then approached the driver's door, fiddled with it for a moment, and pulled it open. The lights flashed, and for a moment you could hear the alarm, but he climbed in and after a couple of bleeps the alarm stopped. The two other guys then stepped up to the rear doors, and whoever was filming zoomed in on them. The picture became more grainy, but the nearside guy, the one who must have shot at us, turned and looked up and down the road just before he opened the door and got in.

I said, "Back up and freeze on his face . . . Just there!"

Dehan spoke through clenched teeth, "Got you, you motherfucker!" She glanced at Newman's astonished face, but she didn't apologize. Instead, she said, "Jay Guzman. He's from the hood. Started out as muscle for the Sureños. Then did his degree at Attica and graduated with honors in various forms of murder. There were three hits attributed to him at the correctional facility, then a string more over the last few years, mostly for the Mob."

Newman looked impressed. "Any doubt?"

She shook her head. "None."

I said, "Let's go get the son of a bitch."

"Take a SWAT team." He stood. "I'll come down for the briefing."

While Newman gathered the team in the briefing room, Dehan found Guzman's number. He had a nice house out near Eastchester Bay. She called and waited while it rang. Then she suddenly cocked her hip and flopped her head on one side with an idiot grin. The accent was straight out of the Deep South.

"Oh, good morning! I represent the Exclusive New York Fine Food and Wine Company. We have been asked to extend an invitation to Mr. Guzman to be among our very select group of members. I wonder if Mr. Guzman is there? Could I speak to him possibly?" She waited, listening, with a bright smile on her face, then said, "Oh, he's sleeping? Oh, heavens no! Don't wake him!" She laughed out loud. "I'll call back at a more convenient time. Five o'clock? I'll be sure to call then. You have a super day, y'hear!"

She hung up and strode into the briefing room. Newman was talking but she interrupted him.

"Guzman is at home right now sleeping. Apparently he was up late and will sleep till about four. But we need to act now. There is too much riding on this."

Newman glanced at me. I smiled and nodded. He turned to the SWAT team. There were six of them.

"Okay, like I said, this guy is very dangerous. We are going into his home. We don't know what we are going to find in there, but we have to assume the worst. Our latest intel is that he will be in his bed asleep, but you need to be ready for him to be awake and armed. He has a wife and two kids. So you will need to be aware of them and keep them out of harm's way. The wife may be in bed with him. Be prepared for that.

"Jones, Smith, Patel, and Philips, you go in the back. Dehan, Gunther, and Sanchez, you go in the front. Dehan is in charge of this operation. Get him *alive*! Okay? We need this man *alive*! Go!"

He stood and put a hand on my shoulder. "You sit this one out in the car with me, Stone." He grinned. "How does it feel to be getting old?"

I raised an eyebrow at him. "I wouldn't know, sir."

He laughed and we made our way out to the cars.

TWENTY-ONE

THERE IS NOTHING IN THIS WORLD MORE FRUSTRATING that having to sit in a car and watch your partner lead a SWAT raid on a house where you know there is an armed man who has put two slugs into your body. It doesn't get much more frustrating than that.

We sat in silence as they deployed in their body armor, four around the back and Dehan and two more entering through the front garden, flattened against the walls. The two guys with her, Gunther and Sanchez, looked big and tough. Beside them Dehan looked delicate and frail. I knew she was as tough as nails, I'd seen her in action and I knew she was fast and lethal, but to me right then, with two bullet holes in my chest, she looked like a young girl that I should be protecting.

"It should be me going in there, not her."

Newman looked at me curiously. "In your condition you'd be a liability, John."

I sighed. "Yeah, I know."

"It was very brave, what you did. Well beyond the call of duty."

I shrugged. "No, it wasn't. I didn't think. Any one of us would have done the same for a partner."

He grunted. There was a shout. Dehan's voice. Then they were battering the door and the three of them were storming in, hollering. I strained my ears, listening for gunfire, then climbed out of the car where I could hear better. The only sound was the distant sigh of mundane traffic, the whisper of the breeze among the cold, naked branches, and far off, muffled, the occasional shout. I stood staring, knowing that people might be dying, that in that house was the intention to kill, and Dehan was the victim of choice.

I heard Newman shout, but I wasn't listening. I didn't even know that I was running. I crossed the lawn and I was up the stairs to the porch and busting in through the doors. A woman with two kids sitting on a sofa in the living room. A cop in a helmet and body armor standing over her. He glanced at me and frowned but I was already on the stairs. Voices, shouting, barking, hollering. Dehan's voice, harsh, aggressive. I smiled and began to laugh as I ran up the stairs. Three guys in the bedroom doorway with their weapons drawn.

"Sir! You cannot come in here! *Sir!*"

Inside the room, Dehan's voice bellowing, "*On your face, motherfucker!*"

I pushed past, muttering, "Out of my way, goddamn it!"

And there was Dehan, a half-naked man on his face on the floor, with his arms behind his back, and her kneeling on him, holstering her piece with one hand, cuffing him with the other. One guy covering her and a second moving toward me with his hand stuck out, shouting, "Stay outside!"

I pushed his hand away and snarled at him, "Get out of my face!"

Dehan looked up and grinned. "Glad you could make it, Sensei. I got a late present for you. Merry Christmas."

Behind me I heard feet lumbering up the stairs. Next thing, Newman was bursting in. He didn't say anything, but I wasn't looking at him. I was staring at Dehan's grinning face as she dragged Guzman to his feet.

She stared back for what might have been a second or an hour. I heard myself saying, "Good work." She nodded and I looked around at the SWAT guys who were watching me like I was crazy. I said, again, "Good work."

Newman was scowling at me like he wanted to can me right there and then. He said, "Dehan, take the prisoner down to the station. Book him and take him to the interrogation room."

I growled at him, "I interrogate this suspect with Detective Dehan, sir."

Dehan and the SWAT team dragged Guzman from the room. One of them grabbed his clothes and a dressing gown. After a moment of commotion, Newman and I were alone in the room, with the receding sound of voices downstairs. We stared at each other for a long moment. Finally, he said, "Is there anything you need to tell me, Stone?"

I said, "No."

"You are an experienced officer. You have the best track record in the Forty-Third. You have almost thirty years of experience. What the *hell* did you think you were doing?"

I chewed my lip, but I couldn't answer him. Finally, I said, "I don't know."

"Talk to me, John! Twice, in almost as many days, you have acted irrationally!" He took a couple of steps toward me. "Quite aside from the fact that Detective Dehan was probably not the target in the shooting, she was in a position to take cover. You ran around the car and put yourself in the line of fire!"

I sighed and looked away from him. "I acted without thinking to protect my partner."

"And now? What is your explanation for this?"

"I . . ." Again, I had no answer. Lamely, I said, "It should have been me."

He came up close to me. "Stone, I am going to ask you one more time. There are rumors. My policy with rumors is to ignore them. Do I need to be listening to this one? Is there anything that you need to tell me?"

I stared at him a long time. "I don't know."

"Figure it out. But understand this, one more display like this and I will suspend you. Do you understand that?"

I nodded. "Yeah. I understand it, sir."

He kept looking at me. "So? What now? Can you handle this?"

"Yes. I need to interrogate Guzman, sir. I will hold it together."

"Fine. I'll be watching. But, John?"

"What?"

"I am not just the inspector. I'm your friend. If you need to talk, talk to me."

"Yes, sir. Thank you."

He smiled. "Or talk to her."

I didn't answer. I walked past him and went down the stairs, thinking about Guzman.

When I got outside, Guzman was in the back of a patrol car. It pulled away and headed north, toward the station. The SWAT cars were pulling away after it. Dehan approached me. She was still grinning and came and stood close to me. "Hey, pardner. You arrived a little early there, didn't you?"

"Yeah. And I just got hauled over the coals for it."

She looked past me, and I was aware of Newman exiting the house. He spoke to a couple of guys from the SWAT team who were climbing into their vehicle. Then he headed toward his own car without saying anything to us. She examined my face a moment and said, "Ride with me."

"Dehan . . ."

She narrowed her eyes. "What is it?"

"We need to talk."

She squinted. "*Now?*"

I drew breath, hesitated. "No. I guess not now. Let's go interrogate this son of a bitch."

WHEN WE GOT to the station, Maria told me he had been booked and was in interview room one, waiting for us. We went straight up. As soon as we stepped in, he started mouthing off.

"What the fuck? You come stormin' into my house! Threatening my family with weapons! Abusin' me and my family! My wife! My children!"

We sat opposite him and I said very quietly, "We have you on film."

He paused. "What?"

"We have you on film. The car was caught at the gas station where you stopped after you tried to kill me. We traced the car to the owner. One of his neighbors caught you stealing the car on his cell."

"That's bullshit . . ."

"Don't waste your time, Guzman. How the fuck do you think we found you? The sooner you start cooperating, the easier it's going to be to cut a deal."

He stared hard at us for a long moment, first at me, then at Dehan, then back at me again. His simple brain was struggling with the equation I had given him. I sighed. I felt real tired.

"Guzman, you're going down for the attempted murder of two police officers. The story is over for you. At your age, you'll be lucky to get out before you're dead. The proof is conclusive. There isn't a jury on Earth that would not convict you within five minutes of seeing the evidence. It's a slam dunk. Am I getting through to you?"

"I wanna see my lawyer."

"Don't worry, he's on his way. I am not interrogating you. I am just talking."

"Okay."

"You've already been told. You don't need to say anything. But you'd be smart to listen. Because there is a way for you to be able to see your family again, and be with them."

"There is . . . ?"

I put my finger to my lips. "Shshshsh . . . Don't talk. Just listen. I am not interested in you, Guzman. I would happily waive all charges against you. I would happily recommend a deal to the DA. Witness protection could put you far away, in Cali, in a nice house with your family. A new life." I sighed again. "You know what I want, Guzman, don't you?"

He puffed his cheeks and blew. "Man, I don't know . . ."

"Don't talk. Just listen. The way it is now, you are going away for the rest of your life and nobody—*nobody*—is even going to try to help you. You will become an old man in prison. And you will probably die in prison." I paused, watching his stupid, simple face. "But you give me what I want, Guzman, and you will spend the rest of your life enjoying the blessing of your wife and your children, on a beach in California. Not many people get a second chance, Guzman. God has seen fit to offer you a second chance. What do you think the smart move is? Huh?"

There was something like awe in his face.

"They would kill me, man?"

I burst out laughing, leaning back in my chair and throwing back my head. "Jay! Jay! Do you *really* think they are *not* going to kill you? You *really* think they are going to let you reach two years in jail? Do you have *any* idea how dangerous you are? Do you understand the people who you will bring down if you talk to me?" I paused and shook my head. "The information you have is so important, Guzman, that even if you decided in five years to come clean, it could reduce your sentence." I laughed again. "But don't get ideas, because your employers, the people you can bring down with what you know, are aware of that, and they will not let you get to five years. You won't last three months, pal. Your smart move is talk to me. Make a deal. Get on the witness protection program. It is your best, last hope."

He swallowed. He was terrified. He was not intelligent, but he was shrewd and cunning enough to know that I was telling the truth.

"Your lawyer will be arriving in a few minutes, Guzman. Listen to him, see what he says to you. My bet? He will tell you to plead guilty and keep your mouth shut. That's because the people paying his fees are your employers—the people who will go down if you talk. You'll stand trial, you'll go to prison, and after a few weeks you'll be executed in the showers. And the buck will stop with you, and all of those sons of bitches will laugh and piss on your grave." I shook my head. "No, that's a lie, Guzman. They won't piss on your grave, because they will have no idea who the hell you are, or where you are buried."

"You would say that . . ."

"I'm not going to try and persuade you, Jay. I'm going to take them down sooner or later, one way or another. This way is quicker, and though I would be happy to see you rot in a cell for the rest of your life, or get knifed in the showers, you son of a bitch . . ." I showed him my arm in a sling. "I would be just as happy to see you give your wife and kids a decent life in exchange for seeing your bosses get what's coming to them, sooner rather than later. But in the end?" I shook my head. "It's all the same to me."

There was a commotion outside and the door burst open. A big guy in an Italian suit wearing a fedora and an expensive coat came in. "We're done here! I am Mr. Guzman's attorney. He has nothing to say. This interview is over!"

I kept my eyes fastened on Guzman's. I said, "Yeah, we're done here."

Dehan turned and shouted, "Sergeant!" The sergeant poked his head in the door. "Take Mr. Guzman down to the holding cells when he's finished talking to his attorney."

"Sure thing, Detective."

We stepped out of the interrogation room and walked down the stairs. As though of a single mind, instead of going into the detectives' room, we stepped into the street. It was late afternoon and the sun had slipped behind the buildings and the bare trees, casting long, wintry shadows.

Dehan stopped, breathing plumes of condensation, and watched my face with a frown. She said, "I think we're done for today, Stone. You look beat. Let Guzman stew for the night. He'll talk to us in the morning. You scared the bejesus out of him. I think we got him."

In my mind I told her to go home. I'd get takeout, watch a movie, and see her in the morning. I told her to stay at the station, go out to dinner with some guy, any guy! Do whatever she had to do. I'd take care of myself, the way I always had. But not a single one of those words could make it out past my throat. My jaw was locked shut. She watched me a moment longer, then made a face like a firm decision. "Come on. You shouldn't even be here. I'm going to get the key and our coats. We're going home."

I nodded. She went inside and I walked across the road to my car. I leaned on the roof and covered my face with my hands. I smiled and laughed softly to myself.

We're going home.

Home.

TWENTY-TWO

I STOOD FOR ABOUT FIVE MINUTES WATCHING DUSK gather around the station house, watching the late sun turn from gold to burnished copper as the shadows deepened and the cold bit through my jacket into my skin. Then I saw Guzman's attorney step out of the station house door, swinging his attaché case, and walk quickly toward Story Avenue. A moment later, Dehan appeared, wearing her coat and carrying mine. She took the two stairs in one long stride and was just looking to cross the road when I saw her stop and look back. Maria, the desk sergeant, was at the door saying something, pointing back with her thumb, like she was hitchhiking.

I pushed myself off the car and walked to where Dehan was standing. As I approached, she turned to me. Her face was a vivid mix of pity, compassion, and wanting to hit somebody.

I asked, "He wants to see us now?"

She nodded. "He's going crazy."

"Let's strike while the iron is hot, Dehan. Let's reel it in."

She sighed and followed me into the station. As we walked, I said to her, "I'm going to get Newman. We'll call the DA. You go and get Guzman. Take him to number three. Take two armed guards with you and post them outside the door. I want the whole damned station on red alert. If anyone or anything comes near him, shoot it."

"You got it, Sensei."

As I climbed the stairs, I could hear her bellowing like a marine gunnery sergeant rallying his troops.

Upstairs, I pushed into Inspector John Newman's office without knocking. He looked surprised but not upset.

"John . . ."

I raised an eyebrow and almost smiled. The pain in my shoulder didn't let me see it through. I said, "John, you're going to want to see this. Guzman is about to give us Hennessy and her hit man."

"Holy . . ."

"Shit is the word you're looking for, and a ton of it is about to hit the fan."

"Is it time to call in the Feds?"

"No." Then I shrugged. "It's your call, Inspector, but as of right now we still have no evidence. Let's see what Guzman gives us. But call the DA. We need her in on this interrogation. We need her to authorize the deal, and we also need a safe house for him. Because after tonight, he is going to have some very powerful and very dangerous enemies." I hesitated. "And so are we."

Half an hour later, Newman and Jane Anderson, the very worried district attorney, stepped into the observation cubicle attached to interview room three, and I went in to join Dehan and Guzman. I sat down, told Guzman that we were being recorded, and then recited the date and the time, stating who I was and who was present. Finally, I said, "Okay, Guzman, what have you got to say to us?"

He was watching me with fearful eyes. A couple of times he glanced at Dehan. His breathing was shallow.

"First I need guarantees, man. You don't know how dangerous these people are."

"What guarantees do you need?"

"What you said before. I need indemnity. I need protection,

and I need the witness protection program for me and my family."

"What do we get in exchange for that, Guzman?"

He kept trying to talk, but all he could manage was to swallow and lick his lips. Finally, he said, "I can give you the name of the guy who paid me to whack you and Detective Dehan. I can tell you where the order came from. And I can give you a name . . ."

"What name?"

"The name you're looking for. The name of the guy who was talking to Thorndike. The big shot hit man."

"How do you know that name?"

"Fuck you. Gimme the deal, then I talk."

I stood and walked out. Newman and the DA joined me in the corridor. Jane said, "Give it to him. I'll call the office and get them drafting it. If there is the slightest chance that what he is saying is true, we need to nail these bastards before they slip out of our grasp. Once the deal is done, you understand this will become a federal case?"

I nodded. "Yeah, I know that. And that worries me."

I turned and went back in. I sat and said, "Okay, Guzman, you have your deal. The paperwork is being done as we speak. This conversation is being recorded. You have all the guarantees you need. Now talk."

I heard the suppressed sigh of relief from Dehan as she flopped back in her chair. Guzman went pale and sagged as he realized the enormity of the commitment he had just made. In that moment, I understood that I owned this son of a bitch. Maybe not for long, maybe only for the next twenty-four hours— until the Feds took over—but for now he was mine to do with as I pleased with. I smiled, like he was now my pal.

"Relax, Jay. Believe it or not, this is probably the safest you have ever been in your life. And the more you commit, the more you give us, the more we'll want to keep you that way. As of the last two minutes, you have the biggest law enforcement machine in the world focused on keeping you alive. We're friends now, on the same side."

He stared at me for a long moment as he adjusted to the idea that all the people who used to be his friends were now his sworn enemies, committed to his death, and all the people who had until now been his sworn enemies were his friends and allies, committed to his safety and survival. It was like he was dying and being reborn.

"Yeah," he said. "I guess . . ."

Not everybody is moved to profound statements in profound moments. What can you do?

Dehan said, "So who ordered the hit on Detective Stone, Guzman?"

"A fockin' Italian guy, name of D'Angelo. He's Senator Hennessy's personal sec'atery. He paid me twenty grand, cash. He brought it in a paper bag. I still have the bag. I always keep 'em." He grinned. "You know why I keep 'em?"

I said, "Tell me."

He pointed at me with a big sausage finger. "I ain't as dumb as I look. I read somewhere that paper is one of the best surfaces for keeping fingerprints. Did you know that? So this schmuck D'Angelo—I never did like the fockin' Italians, you know? They give me a lot of work. The fockin' Jersey Mob operate a lot down here. Did you know *that*? They give me a lot of work. But I never liked 'em, you know? You never know if they're bein' straight with you. Us, the Mexicans, you know where you stand with a Mexican." He turned to Dehan. "*Vos sois Mejicana, a que si?* Am I right?"

She looked at him like she wanted to cut his throat. "Why do you keep the bags, Guzman?"

"Yeah, right, because I figure if I ever need an insurance policy, I got proof, right there, that this fockin' Italian schmuck has been payin' me."

I smiled. "You're a smart man, Jay. So you keep these bags in your house?"

"Right there, in my wardrobe."

I knew that as he was saying it, Newman and the DA were applying for a search warrant for his house. D'Angelo didn't know it, but right then, wherever he was in his sharp, two-thousand-dollar Italian suit, he was going under.

"Was D'Angelo working on his own?"

"You kidding? That schmuck ain't got the brains to act on his own. Me? I been an independent operator all my career. You know? The fockin' Sureños wanted me in the gang. I told them, 'Fock you!' I make the hits, I set my price, they pay. The fockin' Mob wanted me to join, not as a fockin' soldier, you know what I'm sayin'? They wanted me as a made man. You know what I told them? I told them, 'Fock you. *Fock* you!' I ain't no wise guy, I ain't no Sureño. I'm my own man. So they offered me work, I charge my fee, they pay. Everybody happy. An independent contractor. That was me."

Dehan sighed. "So about D'Angelo . . ."

"Yeah. No, he worked for Hennessy. You nail him and he'll deny it. That is one big, scary organization, you know what I'm sayin'? The Mob is Little League compared to that firm. It's not just her, neither. Her husband is the big honcho. Those guys are above the law. They are untouchable."

I felt a surge of hot anger in my belly, but I spoke quietly. "Nobody is above the law, Guzman. That's why it's the law. Sometimes people forget that, but the bigger they get, the higher they climb, the harder they fall."

He shrugged and made a face. "Maybe. Either way, D'Angelo was the go-between. He gets his hands dirty so she don't have to. If things go bad, she washes her hands and he takes the fall."

"Can you prove that?"

"No. I can tell you about a hundred conversation I had with D'Angelo where he *said* he was workin' for Hennessy, but that ain't worth shit to you. What I can do is give you the name of the guy who can nail Hennessy."

I could feel my heart pounding. Dehan leaned forward and

put her elbows on the table. Her voice was little more than a whisper. "Who's that?"

"He was the fockin' Terminator, man. I got so much fockin' respect for this guy, you know what I'm tellin' you? This guy is a fockin' *ninja*, man. I call him the Aspirin Guy. You know why I call him that? Because Hennessy used him to get rid of all her fockin' headaches. Then he fockin' retires. He disappears. Is he dead? Nobody knows. And every fockin' day of their fockin' lives they are wondering, 'Is he gonna come back? Is he gonna spill the fockin' beans on me?'"

He threw his head back and started laughing.

I said, "And that's what happened."

"Too fockin' right it happened. There ain't never been so much fockin' nervous dia-fockin'-rrhea in Washington!"

He roared with laughter again and I couldn't help smiling. I glanced at Dehan and saw she was smiling too.

"So D'Angelo ordered you to hit Thorndike."

He nodded. "That's right. Paid me twenty grand to kill him."

I shook my head and narrowed my eyes. "How did you get him to let you in? Why did you use his gun? And how did you even know where his gun was?"

He made a face like my stupidity offended his sensibilities. "No, man! You don't know nothin'! I didn't kill him! I don't know who the fock killed him. I was at the plannin' stage, just observin' him, know what I'm saying? Like all good jobs, the important thing is the planning and the preparation." He turned to Dehan. "Am I right? Before I could get to him, somebody else did the job for me." He held up his hands. "But I kept the fockin' dough. They want him dead. He's dead. The fee is the fee."

I closed my eyes and tried to think through the cloud of pain. It didn't make any sense right then, so I filed it away and asked the billion-dollar question.

"So what's this Aspirin Ninja's name?"

He chuckled. "Mr. Fockin' Anonymous. Adrian Philips."

Then he said with more emphasis, as though correcting himself, "Adrian Simon Philips. It's like the name of a nobody, right?"

My heart sank. "Adrian Philips is dead, Guzman. He died in 2007."

He gave a big shrug and spread his hands. "I don't know what to tell you, Detective Stone. That's the guy. Adrian Philips, Mr. Anonymous."

Dehan sighed loudly and ran her fingers through her hair. "How do you know this? Why are you so sure?"

"Because I often talked to D'Angelo about him. In the beginning I used to complain that this guy got all the class A jobs and the big bucks. Then when I saw how he operated, I saw why. He was good, know what I'm sayin' to you? Never no comeback from one of his jobs. He was a fockin' *ghost*, man! A suicide, a fockin' accident, a house invasion. Always untraceable.

"Then, when D'Angelo hired me to kill Thorndike, he wanted me to go after Philips too. I told him to go fock himself. I ain't no fockin' suicide!"

I sat forward and stared at him. "They wanted you to kill him?"

"That's what I'm tellin' you."

"Where? Where was he?"

He held up his hands and shook his head. "Oh, no! No way, man! *No fockin' way!* I didn't want to know. I told D'Angelo, 'Don't you fockin' tell me where he is or nothin' about him! No way, man!' I'll whack the reporter, but I don't want to know nothin' about that fockin' guy."

I thought for a moment. Suddenly, I needed to be out of there, in the cold evening air, to think. I had all the pieces, now I needed to put them together.

"Okay, Guzman. You're going to be taken somewhere safe now. The inspector will take care of you."

He grinned. "So, I guess we're on the same side now, huh? I joined the other family!"

He laughed and I left, with Dehan close behind me. Newman and the DA were in the corridor waiting for us. Neither of them said anything. They just stared at me.

I said, "I'm going home. I need to think." I looked at the DA. "Just give me twenty-four hours. The interview was inconclusive. We need to nail this . . ." I shook my head and sighed. "We need to nail this Aspirin Ninja before we hand it over. At the moment, his testimony barely gives us D'Angelo."

She nodded. "I'll give you more than twenty-four hours, Detective. I want the results from the prints on those paper bags before I call in the bureau. I have given that top priority at the lab, so you have a couple of days. Find out if Philips is alive or dead. Do it fast."

"Thanks."

We left them there and went down the stairs. It had gone dark, and as we stepped out, I searched the sky for stars, but I couldn't find any. When we got to the car I leaned on the roof while she unlocked it.

"You want to drop me off and take the car? You can pick me up in the morning."

She stared at me a moment, then did a comic imitation of Guzman: "Fock you! You know what I'm saying? You onerstand me? *Fock* you!"

I laughed. "Come on, Dehan. You have an apartment and a life. I can't expect you . . ."

"What?" She jerked her head at me. "You don't like having me around? *Fock* you! I'm a pain in your ass? Tough shit! You think I don't know what you'd do if you were alone? Eat takeout and drink whiskey. You can do that when you're healed. Meantime I'm making sure you eat. Like my great-grandmother used to say, 'You'll die, but first you'll eat.' Now get in the fockin' car. We're going home."

She got in and slammed the door, and I climbed in after her.

"Every time you quote that story, it's a different person."

"Yeah, well . . ." She turned the key and the big engine growled. "They all said it. And now I say it."

She pulled out of the bay in the parking lot on Fteley Avenue, switched on the headlamps, and we headed home.

TWENTY-THREE

SHE STOOD IN THE KITCHEN, STILL IN HER COAT, looking down at the screen of her phone, while I lowered myself carefully onto the sofa. She had an open bottle of beer in front of her on the breakfast counter, and I had a glass of Bushmills on a small table beside me. When I'd finished wincing and easing myself into position, I said, "Everything okay?"

She looked up. She looked like a person who has just been awed into silence. Finally, she said, "It's an email, from the stupa at Jetavanaramaya. It says that Ananda is no longer there. He hasn't been for a long time."

I groaned. "Shit! Do they know where he is?"

She nodded. "Yeah, he's on a mission."

"A mission? What is he, some kind of Buddhist secret agent?"

"Don't be stupid. A mission, like the Christians had missions."

"Oh, yeah. Okay. So where is he?"

"At the Top-of-the-World Stupa . . ."

"Where? What? The Top-of-the-World . . . ?"

"The Top-of-the-World Stupa. Stone . . . it's eighty miles outside Phoenix, Arizona."

I smiled and closed my eyes. After a moment I reached in my

pocket and pulled out my cell. I opened my eyes again and Dehan was staring at me.

"What does it mean?"

"It means you have to book us onto the first flight to Phoenix in the morning. Get a car too." I smiled. "I'm going to call Newman."

She stood staring at me while I dialed. Then she opened her laptop and started rattling at the keys.

Newman listened in silence while I explained about the Buddhist temple. He stayed silent for a while after I'd finished too. Then he said, "This is it, isn't it, Stone?"

I nodded even though he couldn't see me. "Yeah. This is it."

"Good luck. You're there unofficially, you understand."

"Yes."

"You think Philips is dead?"

"I think so. I'm not sure."

"Okay, keep me posted."

I hung up and Dehan said, "Seven fifty-five tomorrow morning. We get in thirty-five minutes after eleven. I booked a Mustang Cabrio convertible too."

"Good." I closed my eyes again. I felt suddenly drained. I spoke as though I was half-asleep. "You better get us a room too. We don't know how long this is going to take."

"A room?"

I opened my eyes and looked at her. She was smiling with hooded eyes.

"Yeah, in case we have to stay over a couple of nights."

"I'll get us a couple of rooms, shall I?"

"Yeah—that's what I meant, Dehan!"

"Dirty old man."

"Shut up. I'm wounded."

"Dirty old man."

"You wish."

IT WAS sunny and warm in Arizona.

We picked up the Hohokam Expressway just outside Phoenix International Airport, under a brilliant, clear blue sky, and headed south till we came to Highway 60 and then turned east through the heart of town. Highway 60 through Phoenix is kind of weird, because it is bounded most of the way by high walls, so you can't see the acres of low houses with their swimming pools and desert gardens. All you can see is the long, straight highway, and the high, concrete walls with tall, thin palm trees towering over them against the perfect, azure sky.

After about half an hour, we finally emerged into the desert, the road veered south and east, and we began to rise steadily through Gold Canyon, toward the Superstition Mountains. After ten minutes, we turned east again and began to climb through wide desert scrubland populated with small, gnarled bushes and tall saguaro cacti. After another half hour, the desert landscape began to be replaced by pine woods, steep mountainsides, and deep gorges. Finally, we came to the small town of Top-of-the-World. There we turned onto a dirt track that claimed to be North Pinal Ranch Road and led us through pine forests on a steady climb toward a weird, fantastical, gleaming white temple at the top of a high ridge overlooking the town.

We wound our way up the dirt track for another five minutes and finally came to a large, modern complex of concrete-and-glass buildings surrounded by lush gardens. Palms, cacti, and abundant exotic flowers had been arranged around a network of fountains, ponds, and streams with small wooden bridges. A series of sign-posts directed us to a near-empty parking lot. Dehan killed the engine and we climbed out.

We stood looking at the surreal arrangement of structures and gardens. The track went right through it and continued up a smaller hill to the vast, domed, gleaming white stupa. It was crowned with a golden spire that shone in the winter sun and pointed up to the vast, clear dome of heaven.

Dehan took hold of her long, black hair and tied it in a loose knot at the back of her neck. "What is this place? It's like something out of one of those weird 1960s science-fiction movies."

"I think it's a monastery."

"So you think they have a reception desk or something?"

"Let's go and find out." We followed a footpath through gardens and over a bridge that spanned a narrow stream to a large building with broad, glass doors into a cavernous room with no windows. The floor was tiled in marble, and the walls were painted in elaborate frescoes that seemed to depict scenes from Buddha's life. Stacked in a corner was a pile of mats and small cushions. Dehan removed her aviators and muttered, "It reminds me of a dojo."

"I think you're not far off. I think this is where they meditate."

We stepped out again and crossed a paved area, past a large pond, and headed toward another building which was almost as long but was on two floors and had plenty of windows. It had "administration" written all over it. As we approached, the door opened and a young man with very short hair, jeans, and a sweatshirt came toward us, smiling.

"You look lost," he said with all the subtlety of a man in his twenties who has just discovered a spiritual path. I ignored him with all the subtlety of a man in his forties who has met a lot of men in their twenties who have discovered a spiritual path.

Dehan asked him, "Do you work here?"

"I have some duties here," he answered, as though he was gently correcting an error in her perception of truth.

I said, "Good. We are looking for somebody. Maybe you can help us find him."

"Who are you looking for?" He clasped his hands together, like he was going to pray for us to find what we were seeking.

Dehan said, "His name is Ananda Sri Pannasiha. He's from Sri Lanka."

He smiled beatifically and nodded several times with his eyes closed. "Sangha Nayaka Ananda Sri Pannasiha is the senior monk

here. He is up at the stupa at present, tending the gardens. Please .
. ." He bowed slightly and gestured with his hand for us to follow
the path up to the temple. "He will be pleased to see you and
answer your questions."

I frowned at him. "How did you know we had questions for
him?"

"Everybody who comes here has questions for Nayaka
Ananda."

"Thanks."

He bowed and withdrew like someone auditioning for one of
the sillier parts on *Star Trek*, and Dehan and I started our own
trek up the path toward the temple. It was slightly more than
three hundred yards, but it was uphill, and it took us about ten
minutes to reach the steep, white steps that led to the temple
doors. The structure was magnificent. It inspired both awe and
peace at the same time. Broad gardens surrounded it with palms,
cacti, bright flowers, and sand and stones of remarkable colors,
arranged in patterns that were startling and evocative.

At the back, we found a stream with a red, wooden bridge
over it. Beyond the bridge, there was a man in a saffron robe,
down on his knees tending to a bed of flowering shrubs. As we
approached, I began to see him more clearly. He looked as though
he was in his early sixties. His skin was dark and weathered from
the desert. His hair was cut very short and seemed to be turning to
gray. From what I could see he was slim and lithe, and strong.

We crossed the bridge and stood at the edge of the garden
looking down at him. He turned to face us and shielded his eyes
from the sun, which was low in the southern sky. I smiled at him
and said, "Adrian Simon Philips?"

He smiled and stood, stepping out of the garden so that the
sun was no longer in his eyes.

"I'm sorry," he said, "I am blinded by the light." He laughed.
"I'm afraid Adrian Philips is dead. I am Ananda. Can I help you?"

He spoke what the Brits call cut glass English. The English of
the upper classes, Oxford dons and High Court judges.

"I hope so," I said. "You sound and look more English than Sri Lankan."

He chuckled. "Karmapa once said, 'Anyone who thinks that reality is an illusion is an idiot. And anyone who thinks it isn't, is an even bigger idiot.'"

"That's cute. It also doesn't mean anything and neatly avoids answering my question."

"I am sorry, I wasn't aware you had asked a question. I thought you had simply made an observation. Who are you?"

"My name is John Stone, and this is Carmen Dehan. We are detectives with the New York Police Department. We have no jurisdiction in Arizona, so we are not here in an official capacity."

"Oh, yes, I understand. And you are looking for Adrian Philips because you are reopening the investigation into David Thorndike's murder, and *his* investigation into Carol Hennessy."

"You're well informed."

He laughed. "Oh, yes! Yes, I am very well informed." He pointed at an oxblood pagoda where there was a round table with some chairs. "If you'll join me in some tea, I will try to answer as many of your questions as I can."

We followed him along the short, graveled path and climbed the steps into the pagoda. There he produced from somewhere, it may have been in his robes, a brass bell, which he rang vigorously just before he sat. We sat too, and a few moments later a young girl in her early twenties appeared. She had a stud in her nose, faded jeans, and a gray sweater. She ignored us and bowed to Ananda.

"Nayaka Ananda."

"Bring us some tea, would you, Betty? Thank you."

She left, and he looked at Dehan and then at me. "What would you like to know?"

"Was Adrian Philips employed by Senator Carol Hennessy to murder these people?"

I reached in my pocket and handed him the list that we had

been sent. He took it and examined it carefully, name by name. Then he nodded and handed it back.

"Yes, these and a few more. I would be happy to provide you with a complete list."

Dehan shook her head. "If you are not Adrian Philips, why have you got that kind of detailed knowledge?"

His look was direct and unwavering. He seemed to hold her face in the invisible grip of his mind as he answered, "Don't ask why, Carmen. It's an impossible question to answer. How do I have this detailed knowledge about Adrian? Because I know Adrian very intimately. We were very close. When he died, I . . ." He took a deep breath and paused, like he was scanning a list of possible verbs. Finally, he said, "I inherited his files and documents, and a great deal of information."

"Did Adrian die in Pakistan, in 2007?"

"That was one of the places where he died."

"What is that supposed to mean?"

"We die and re-become at every instant, Carmen, in a million tiny ways. But some people die in major ways, at major points in their lives. They experience catastrophic change, which annihilates their identity, such as it was, and they become something, or someone, new. That happened to Adrian several times. The last was in a very appropriate bomb blast in Pakistan." He smiled at her. "But your pursuit of Adrian will not move you along in your hunt for David Thorndike's killer. It will only tantalize your curiosity, lead you astray, and fail to satisfy you."

Betty appeared with a tray, a teapot, and three cups. She set it down on the table and poured for us. The tea was pale green and smelled slightly of rosemary and fennel. She bowed to Ananda and left.

I said, "Did you supply David with documentary, video, and audio proof of Adrian's work for Hennessy?"

He nodded. "Yes, I did. I gave him copies of the originals, which I have here." He paused for a moment, as though thinking. Then he said, "Adrian Simon Philips, had he ever had the good sense to go to a psychologist, would probably have been diagnosed as a sociopath. He was completely devoid, at least as far as he was aware, of any capacity for compassion or empathy. He could look on the suffering of others without any feeling at all. In that sense he was the mirror image of the Buddha, whose entire motivation in life was to help people to stop suffering. That is what is at the heart of Buddhism.

"Adrian was physically very strong and very healthy. He realized in his teens that he could make a lucrative career out of killing, because it was something that commanded a very high price and which very few people had the skill and the emotional capacity to do. So he joined the SAS, became highly skilled, and also well connected. When he was ready to move on, into the private sector, he set about torturing a prisoner. The British Army frowns on that kind of thing, so he was dishonorably discharged. This, of course, in the market that he was looking to open up, was like having a PhD. It demonstrated exactly what he wanted his clients to know—he had no compassion. He would go well beyond where most other people would pull back.

"He did a number of jobs for the Russian Mafia and a few Middle Eastern and African governments. His specialty was the untraceable kill, and that soon got him noticed by the Hennessys. They employed him, and set about systematically eliminating all of their enemies, both in industry and in politics. His instructions were not only to kill them, but to strike fear deep into the hearts of all of those with whom the Hennessys had dealings. This he did, very successfully.

"Unlike most killers, Adrian had a very good intellect. His IQ was up in the hundred and fifties. He was a genius, and he was blessed with a total lack of respect for authority, as well as a total absence of fear where other men were concerned. It was not difficult for him to manipulate the Hennessys. His supreme arrogance and his ruthlessness fascinated them. He arranged several meetings with them in which they discussed in depth the jobs he had done, and the jobs he was in the process of doing for them, in the context of their long-term plans. He filmed and recorded all of those meetings. His intention was to blackmail them and become immeasurably rich and powerful by controlling these preeminent figures in world politics.

"But, after about six or seven years, it is hard to be precise, he began to die. He began to realize something very important about himself. It was not that he was incapable of compassion and empathy, but that he had simply buried those processes, those mechanisms of the psyche, those *emotions* in his unconscious mind. In much the same way that we are usually unaware of the backs of our knees because we never think of them. We are only ever conscious of what we focus our mind on. What we don't focus on, we are not aware of. And gradually Adrian began to focus his mind, his *imagination*, on other people's pain. And in so doing, he started to become aware of it.

"The full extent of this horror is something that very few people could ever comprehend. Because the fear, pain, and emotional agony of every one of his victims, and their loved ones, began to haunt him. And his imagination made him more vividly aware of them every single day. Until he believed he was going insane. Not losing his mind, because losing his mind would have been a blessing, but sinking into his mind, as though his mind were hell itself.

"He had studied Zen Buddhism for many years as part of his training in the martial arts. And now, much like the samurai of old Japan, he turned to Buddhism, and in particular, Theravada Buddhism. Because this branch of Buddhism is most concerned with the doctrine of kama, or, as you probably know it in Sanskrit, karma. Action and intention, and the consequences thereof.

"He found a degree of peace and set about trying to improve his very dark kama by meditation and by helping as many people as he could to move out of suffering and into joy.

"Then, in October of 2007, he was destroyed in a bomb blast. But, as I say, he left me all his knowledge and all his documents, electronic and otherwise. To which, you are most welcome."

For a moment, looking into his extraordinarily direct, honest eyes, I felt a cold chill run down my back, as though I was in the presence of something that was not entirely of this world. It was as though I knew that he and Adrian Philips were both the same person, and yet also two entirely different people.

I dismissed the notion and said, "Thank you, Ananda, that would be really very helpful."

"Not just for you," he said and smiled. "But for this poor, beleaguered nation."

I frowned. "Yes, I guess so."

He turned and gazed at Dehan's face for a long moment, then he turned and gazed at me. He smiled and said, "May I suggest that you take the afternoon to rest and relax? You are welcome to walk in our gardens if you like. I have some chores I need to finish. This evening, I will gather together all Adrian's belongings, and, if you will drive up here tomorrow morning, I will hand them over to you. If you need me to come to New York at any time, to give a statement or testify at trial, I will be happy to do so." His smile broadened. "But for now, John, I think you really need to rest that shoulder. And your heart. The heart is not an organ we should neglect. Look what happened to Adrian when he neglected his." He stood and moved toward the steps. "Enjoy your tea. I'll see you tomorrow."

And he walked with quiet, vigorous steps back toward the garden where we had found him. I turned to Dehan and spread my hands. She shrugged.

TWENTY-FOUR

"HE IS ADRIAN PHILIPS."

We were sitting in Séamus McCaffrey's Irish Pub and Restaurant on West Monroe Street. She had a Bud, and I had a pint of the kind of beer that puts wiry red hair on your chest. We had been quiet for a while and she spoke suddenly, looking at the interlocking wet rings she was making on the tabletop with the base of her bottle. Then she glanced at me, like she thought I would disagree. "Adrian Simon Philips, ASP, the snake, the deadly killer, Ananda Sri Pannasiha. ASP."

"You're probably right."

"So, what? He gets to kill all these people, what is it, twenty? Thirty? More? He has a spiritual epiphany and just walks away from his past? 'I'm not that man anymore, so I am not guilty.' Hennessy goes down, D'Angelo goes down, whoever else is involved gets taken down too, and he just smiles and walks away."

"That seems unlikely, don't you think?"

"Well, what are we going to do about it?"

I took a long pull on my beer and gave a big sigh. "Well, before we decide that, we need to have a clearer understanding of what the hell is going on. And we should get that when he gives us all this material tomorrow." She drew breath to complain and I cut her short. "But! There are a couple of things that have me a bit confused. For a start, if we are assuming that he is Adrian Philips, and he has had this great epiphany, that would explain why he wants the whole story to come out, and why he wants some form of justice done. But what it doesn't explain is—one, why he did nothing for ten years after David was killed, and two . . ." I stared at her and frowned. "How the hell he expects to get away with it! He says he's willing to testify at trial. But if he does, and he is Philips, D'Angelo and Hennessy will recognize him. There must be British officers who can identify him. There must be photographs of him at his old regiment. Once Hennessy's team sets out to show he is Philips, they will find proof. He's not stupid. He is anything but stupid. So how the hell does he plan to pull it off?"

She thought about it, staring at the table and making Olympic symbols with her drink. "I don't know. He's playing mind games. All his clever philosophical bullshit, but in the end all he's doing is trying to get away with murder."

"Like I said, Dehan, you're probably right."

"And how the hell did he know about your wounds? He gives me the creeps, Stone. This guy is weird."

"He's very observant. I wasn't moving naturally. My arm was stiff . . ."

"And the heart?"

"Like you said, mind games. Either way, we take the material back and, if it's as good as he says it is, it becomes a federal case and we hand the whole thing over to the bureau. And they get to decide what they want to do with ASP."

"I guess . . ." She went to take a pull from her bottle and found it was empty. She sat forward and pointed at my glass. "You want another?" I shook my head, and she made to stand, hesitated, and then sagged back in her chair again.

"So who killed Dave?"

I nodded. "I have been sitting here wondering the same thing. We've been on this crazy wild goose chase." I smiled in a way that was rueful. "Which makes Carol Hennessy rather appropriately the goose who is going to get cooked, but we are no closer to answering those simple questions which we started out with."

She stood and went to the bar, and I sat staring at nothing but seeing David's astonished face looking at somebody who was holding his gun with a steady hand. Somebody ruthless, cold, and deadly accurate. Somebody who had killed him with a single, well-placed shot, and had then left the gun right there on the bookcase and walked away.

Without the article.

Dehan came back with another Bud and another pint of Murphy's bitter, which she put down in front of me.

"If you don't want it, you can throw it in my face. But I ordered bacon sandwiches and fries, so I figured you'd want a drink."

"Thanks."

"So here's what happened. Don't interrupt. Just listen."

"Yes, Memsahib."

"2007, after a lifetime of killing, Adrian Philips has an epiphany and decides he wants to make things right. He turns to Buddhism as a way of dealing with his conscience or his karma or whatever you want to call it. But he doesn't want to spend the rest of his life in jail, so he stages his own death in Pakistan and moves to Sri Lanka, where he becomes a monk and calls himself Ananda Sri Pannasiha. And in this new identity, he does two things. One, he requests a transfer to the monastery here in Arizona, and two, he contacts Dave Thorndike of the *New York Telegraph*, a paper that is not afraid to get down and dirty and take on the big boys."

"Good."

"I said don't. Now, thanks to the material that he is able to give Dave, Dave's article progresses fast, and in February, he contacts Lee and tells him what he has. Lee freaks out and goes to Hennessy and tells her what Dave is going to do. Ordinarily, she would order Philips to deal with this kind of problem. But now Philips *is* the problem. The aspirin has become the arsenic."

"And now you are going to run into a problem."

"Shut up. No, I'm not. You were going to say, why would Lee kill Dave if Hennessy had already ordered Guzman to do it? Well, that's simple. She's a careful woman. She takes Lee's information and she says nothing to him. She goes to D'Angelo and tells him to take care of it. He dispatches the order to Guzman.

"But meantime, Lee, keen to get in good with the powerful Hennessys, takes matters into his own hands."

I nodded. "That's possible. And the article and the laptop are not there because Dave has already given them to Lee, who now hands them over to Hennessy."

"That was my big finale, and you stole my thunder."

"Sorry. Do it again. I'll pretend."

"Take a hike."

The bacon sandwiches arrived, and I realized how hungry I was. We ate in silence until there was nothing left but crumbs on our plates, and she sat picking at those with her fingers.

I said, "You figure Lee for the kind of man who would kill somebody like that?"

"What do you mean?"

"It was cold. Steady hand, took aim, looking right into his face. Didn't flinch. It takes real cold blood to do that. I wouldn't be able to shoot someone in the head while they were looking me in the eye." I shrugged and smiled. "I just don't see that in Lee."

She made a face. "He was ruthless enough to shop his friend to Hennessy. Greed and ambition can do crazy things to a person."

I shrugged. "I guess."

She frowned. "You think Philips did it?"

"If that is Philips, he is certainly cold and professional enough to do it."

"But that doesn't make any sense."

"No, it doesn't."

WE STAYED the night at the Hotel Don Carlos next door, and the following morning, under fresh, blue skies, we drove out again to the Top-of-the-World Stupa, to meet with Ananda again. The unenlightened being on reception smiled beatifically at us and told us that Nayaka Ananda was waiting for us at the pagoda behind the stupa, where he had met us the day before, and we retraced our steps up the long track.

He was seated on the floor in the lotus position and appeared to be meditating. When we were crossing the bridge, he opened his eyes and watched us approach. As we climbed the steps, he stood, in a single fluid movement, and bowed to us.

"Good morning, Carmen; good morning, John. Please, will you sit?"

We greeted him and sat, and he picked up from the floor a military rucksack and placed it on the table in front of me.

"I think you'll find everything you need to close your case in here. If you have any questions, feel free to ask me. I have no secrets."

I opened the sack and extracted a number of A4 notebooks, a case of rewriteable CDs and DVDs, and an album of photographs. While I was doing that, Dehan said, "I have some questions."

Ananda smiled. "I thought you might."

"I think you're full of shit. I think your story is bullshit, I think you are Adrian Philips, and I think you got religion as part of your midlife crisis and now you want to clear your conscience of all the murders you've committed without having to face the music. So you've invented this cock-and-bull story about how Adrian Philips is dead but you knew him intimately, but it's bullshit. You *are* Adrian Philips, and you can't run away from yourself."

He held her eye throughout her speech with no expression at all on his face. When she'd finished, he waited a moment, then said, "That isn't a question, Carmen. That is just a statement of your perception."

"More bullshit."

Now he smiled. "Frame your question. What is it, exactly, that you want to know?"

She was struggling and looked at me for support. I said, "I want to know how you expect to get away with it. You have offered to be a witness at the trial. You told us yourself that Philips met with Hennessy and D'Angelo several times. If you go into the witness box, they will see you and recognize you. You're on the FBI's wanted list. Once Hennessy and D'Angelo finger you, the FBI will be all over you like a rash. There must be photographs of you back in England, with the regiment. How do you think you are going to pull this off?"

He looked a little bit amused and again waited for me to finish. When I was done he said simply, "I am not Adrian Philips. Adrian Philips is dead. So there is nothing for me to get away with or pull off. And it seems to me that you are wasting valuable time and effort in attempting to prove that your perception is the truth, rather than seeing things as they really are. When I give evidence at the trial, you will have your answer."

A small white bird with a bright yellow face landed on a rock in the pond opposite the pagoda and started to peck at the water. He watched it for a moment, and I couldn't shake the feeling that I was looking at a man who was deeply at peace with himself. I asked him, "Did you kill David Thorndike?"

His face creased up and he started to laugh. "No, John, of course not." He thought for a moment. "He was killed, probably, on the night of Friday the fifth of March, 2008. You are welcome to check the records of the stupa. You will find that that Friday, as every other Friday for the last ten years, I was in meditation at the meditation hall for the whole evening."

Dehan said, "When you heard that Dave had been murdered, why didn't you come forward and inform the authorities that you had all this information?"

He listened to the question, then gazed at the bright morning, at the pond, and at the tiny bird, still standing on the rock.

"Carmen, I know you don't trust me or believe me, and there is no reason why you should. But trust yourself, trust what you know to be truth. The last person whom I offered this information to died because he had it. Kama is a real thing. It is not a theory or a hypothesis, or a mystical force. It is a true system, a process, that responds to our actions and our intentions.

"So, if I had come forward and offered this information, which is so loaded with cruel, destructive intentions—if I had come forward and offered it to some investigator, what would my purpose, *my* intention, have been? To bring peace? To bring joy?"

She scowled. "Justice! To bring justice!"

"What is justice, Carmen?"

"More philosophical bullshit!"

He smiled and nodded. "Yes, that's what I think it is too." She opened her mouth, but he raised a hand and stopped her. "I have asked you a question. What is justice? You have answered me with ugly noises and implied insults, but with no reasoned thought. I am going to ask you to think about the question, for yourself, and answer it. You have committed your life to the pursuit of justice; it might be a good idea if you had a clear understanding of what it is. In the meantime, unless you have any other questions for me, I think it is time for us to part."

I nodded. "Thank you, Ananda."

"Thank you, John. Please be careful with your cargo. It is dangerous." He turned to Dehan, who was looking at him like he had sprouted antennae from his head. "Carmen, I hope you find what you are looking for."

And a moment later, he was down the steps and striding along the path toward the bridge. I watched him go, and I wasn't sure whether to smile or not. I had seen the tattoo he had on his forearm. It was half-concealed by his saffron robe, but at one moment, while he was talking, the robe had slipped. He had made no effort to hide it. It was a winged dagger with a motto across it: *Who Dares Wins*. The emblem and the motto of the British SAS.

In the end I smiled, shoved the files back in the rucksack, and stood. "Come along, Little Grasshopper. Let's get back to the Big Apple and cause a bit of mayhem and pandemonium."

We walked slowly through the peaceful sunshine, listening to the faint twitter of distant birds and the ripple of water from all the streams and fountains that played here and there throughout the complex. And somewhere, nearby, there was the deep, resonant chime of a large, tubular bell.

TWENTY-FIVE

WE CAUGHT AMERICAN AIRLINES OUT OF PHOENIX International at twenty-five after four that afternoon, and landed at LaGuardia five hours later, at fifteen minutes after eleven, New York time. I slept all the way and arrived feeling exhausted, with a hellish mixture of numb aches and shooting, stabbing pains in my shoulder.

The airport was practically empty as we came out of arrivals, and I was suddenly acutely aware that our weapons and our badges were locked in the Jag in the secure parking lot. We crossed the echoing, cavernous hall, looking over our shoulders, and stepped into the cold, New York January night. Like me, Dehan was scanning every corner and every shadow, every car and every pedestrian. But nobody knew we were there. Nobody knew where we had been. Not yet.

We got the shuttle to the parking garage and finally made it to the car. Dehan drove, and neither of us spoke all the way home. My shoulder was killing me. When she finally pulled up and killed the engine, she looked at me.

"It hurts, doesn't it?"

I nodded and reached for the handle to open the door. She put her hand on my knee. "Wait."

She pulled her Glock, cocked it, and climbed out of the car, scanning the street in both directions. I swore to myself, drew my weapon, and got out too.

She said, "We're clear."

Condensation billowed from her mouth, luminous under the streetlamps. I opened the trunk and took out our bags, hiding the pain as I lifted them. I carried them up to the porch and she followed, still covering the street. I unlocked the door, flipped on the switch, and we went inside. Then we checked every room. When we knew we were safe, she smiled at me and said, "Weird, huh?"

"Yeah." I watched her go to the kitchen and get a glass of water and two painkillers. She brought them to me, and I took them and sat. "I'll tell you what it brings home to me, Dehan. We can't hang around for the Feds. We have to act and act now. I've got some pizzas in the freezer. We stick them in the oven, make a gallon of coffee, and spend the next two or three hours, however long it takes, going through the evidence. When we know it's watertight, we tell Newman—I don't care if it's four a.m., we wake him up. And first thing in the morning, we make our arrests. Then, when the DA is primed and the suspects are in custody, we hand it over. Right now we are sitting ducks, and the longer we wait, the greater the risk."

She nodded. "Yeah, let's do it."

And for the next four hours, we ate pizza, drank a gallon of coffee, and waded through reams of evidence, photographs, DVDs, and CDs. The evidence was not compelling, it wasn't damning. It was conclusive. There was absolutely no question that D'Angelo and Carol Hennessy had conspired in the murder of every name on the list and a few besides. There was no doubt, reasonable or otherwise, that Carol Hennessy had ordered their assassinations. David had been right. This was not dynamite. It was nuclear, and when this shit hit the fan, it would be the biggest scandal of the century. Questions would be asked from the lowliest barstool in Hunts Point to the Senate, in every newspaper and on every talk show around the world: How was it possible for this woman to get away with what she had done for so long? Where were the checks and balances? Where was the constitutional machinery that was supposed to make this kind of thing impossible?

When we had finished, Dehan flopped back in her chair and rubbed her face with her hands. Then she sat and stared at me for a long moment. "Stone, however many we put inside, or the Feds put inside, how many will get away?"

"I don't know, Dehan, but after this is over, it is going to be much, much harder for these parasites to do this kind of thing. For that much at least, we need to thank Ananda."

She grunted, and I grabbed my phone and called Inspector John Newman at his house, where he was sleeping. It was five in the morning.

―――――

By fifteen minutes after six we were in the briefing room at the station. We had four teams plus myself, Dehan, and the inspector, who turned to me now and said, "Detective Stone, this is your show."

I stood and faced the room. Sixteen cops, twelve uniforms, and four detectives specializing in company fraud all looked back at me, frowning, aware that something extraordinary was happening, but not sure what.

"First, let me say that what is discussed in this room this morning stays strictly among us. People's lives are at stake. One careless comment or phone call, and people could die. Us included.

"Now, we have to act fast, and there can be no mistakes. This has got to go like clockwork. Team one, you will go with Inspector Newman and make the arrest on Senator Carol Hennessy." There was a muffled gasp. I stared hard at them. "If she has prior warning that we are coming, I will hold each one of you responsible. You will proceed directly from this room to the cars, you will speak to no one, and you will make the arrest.

"Team two, you will go with Detective Dehan and make the arrest on Anthony D'Angelo, Carol Hennessy's personal secretary. Team three, you will come with me and make the arrest on Jackson Lee. Team four, detectives, Inspector Newman will give you the warrant to go into the Hennessy Foundation offices, freeze their assets, and conduct a far-reaching investigation into their financial activities. The warrant was granted at five forty-five this morning, and the judge wasn't too happy. So your powers are extensive."

There was some muted laughter. I looked at the clock on the wall. It was twenty after six. "Okay, let's go!"

And we scrambled.

Within half an hour, shortly before seven a.m., Newman and his four patrolmen had stormed into Senator Carol Hennessy's apartment in Manhattan, dragged her from her bed, cuffed her, and marched her downstairs to the waiting cars.

Almost simultaneously, D'Angelo, four blocks away, was intercepted while doing his morning run along the banks of the Hudson. He struggled and tried to run, was restrained, and Dehan cuffed him and read him his rights.

Lee was also out running, in Morningside Park. We waited in the cars, in the dark, cold morning before sunrise, and as he exited onto Manhattan Avenue, intending to cross to his apartment block, I climbed out of the car and approached him. He stared at me in astonishment.

"Detective Stone? What on Earth . . . ?"

"What's the matter, Mr. Lee? Had you heard rumors of my death? They were greatly exaggerated."

He stammered a moment. "No! I . . . it's just, at this time of the morning . . ."

"There is no good time for being arrested, Mr. Lee."

"*What?*"

I pulled out my cuffs, and the team climbed out of their cars.

"I am arresting you for the murder of David Thorndike, Mr. Lee, for conspiracy to murder an officer of the law, and for concealing evidence of murder and conspiracy to murder."

He was shaking his head and staring at me goggle-eyed.

"No! No, that's not true!"

"Turn around!" Two patrolmen spun him around, and I cuffed his wrists behind his back. "Okay, let's get him to the station."

It went like clockwork, and as we drove away from Morningside Park back toward the Bronx, the team of detectives were taking control of the Hennessy Foundation and starting their long, methodical investigation into one of the most corrupt institutions ever to be created.

By eight o'clock, we had our three major suspects in custody, and Lee in interview room three. Dehan and I were sitting in Newman's office. The expression on his face said he was somewhere between elation and terror at what he had just done.

"I don't mind telling you, Detectives, that I will be very glad to hand this over to the bureau."

I nodded that I understood, but said, "Can you give me an hour, two at the most, sir? I need to talk to Jackson Lee."

He shook his head. "He'll lawyer up, John. Hennessy and D'Angelo did it straightaway."

"I know, sir. But I think I can get to him. And if we have a confession, that will clinch it."

"Well, I suppose I owe you that much. But the fallout has started already. We're going to have the White House and the Feds all over us before very long. You'd better make it quick."

"Thank you, sir."

We grabbed some coffee and made our way to the interrogation room. Lee's attorney was already there with him. He was a big man in his fifties who looked like he'd been around the block a few times and knew his way blindfolded. He drew breath, but I raised a hand as I sat down and Dehan sat next to me.

"Please, Counselor, we haven't much time, and you and your

client need to hear what I am going to say. Pretty soon the Feds are going to claim jurisdiction over this investigation. When they do that, Hennessy is going to start pulling strings, and your client and D'Angelo are going to have the buck passed firmly into your hands. This is a onetime opportunity for you to get in first, before the big Hennessy machine starts rolling."

They exchanged a glance. They must have been telepathic, because his lawyer looked at me and said, "What do you want, and what are you offering?"

"I want the full story: What happened to David's article? Where is it now? What happened to his laptop? Where is it now? Exactly how he killed David and, above all, his motivation."

Jackson leaned forward. His counsel put a hand on his arm, but he ignored him.

"I can tell you about the article and the laptop, but I don't know who killed David."

Dehan said, "Bullshit."

The counsel said, "Jackson, stop talking."

I leaned forward and looked into his face. "He told you about his investigation. He told you he had met the hit man, Philips; he told you Philips had given him everything and Hennessy was going down . . ."

Jackson was nodding. "Yes, yes, that is all correct. I asked to see the material. Obviously, it was a bombshell. The repercussions were going to be seismic. I told him I needed to review it. He brought it to me, left it with me, and when I read it . . ." He shook his head and laughed. "It was beyond anything I had imagined."

"So you went and warned Hennessy . . ." But even as I uttered the words, sitting there looking into his deceitful, slippery face, the truth dawned on me. He was watching me, reading my expression. I stopped dead. "Son of a bitch! You didn't go to her at all, did you? The directorships, they weren't gratitude. You were blackmailing her!"

"But I didn't kill Dave."

The counsel sighed. "For God's sake, Jackson. I can't help you if you keep talking."

He ignored him and stared at me. "I'll talk, but I want a deal. And I did not kill Dave, Detective Stone. You have to understand that."

Dehan said, "Where are the documents?"

"Have I got a deal?"

I said, "I'll recommend it to the DA. Do I need a search warrant for your house? The minute I pick up the phone to get a warrant, the offer is off the table."

"They are in my safe at home in Oyster Bay. I will hand them over to you along with everything I know. But you have to believe me. I did not kill David."

I shook my head. "You had a multimillion dollar scam. You were going to be rich beyond your wildest dreams, but as long as David was alive and wanting to publish his article, you couldn't pull it off. He *had* to die so that you could blackmail Hennessy."

He was shaking his head. "No, for God's sake, Detective! I didn't decide to blackmail Hennessy until I heard he was dead! He was my friend! I couldn't have looked him in the face and shot him in the head like that! I couldn't do it to a perfect stranger, much less Dave!"

His attorney spoke up. "Okay, now that's enough. Do not say another word, Jackson, until we hear from the DA." He turned to me. "And if you want my client to incriminate Hennessy and D'Angelo, forget about the murder charge. You heard the man, he did not kill his friend. Now, this interview is over."

We left them to confer, and Dehan and I went to our desks. She looked exhausted and I felt wrecked, but my mind was racing. Suddenly, things were beginning to slot into place. I sat in my chair and saw David's notebooks and diary that Samantha had given me. I picked up the diary and started leafing through it. The question that Ananda had asked Dehan was scrawled across one page. "What is justice?" And below it, "Morality does not exist in nature. It is a human construct."

Dehan had her eyes closed. I said, "David was going through a moral crisis."

She opened her eyes and looked at me. "Yeah, you said."

I nodded. I thought a moment, then sighed. "Well, I guess this is all just about sewn up. Whatever I recommend to the DA, she is not going to offer Lee a deal. Not now that he has confessed to blackmailing Hennessy. His motive for killing David is too strong. The Feds will wrap it up."

She nodded. "I need to sleep. Are we about done?"

"Just about."

I picked up my phone and called Frank at the lab.

"Hey, Stone, how's it hanging?"

"Pendulous. Listen, remember the letter I sent you?"

"Yup."

"Did you look at it? Was I right?"

"Aren't you always? Yes. You were right."

I sighed. "Thanks, Frank."

I hung up. "Okay, Dehan, my friend, let's go home. But can we go and see Katie on the way? I'd like to fill her in, give her some closure."

"Sure. You're a kind man, Sensei. Let's do that."

So Dehan phoned Katie to see where she was, and I phoned the district attorney to give her my recommendations on offering Lee a deal, and as we half staggered out to the Jag, political pandemonium broke out behind us and the case slipped from our hands and into the hands of the Federal Bureau of Investigation.

TWENTY-SIX

THE BRIEF RESPITE FROM THE RAIN WAS OVER AND AN armada of low, sagging clouds in various shades of gray, heavy with water, were moving in from the Atlantic. Droplets accumulated on the windshield, and occasionally the wipers stirred into life and pushed them to one side. We were headed for Vincent Avenue in Randallfield, where Katie had a house.

Dehan shook her head and gave a small laugh.

"So it was that simple all along. You know? Sometimes I think that things are never complicated, it's just that we can't always see that they are simple, because of the way we are looking at them."

I gave a couple of nods. "You may well be right, Dehan."

She thought for a minute longer. "Dave had entrusted the stuff to his childhood friend, who saw the potential to become fabulously rich. He killed Dave and blackmailed Hennessy. We had it there, right in front of our eyes, all along."

We came off the Cross Bronx Expressway and onto East 177th. As she turned left onto East Tremont, she said, "But you know what's still eating me, don't you?"

"Yes."

She glanced at me. "Is he? Is he Philips?"

I thought about that for a long moment as she accelerated

toward Randall Avenue. With anybody else in the world, it would be a simple question of identity, but with him it was somehow impossible to consider it on that level. It became a philosophical question about the very nature of identity itself, even if you didn't want it to be. In the end, I shrugged. "Logically, it's him. But I never saw anyone so certain of the fact that they were *not* somebody." I spread my hands. "And it does not seem to faze him at all that he is going to face Hennessy and D'Angelo in court."

She turned onto Randall Avenue and we crossed the bridge, and next thing, we were turning into Vincent Avenue, heading north and looking for Katie's house.

It was a large, white, double-fronted clapboard affair with black gables and black shutters. We parked out front and climbed the stairs to her porch. She opened the door before we had time to ring and led us to a spacious, comfortable living room, where she gestured us to a couple of sage-green armchairs. We refused coffee, and she sat on a matching sofa.

I watched her a moment. She looked anxious. I smiled and said, "Should I call you Katie or Kathleen?"

Her answer surprised me. She smiled back and gave her head a little shake. "Kathleen is dead. I am Katie."

I gave a small bark of a laugh. "So it is possible to die and be reborn within a single lifetime."

"I guess it is."

"Katie, we tracked down David's source. He may be Adrian Philips, the man who killed your family, or he may not. At the moment we have no way of knowing for sure. It seems Philips repented for the things he had done, and turned to Buddhism as a way of atoning. It also looks as though he was killed in a bomb blast in Pakistan in 2007. If that is the case, then this man, Dave's source, was his spiritual teacher."

She made no expression with her face, just blinked several times. "So, the man who broke into our house . . . He might be dead?"

"There is a good chance. The case is now in the hands of

the FBI. They have the resources to find out for sure. If the source we have found is in fact Philips, he will be arrested and tried."

She seemed to digest that information for a bit, then asked, "And what about Hennessy?"

I smiled again. "She has been arrested. So has D'Angelo."

She stared at the carpet for a while, then turned to look out at the gray rain that had started to fall outside, leaving long streaks like tears on the panes.

Dehan had frowned at me briefly, and now said to Katie, "We also arrested Jackson Lee, Dave's friend."

Katie looked surprised. "Really?"

"Dave had entrusted the article to him, along with all his notes and his research, everything he had learned from his source. Lee stole it and murdered Dave, so that he could use it to blackmail Hennessy."

An expression of dawning realization washed over her face, and she slowly leaned back on the sofa. In a very small voice she said, "After all these years . . ."

I spoke quietly. "Does it make sense at last?"

She nodded.

"Something that intrigued me for a while," I went on, "was the way, in his diaries and his notes, he went on and on about these moral quandaries, questioning what was right and wrong, what morality was."

She gave a small, sad sigh. "In his own, twisted little way, he was a very moral man. Trouble was, he could only think of morality on the grand scale, how it affected society, history, culture. He was all about the law, democracy . . ." She trailed off, looking at the rain again. "But when it came to individual human beings, he was blind. Hennessy had to be brought to justice, not because she had killed a little girl's father, not because she had robbed a good man of his life and a wonderful woman of her husband, no. She had to be brought to justice because she had betrayed her sacred office as a secretary of state, as a congresswoman. Because she had betrayed democracy. He was a very moral man, in his own, twisted way."

We were all quiet for a moment, listening to the patter of the rain in the street. My voice sounded too loud when I spoke.

"And then he met Ananda Sri Pannasiha. Or it may be Adrian Simon Philips, the poisonous ASP. And he began to question all his morals, everything he had ever believed in, didn't he?"

She nodded. "Yes."

"And the only reason you were with him began to dissolve."

She nodded again.

"And the one hope you had cherished, that your father, your sister, and your mother, and you, might finally get justice, began to slip through your fingers."

It was almost a whisper. "Yes . . ."

"There is one small piece that I am missing, but I think I can hazard a guess. He fell in love with you, didn't he?"

She nodded.

"Ananda, Philips, whoever he is, had a deep impact on him. He is that kind of man. And I think David started to question just about everything. But two things were clear for him, I think. He was in love with you, and he had in his hands the opportunity to become very, very rich. I think what he proposed to you was that he would leave his wife, and you and he could be together, living like kings. Making Hennessy pay."

She sighed. "This monk he was seeing twisted him somehow. He said he had been liberated. Why should we publish the article when we could use it as blackmail and become rich? The Hennessys were billionaires; if we were clever, we could live in luxury for the rest of our lives without ever having to work again. This, according to Dave, was how she should pay for what she had done to me and to my family."

"You tried to reason with him. You wanted justice and retribution."

"I wanted her exposed for the monster she was, and I wanted her punished. But, as ever, he was blind to anything except his own grand visions. I pleaded with him, begged him. But he ignored me."

"And that was why you split up with him. It had nothing to do with his wife."

She shook her head.

"So he handed all the material over to his attorney as the first step in his blackmail scheme. The old standard: if anything happened to him, his attorney was to publish the material and make it available to the FBI."

She smiled without humor and nodded again, more slowly.

"I can imagine that the rage must have been building inside you until it was impossible to control. And the solution seemed obvious. If he wouldn't listen to you, there was only one course of action open to you. You went there on the Wednesday with the pretext of collecting books and CDs . . ."

"I also gave him one last chance and begged him to reconsider. But he was so arrogant and obstinate. He was convinced that once he was rolling in money and had divorced his wife, I would come back to him."

"And you took the gun away with you. Then, on the Friday, you returned late at night. I am guessing you were wearing surgical gloves. When he opened the door, you stepped in and shot him once in the head. Then left the gun on the bookcase and walked away. In your mind, this would trigger the instructions he had given to his attorney, to release the material for publication and an investigation by the FBI. What you could not possibly have imagined was that his attorney would go ahead with the blackmail, and there would be no investigation."

"All these years I have been wondering what happened, what went wrong. I assumed she had people in the FBI who sat on the evidence. Then when you came 'round . . ."

"And that's why you sent the anonymous letter. That's why you couldn't let us know who you really were or how deeply involved you were in his investigation, because it could end up incriminating you. But your prints, Katie, were all over the letter, and all over the copy you handled. I found out this morning and confirmed what I already suspected."

Dehan was frowning and shaking her head. "Hang on. You had an alibi for Friday night."

I nodded. "That had me stumped until I remembered something Sammy Gupta, David's landlord, had said." I turned back to Katie. "He said you turned up several times with your sister. Then we discovered that you were Kathleen O'Connor, and your sister had been killed at the same time as your parents. It followed logically that Sammy had seen you on a couple of occasions with a friend who was more or less similar to you. So I'm guessing you invited her and her boyfriend out to dinner, made an excuse for not being able to join them, and gave her your credit card . . ."

"I told her I wanted to thank her for being so supportive when I split up with Dave. She and her boyfriend had been having difficulties. I suggested an early Valentine's dinner for them and gave her my card. I trusted it would be enough to confirm my alibi."

"You know I have to arrest you now, Katie."

"I know. But at least Hennessy will finally be exposed for the murdering parasite that she really is." She looked around at her living room. "I inherited this from my parents, you know." She sighed and stood. "Shall we go?"

And outside the gray rain persisted among the cold, naked trees.

EPILOGUE

NEWMAN HAD ORDERED US BOTH TO TAKE AT LEAST A couple of weeks holiday, more if we needed it. I think he was terrified of what we might turn the next cold case into, and it was he who needed a holiday from us.

I had managed to light the fire, and Dehan had put a chicken in the oven and fixed us a couple of very dry martinis. I was lying on the sofa with my eyes closed, listening to the soft patter of raindrops on the sidewalk outside and the occasional, desultory rustle of paper as Dehan turned the pages of the magazine she was reading.

After a while, I heard the magazine drop to the floor. She stretched and yawned, and I counted back from five to one. I knew she'd talk on one.

"Say, Stone. Aren't you sick of the rain?"

I nodded. "Mm-hm . . ."

"Wouldn't it be nice to go somewhere with sunny beaches, nice restaurants, big steaks . . ."

"Yup."

"And god knows you've earned it!"

I shrugged. "Nyah . . . I'm no good at going on holiday on my own. I get bored."

She was quiet for a while. She was behind me and couldn't see me grinning to myself. I heard her pick up the magazine again and turn a couple of pages. "I could keep you company. I don't mind . . ."

"Oh . . . well . . . I guess that would be okay . . ."

"Dork." She was quiet a little longer, then said, "I always wanted to go to Goa."

"You want to go to Goa?"

"It's in India. It looks amazing."

I shrugged. "Okay. Book it. My card is in my jacket."

There was a stunned silence.

"*Seriously?*"

She sounded so much like an excited kid I had to open my eyes and turn to look at her. Her face was radiant. I laughed. "Seriously." I flopped back and closed my eyes. "I learned in the last week that you can't take anything for granted in this life. Let's do it. Goa, here we come!"

She jumped up and astonished me by kneeling beside me and planting a big, messy kiss on my cheek. Then she was off to get my wallet and her laptop. A minute later, she was back in her chair rattling at the keys on her computer. I lay, with my eyes open, looking over at the breakfast bar and the kitchen and smiling, enjoying the sound of her.

"You know how long I have wanted to go to Goa? *Years.*" She rattled a little longer, then went on, "Say, Stone, the other night, just before you got shot . . ."

"Uh-huh . . ."

"You said you wanted to talk to me about something. Something Shelly had said. What was that?"

I didn't answer for a moment. Then I smiled. "Nothing important. Maybe I'll tell you in Goa."

Don't miss UNNATURAL MURDER. The riveting sequel in the Dead Cold Mystery series.

Scan the QR code below to purchase UNNATURAL MURDER.

Or go to: righthouse.com/unnatural-murder

NOTE: flip to the very end to read an exclusive sneak peak...

DON'T MISS ANYTHING!

If you want to stay up to date on all new releases in this series, with this author, or with any of our new deals, you can do so by joining our newsletters below.

In addition, you will immediately gain access to our entire *Right House VIP Library*, which includes many riveting Mystery and Thriller novels for your enjoyment!

righthouse.com/email

(Easy to unsubscribe. No spam. Ever.)

ALSO BY BLAKE BANNER

Breath of Hell (Book 8)
Invisible Evil (Book 9)
The Shadow of Ukupacha (Book 10)
Sweet Razor Cut (Book 11)
Blood of the Innocent (Book 12)
Blood on Balthazar (Book 13)
Simple Kill (Book 14)
Riding The Devil (Book 15)
The Unavenged (Book 16)
The Devil's Vengeance (Book 17)
Bloody Retribution (Book 18)
Rogue Kill (Book 19)
Blood for Blood (Book 20)

DEAD COLD MYSTERY SERIES
An Ace and a Pair (Book 1)
Two Bare Arms (Book 2)
Garden of the Damned (Book 3)
Let Us Prey (Book 4)
The Sins of the Father (Book 5)
Strange and Sinister Path (Book 6)
The Heart to Kill (Book 7)
Unnatural Murder (Book 8)
Fire from Heaven (Book 9)
To Kill Upon A Kiss (Book 10)
Murder Most Scottish (Book 11)
The Butcher of Whitechapel (Book 12)
Little Dead Riding Hood (Book 13)
Trick or Treat (Book 14)
Blood Into Wine (Book 15)
Jack In The Box (Book 16)
The Fall Moon (Book 17)
Blood In Babylon (Book 18)
Death In Dexter (Book 19)
Mustang Sally (Book 20)

A Christmas Killing (Book 21)
Mommy's Little Killer (Book 22)
Bleed Out (Book 23)
Dead and Buried (Book 24)
In Hot Blood (Book 25)
Fallen Angels (Book 26)
Knife Edge (Book 27)
Along Came A Spider (Book 28)
Cold Blood (Book 29)
Curtain Call (Book 30)

THE OMEGA SERIES
Dawn of the Hunter (Book 1)
Double Edged Blade (Book 2)
The Storm (Book 3)
The Hand of War (Book 4)
A Harvest of Blood (Book 5)
To Rule in Hell (Book 6)
Kill: One (Book 7)
Powder Burn (Book 8)
Kill: Two (Book 9)
Unleashed (Book 10)
The Omicron Kill (Book 11)
9mm Justice (Book 12)
Kill: Four (Book 13)
Death In Freedom (Book 14)
Endgame (Book 15)

ABOUT US

Right House is an independent publisher created by authors for readers. We specialize in Action, Thriller, Mystery, and Crime novels.

If you enjoyed this novel, then there is a good chance you will like what else we have to offer! Please stay up to date by using any of the links below.

Join our mailing lists to stay up to date -->
righthouse.com/email
Visit our website --> righthouse.com
Contact us --> contact@righthouse.com

 facebook.com/righthousebooks
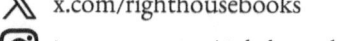 x.com/righthousebooks
instagram.com/righthousebooks

EXCLUSIVE SNEAK PEAK OF...

UNNATURAL MURDER

CHAPTER 1

WHEN YOU SEE IT ON TV, IT HAS DRAMA. BUT IN THE real, three-dimensional world, the steady throb of the red-and-blue lights in the darkness, the way they wash the walls of the house with their dull colors, the way they make the black windows look hollow and empty, like dead eyes—that has no drama. And the pain and the convulsive weeping of the girl who loved the victim and now sees him lifeless and gaping behind the wheel of his cheap Toyota, the numb, expressionless faces of the uniforms who have seen it all before, the ME and the CSI team, who just want to go home to bed—all of that, all of it, it has no drama. The true horror of that scene, of all the scenes like it, lies in the fact that it is banal, it is horrifically ordinary.

We climbed out of Dehan's Focus and ducked under the yellow tape that hung across Bryant Avenue, segregating two houses from the rest of the world, because here somebody had been killed, murdered. Sergeant Solano met us as we crossed the line. Dehan was frowning at him; at three a.m., she'd brought her attitude with her.

"You want to explain to me why I'm here, Sergeant?"

Solano made a face like sheepish turning to worried and said, "I wasn't sure what to do, Detective. It's three a.m. and the inspector's not at the station. It ain't a cold case exactly, but it might be connected. And I knew you . . . your mom . . . So I told Dispatch . . ."

He trailed off. The expression on Dehan's face might have made Godzilla trail off. It made intimidating look like a welcome respite. So I said, "You did the right thing, Sergeant. Walk us through it."

He gave me a grateful smile and pointed at the Toyota. It was parked under a streetlamp. I glanced at what lay beyond it: a run-down, terraced house with steps rising to a large veranda behind wrought iron railings, a redbrick wall and peeling green paint on a cheap door and a window frame; a girl, Latina, sitting on a wooden chair, in her twenties, barefoot, wearing shorts and a T-shirt, crying; a female cop hunkered down by her side, trying to comfort somebody who can never be comforted.

Dehan had moved to the window of the car and was peering in. I said to Solano, "Okay, what's the story?"

"Two victims, Detective." He moved toward the vehicle and I went and stood beside Dehan, looking through the shattered window. There was a young man, maybe midtwenties. He was slumped over on his right side. He looked uncomfortable. There was a lot of blood from two bullet wounds in his head, and at least three more in his arm and chest.

Solano was saying, "This is Sebastian Acosta, resident at the Jacobi . . ."

On the other side of the car, crouching by the passenger seat in the open doorway, I could see Frank, the ME, looking back at me. "Good morning, Frank."

"I knew them." He said it in a dead voice that masked his anger.

I turned back to Solano. "Thanks, Sergeant. I'll give you a shout if I need you. You canvassing the neighbors?"

"Yeah, we're on it."

"Okay, I'll talk to you in a minute."

Dehan had moved around the car. Frank stood, and I joined

them. There was blood on the sidewalk and on the stairs leading up to the veranda. Frank looked unhappy.

"Sebastian Acosta, twenty-six, wanted to be an ME." He pointed at the blood on the stairs. "His friend, Luis Irizarry, twenty-five, was going to be a plastic surgeon. He said there was more money in it and you didn't have to watch your patients die."

Dehan voiced the question I was wondering. "Where is he?"

"In a coma, in an ambulance on his way to the Jacobi."

She screwed up her face. "They were both residents?"

He nodded. "They'd been through med school together and they were doing their residency together."

I asked, "How bad is Luis?"

"Pretty bad. We won't know till he gets there. He took two rounds to the chest. Sebastian took the brunt of the attack. He has two shots to the head and three to the body, point blank. There are powder burns on his face." He pulled out his cell. "I'll get Personnel to email you their addresses."

I walked back around to the driver's side and stood where the shooter must have stood, with my arms outstretched as though I was holding a gun. Dehan came and stood beside me.

"I think I remember them."

I glanced at her. "Yeah?"

She nodded. "And that girl." She jerked her head at the veranda. "I think she's Rosario's daughter, Angela."

"Rosario?"

"My mom's friend. Rosario Rojas. That's what Solano was talking about. Rosario was raped and murdered in this house. That's her daughter. When they were kids, she used to hang out with these two."

"How'd Solano know?"

She raised an eyebrow at me. "Station-house gossip. We are paid to snoop, Stone."

I made a face. "I guess you're right. You okay with this?"

"Sure. I'm going to talk to Angela."

The female police officer had given up on her attempts to

console her and now just stood by her side. As we approached, Dehan asked the cop, "Has she made a statement?"

The officer shook her head. "I'm afraid not, Detective."

Dehan nodded. "Okay, we've got this."

She hunkered down in front of Angela and I rested my ass on the wrought iron railing. Angela looked away. Her face was wet with tears and her bottom lip was trembling. Dehan said, "Hey, Angela, you remember me?"

She looked at her sidelong for a moment, then shook her head.

Dehan smiled. "My mom was Marta. She was a real close friend of your mom's."

"Marta . . . ?"

"Yeah." She pointed up toward Garrison Avenue. "We lived up on the corner of Garrison and Faile. We had the café. You remember? My mom was always over here, having coffee with Rosario."

She nodded. "Yeah, I remember."

"Did you make the call?"

Angela nodded.

"Okay, let's get you dressed and take you down to the station. C'mon, I'll give you a hand."

She led her inside and a light came on in the window. I sat a moment, looking at the door. About two feet from the bottom there were what looked like two bullet holes. I logged the fact for later consideration, stood, and looked down at the scene in the street. I wondered where the gunman had come from. I caught Solano's eye and called him up.

He was talking as he climbed the steps. "We got two 911 calls within less than a minute of each other. We were already on the way when the second call came through, reporting shots fired. From what we can make out, the victims arrived, the shooter must have been waiting, approached the car, and fired through the window. Five of the seven shots hit the driver, two hit the passenger. He got out and tried to make it to the house but collapsed on the stairs. Then the shooter must have taken off, because we got here very shortly afterwards."

"What do the neighbors say?"

He sighed and looked apologetic. "So far a few people heard shots—between five and seven—but nobody saw nothing." He shrugged. "This kind of neighborhood . . ."

"I know, Sergeant, there is not a lot of trust. Between five and seven, huh? Okay, you called Crime Scene?"

"They're on their way."

He left, and I went and pushed open the door. It gave onto a hallway with a broad, wooden staircase rising along the right wall and a passage on the left that gave onto a front room, a back room, and a kitchen. I walked back down the steps to the sidewalk. I counted nine of them. Then I turned and faced the door, holding out my arm like I was shooting. The angle was wrong, so I lay down on the road. A couple of the uniforms looked at me and smiled. I ignored them and held out my arm again, like I was shooting from a prone position. After that, I got to my feet again and climbed back to the hall. There I got on my knees and inspected the wall. After a moment I found what I was looking for, a bullet hole. But I only found one.

Outside, the crime scene team had arrived, and I walked down to meet them. Joe, the team leader, was suiting up at the back of their van.

"Stone. I thought you only did cold cases these days."

"Yeah, so did I. Listen, looks like the crime scene is out here, but do me a favor, will you? Have a look at the door. There are two bullet holes at about two feet. Inside, slightly to the left, there is one bullet hole in the wall. To me, none of it looks fresh. I'd like to know how old they are and what caliber we're looking at."

He nodded. "Sure, no problem. Say . . ." He smiled. "How's things with your partner? Still teamed up with Detective Dehan?"

I raised an eyebrow. "Yeah, why?"

He grinned. "Just making polite conversation, John. I'll catch you later."

I watched him walk away toward the car, followed by the three members of his team, all in white plastic suits, like B-movie aliens. He gestured with his hand and said something, and one of them climbed the stairs as Dehan and Angela came out the old, peeling green door.

They joined me and Dehan asked, "We done here?"

I looked up and down the road, still trying to work out where the shooter came from. There were plenty of spaces where a car could have parked. I walked away so I was standing in front of the Toyota, about five yards distant. The streetlamps made an amber glow on the windshield. There was a look of desolation about it.

"Solano!"

He turned to look at me.

I pointed at the car. "Was the engine running?"

"No, Detective. It was just like that when we arrived."

I walked to the nearest space behind the car. Then I looked across at the other side of the road, where a steel fence blocked off a stretch of overgrown garden. Every parking space on that side was occupied. I stared at Dehan. She was watching me, with her right hand on Angela's arm. I said, "Okay, let's go."

Back at the station, we put Angela in interview room three and went to get some coffee. At the machine, I leaned against the wall while Dehan filled the polystyrene cups.

"Did you notice the holes in the door?"

She glanced at me. "No."

"Joe's having a look at them for me. They're low down, about mid-shin. Two of them. Aside from that, any initial thoughts?"

She frowned and leaned against the wall opposite me. "Yeah. The shooter knew his victims, knew their car, it was kind of an execution, but he was real mad too."

I nodded. "Knew them why?"

"Because I watched you. You were checking if you could see in through the windshield, or the side window. He would not have been able to see their faces from the front because of the glare from the streetlamps, or the back simply because it's impossible.

And from where he stood to shoot, unless he was a dwarf, their faces were hidden by the roof of the car. Plus, he shot through a closed window, which, under the lamp, would have made it doubly hard to see them. Ergo, he knew who they were, and he knew their car. Obviously he was waiting for them, popped them when they arrived, and then made off."

I nodded. "What about Angela?"

She shrugged. "I was thinking maybe she's just a random witness. You know . . ." She spread her hands. "Med students, access to chemical substances, tempted to help pay their fees with a little private enterprise. Maybe they thought they were meeting a buyer and instead they met with somebody whose toes they were treading on."

I sucked my teeth. "Mm-hm, that crossed my mind too. And they just happened to meet outside her house."

"But your bullet holes in the door suggest the connection might be more than that." She hesitated a moment. "Especially as they knew each other."

"I agree. Witnesses in the street say they heard between five and seven shots. There were seven shots in the victims. The two in the door would have made it nine. I found a bullet hole in the wall, but no slugs."

"Just one?"

I nodded, then shrugged. "Suggests somebody got injured, but there was no blood. I'm pretty sure those two shots were not fired tonight. If I'm right, there ought to be a police report. I'm interested to hear what Angela has to say about it."

We stared at each other for a long moment. Then she gave a small smile and said, "Let's find out."

CHAPTER 2

SHE DIDN'T LOOK AT US AS WE SAT DOWN. DEHAN placed the cup of coffee in front of her and smiled.

"It's not exactly coffee, but it's hot and sweet and it will help with the shock."

Angela nodded but still didn't make eye contact. After a moment, she said, "Will I be able to go home soon?"

Dehan didn't answer for a moment, then she said, "Of course, whenever you like, but we need to get a statement from you. It shouldn't take long."

Angela went to speak, stopped, then said, "I didn't really see anything."

I scratched my head. "Did you make the 911 call?"

She nodded.

I went on, "What made you call?"

"I heard shooting."

"How many shots did you hear?"

She fiddled with her fingertips, looking at her coffee, like she hoped it would tell her how many shots she'd heard. After a bit, she shrugged. "I don't know."

I bobbed my head slowly a few times, like I was thinking. "More than one?"

"Yeah. More than one."

"Less than twelve?" She nodded again. I went on. "More than three?"

"Yes."

"Less than, say, ten?"

She gave a small sigh and reached for the coffee. "Probably five or six."

"Good, that's very helpful, Angela. Now I'd like to ask you something else. Did the shots come all together, kind of *bang, bang, bang*! Or were they spaced out?"

"All together, like, one after another, real quick. Like, one two three, one two three, and then one. So I guess it was seven."

I smiled at her. "That's very good. That's excellent. Were you in bed?"

"Yes."

"What made you realize that they were shots?"

Now she stared at me, real hard, and swallowed a couple of times. "I don't know what you mean."

I spread my hands. "I'm just trying to get a picture of what happened. You're in bed and you hear what sounds like seven firecrackers going off in rapid succession, right . . . ?"

She gave a very small nod and half-whispered, "Yes . . ."

"And you didn't go and look to see what it was, you immediately went to the phone . . ."

Dehan added, "Downstairs."

"So you must have known they were gunshots. I was just wondering how you knew they were gunshots."

She looked like she was about to start crying again. She started to speak two or three times but stopped herself, and finally said, "Well, I looked *quickly* out of the window."

I smiled kindly. "Oh, that's great. So you did see *something*, just—not very much."

"Yes."

"So you heard the shots, you got out of bed, and peered

quickly out of the window. What did you see that made you call 911?"

Her bottom lip was trembling and tears spilled from her eyes. She covered her mouth with her hands. I reached into my pocket for a handkerchief and handed it to her.

"There is no hurry, Angela. I know this has been very traumatic. We would just really like to get whoever did this to . . ." I frowned at Dehan, like I couldn't remember their names.

Dehan reached across the table and took Angela's hand. "Hey, listen, take it easy. In your own time." She smiled. "What were their names? I remember you guys used to play together, right?"

It was like a trigger. She went to pieces, sobbing violently into my handkerchief, making the ugly, convulsive noises of deep grief. Dehan stood and pulled her chair around so she was sitting next to her, and put her arm around her shoulder. The sobbing lasted a good four or five minutes. Eventually, Dehan persuaded her to have some of the coffee, and that seemed to settle her a bit. Then Dehan said, "Hey, we can do this a little later. Maybe we can come 'round in the afternoon and take a statement from you." She looked at me and I nodded. "But, before we take you back, can you just give me a *rough* idea of what you saw when you looked out of the window?"

Angela stared at the tabletop, but like she wasn't seeing it, like she was seeing something else instead, something that made her scared. Her breathing was ragged. Finally, she said, "There was just a man running to his car. Seb was lying on the seat and Luis was on the steps. The man got in his car and drove away."

I said, "Was his car on your right or on your left?"

"On the right."

"And once you saw that, you ran downstairs and dialed 911?"

She nodded.

I looked at Dehan. "I don't know if you have any more questions, Detective Dehan. I have all I need for now."

Dehan gave Angela a squeeze and said, "We will need a full

statement later on, but right now I'll get somebody to drive you home. You need me to call anyone? A doctor, a friend?"

"No. I'm fine."

They got up and moved to the door. As she was about to leave the room, I had a thought. "Angela?" She stopped and looked at me like she was afraid I was going to make her stand in the naughty corner. "Do you think whoever did this saw you at the window?"

She stared at me for a long while before she shook her head. After that, Dehan walked her downstairs and I made my way to our desks. There I dropped into my chair and sat gazing at the black window that showed nothing of the creeping dawn, but just the orange wash of the streetlamp on the corner of Story Avenue. Dehan came in on her long legs, yawning, and fell into the chair opposite me, leaning her elbows on the desk. We stared at each other for a while and eventually, I said, "From her bedroom window, she could not have seen Sebastian lying across the seat. Neither could she have seen Luis on the stairs."

She chewed her lip and gave three ponderous nods. "She was downstairs."

"I think you are right. First order of priority, Carmen, we need to find out what those boys were doing there at three in the morning. I don't believe it is a coincidence that they were outside her house. They were close friends, you could see that by the way she went to pieces when you mentioned they used to play together."

"I noticed that."

"They were there . . ." I shrugged. "They were there for *her*, for some reason. Which begs the question, how did the shooter know they were going to be there?"

"I told Angela we'd see her again after she'd had time to sleep and get over the shock. She said she'd take a pill." She looked at her watch. "It's just after four. We should go and call on the parents."

I sighed and rubbed my face. "Yes . . ."

"You want me to take Acosta and you . . ."

I interrupted her. "No. I'd like us both to do both. This is going to be a complicated case. My gut tells me there will be subtle emotional nuances all over the damned place. I want you there so we can discuss it. We'll see Luis' family first, then Sebastian's."

"You got it, Sensei."

We took her car because my Jaguar was still at my house. She had picked me up after Dispatch called her. I climbed in the passenger seat and slammed the door. She fired up the engine, and I looked at her profile against the creeping light of early dawn. She was exquisite, and totally unaware of it.

She backed out onto Fteley Avenue and headed for Bruckner Boulevard. The Irizarry family lived not far from me, in Morris Park.

"One thing I am still not clear about," I said, as she pulled onto the freeway, "is how this becomes a cold case."

She grimaced. "I've been wondering that myself. I see it and I don't."

"Explain."

She gave a little sigh and thought for a bit. As we turned onto White Plains Road, she started to talk.

"I'm going back a bit. This must be 2004, maybe 2003, so I was thirteen, fourteen. It was about a year before my parents died. My mom had become real close with Rosario, one of the mothers in the barrio."

"Barrio?"

She glanced at me. "Yeah. My mom wasn't an intellectual, but she liked intelligent people. Rosario was smart. She hadn't had much in the way of opportunities or schooling, but she read a lot and she had opinions. She liked my mom because my mom had broken the rules. You know, defied the church, her family, married a Jewish guy. Anyhow, after a while Rosario starts hanging out with a crowd . . ."

She stopped and made a face like she didn't really approve of what she was going to say. I prompted her, "A crowd? What kind of crowd?"

"My dad described them as 'fast.' My mom wasn't crazy about them either. From what I remember"—she glanced at me again—"and I was only about fourteen years old! From what I remember, there were two couples. One of them was mixed race, which attracted a lot of attention. She was a white academic." She laughed. "She might have been a schoolteacher for all I know! But that was the impression. Radical left wing, making a statement, you know the kind of thing."

I managed to frown and raise an eyebrow at the same time. "Kind of woman who made it possible for you to have your job."

"Absolutely. I'm not criticizing. Shut up and listen. Anyhow, she was married to a black guy, black Puerto Rican, I think. He was also some kind of academic. I remember there was some talk about him being ill, and he may have died. These two were close friends with another couple . . ." She thought for a moment. "Eddie and Maria. This couple were also Puerto Rican. He was a defense attorney. He was just starting out, but he was doing okay. He was becoming successful. I don't remember anything about his wife, except that Mom used to say it was a shame he didn't look out for her rights as much as he did for the crooks he helped set free. That was my mom all over. So those four used to hang out, have barbeques and talk the good talk."

"And these are . . . ?"

She seemed to nod with her whole body while she spoke. "These are the parents of our vics. Now, shut up while I tell you. Mom never hung out with them. They invited her to a couple of barbeques but she never went. And after a while, she stopped hanging out so much with Rosario, because, she said, there was too much *cuchi cuchi*."

"*Cuchi cuchi* . . . ?"

"Hanky-panky."

"So what, there was wife-swapping going on . . . ?"

She raised an eyebrow at me. "Or husband-swapping. I don't

know, Mom was never more specific. She was pretty straitlaced, and it may have been no more than flirting while drunk. Point is, it only took Rosario telling her about a couple of these get-togethers, and Mom stopped seeing her so much."

"So what happened?"

"Give me a chance and I'll tell you. Next thing, Mom doesn't hear from Rosario for a while, it might have been a couple of weeks, I'm not sure, and suddenly she turns up dead. Turns out, according to the cops, she's been raped and murdered."

"And they never caught who did it."

"Not even a suspect."

"And Angela is Rosario's daughter. Where's the dad?"

"She was a widow. I don't remember her husband. He left her a pension or something."

"And she was killed in that house?"

She looked at me and nodded. "In that same house."

I looked out at the limpid light and the sleepy storefronts of Morris Avenue. Sunrise was still an hour away and the cars and the streetlamps seemed to be hung with amber dreams, still warm from the beds where people slept behind dark windows. For a moment, I envied those sleeping bodies. And then I pitied the two we were going to wake, to tell them their son was in the hospital, shot in the chest.

Outside Rosario's house.

"They're connected. That is a simple fact." I turned toward Dehan. Her face was momentarily washed with orange light, then went into shadow again. "But the connection doesn't seem to mean anything. It may well be that the people are connected, but the crimes are not. If they are not, this is not a cold case."

She sighed, then shrugged. "So we inform the families, make some initial inquiries, report to the inspector later this morning, and see what he says."

I nodded absently. My brain said that made sense. My gut said my brain didn't know what it was talking about.

CHAPTER 3

WE PULLED INTO HERING AVENUE. I SAID SOMETHING about it being a fishy address, but Dehan didn't laugh. It was a broad, attractive street with large, detached houses and well-tended front lawns. She pulled up outside a double-fronted redbrick with two horse chestnuts standing guard by some stone steps that made a path through a slightly over-ornate garden. We looked at each other. Dehan heaved a big sigh and we got out. The doors slammed and echoed in the stillness. We climbed the steps to a white door and I leaned on the bell several times. After a minute, a sash window opened above, and an angry voice shouted down.

"Who the hell is it? Get the hell out of here or I'll call the cops!"

I stepped back out into view and looked up at him. I held my badge so he could see it.

"Detectives Stone and Dehan, sir. Are you Eduardo Irizarry?"

He scowled. He was a thickset man of about forty, with a balding head, hairy shoulders, and dark, Hispanic features.

"I am he," he said, rather pompously. "What the hell is this about? Can't it wait to a more civilized hour?"

Hell was a word he seemed to like. I thought sourly that it was a place he was soon going to become familiar with.

"Mr. Irizarry, we need to talk to you, in private . . ." I looked with meaning up and down the street.

He hesitated.

I said, "It's about your son . . ."

He closed the window, and after a moment, a light showed through the glass panels in the front door. Next thing, the door opened to reveal Ed Irizarry wearing a silk dressing gown and a foul expression.

"What the hell is this about?"

I tried to suppress the anger that was beginning to warm my belly but failed. I said, brutally, "Your son has been shot. He is in the hospital in a critical state, but we can come back at a more civilized hour if it's inconvenient now."

Dehan's eyebrows rose high on her forehead and she turned to stare at me. Irizarry went a pasty gray color. "Good God . . . shot? By whom . . . ?"

"Do you think we can come in, sir? This is probably not something you want to discuss in front of all your neighbors."

He nodded once, then again several times and stepped back. "Yes, yes, of course . . . Come in."

He led us through a large, middle-class house that was in fancy dress, pretending to be a rococo palace. Evidently we weren't the kind of people he would have in any of his drawing rooms, so he led us to the kitchen, which was not so much rococo as *Fresh Prince of Bel-Air*. He switched on the lights and stood staring at us with his mouth slightly open, like he'd expected us to be somebody else when the lights came on.

After a moment, I said, "Mr. Irizarry, perhaps you should get your wife."

He frowned. "Mary?"

"Is that your wife's name?"

"Yes, of course it is!"

I nodded. "Then that is who you should get. She needs to hear this. Do you mind if we sit down?"

"Of course . . ."

He turned and walked away, back into the sleeping shadows of his house. The kitchen was brightly lit. The walls were lemon yellow, a vast refrigerator gleamed silver, and there was a large, round pine table with four pine chairs in the middle of a floor laid with big terra-cotta tiles. In the center of the table, there was a bowl brimming with tropical fruit. We sat and waited. I wondered, bizarrely, if he'd notice if I had a banana.

The sound of rushing, unsteady feet on the stairs drove the thought from my mind. We stood as they came back in. Mary was small and dark, perhaps a couple of years younger than her husband. Her hair was in curlers, and she had a dressing gown drawn tight around her, as though she hoped it might protect her somehow. She ran across the kitchen, clutching her gown with her left hand, reaching out to me with her right.

"What's happened? Is he all right? Where is he?"

Eduardo announced in a voice that was too loud, "I'll make coffee!" and stared at us each in turn. I ignored him and guided Mary to a chair. We sat, and Eduardo left the coffeepot by the sink and came to sit with us. He looked for a moment as though he might start weeping.

I put my fists on the table and spoke. "Mrs. Irizarry, Mr. Irizarry, we do not know all the details yet, but in the early hours of this morning, at about three o'clock, Luis and his friend Sebastian were parked in a car in Hunts Point . . ."

Eduardo's eyes went wide. "*Hunts Point? What the hell . . . ?*"

Mary covered her ears and screwed up her face. "Ed, *please!*" It was an eloquent gesture that spoke of a hypersensitivity developed over years of enduring his unquenchable outrage at everything he encountered.

I ignored them both and went on. "It seems they were approached by an unidentified person and shot point-blank. Luis was in the passenger seat and managed to exit the car. He received two bullet wounds to the chest. He is in critical condition at the Jacobi."

Ed's mouth was sagging open. He kept staring around the room, as though he was following a slow-moving fly on its journey around the kitchen. Mary had both hands over her mouth. Her eyes were huge with horror as she stared at my face, struggling to give some meaning to what I had told her.

It was Ed who spoke first. "What was he doing at *Hunts Point?*"

Dehan answered him. "We were hoping you might be able to shed some light on that, Mr. Irizarry."

He glared at her. "*I?* How the hell would I know?"

"Ed, *please!* These people are here to help us . . . !"

"*Cops? Help us?* Just shut up, Mary!" He turned back to Dehan. "I have no idea what he was doing there . . ."

Dehan's eyes were hooded when she cut him short. "There were two of them, Mr. Irizarry. He was with his friend Sebastian. You know Sebastian, don't you?"

Mary said, "They've been friends since they were tiny. Is Sebastian badly hurt?"

"He received five shots. Two to the head and three to his arm and chest. He is dead."

Her face twisted with grief. "Oh no . . ." Her voice was the voice of infinite sadness. She said it again. "Oh, no, no . . . Poor Sue. Poor Sue . . ."

She took a handkerchief from her pocket and began to sob into it. She cried silently, with her shoulders shaking in small spasms. I was struck with the impression that crying silently and unnoticed was something she had learned to do over the years. Dehan turned back to Ed, who was staring at the tabletop.

"The reason we thought you might be able to shed some light on why they were where they were, Mr. Irizarry, is that they were parked outside Rosario's house. You remember Rosario, right?"

He didn't do anything. He didn't react. Only, his eyes stared a little harder, and it was his motionlessness that was so striking.

Mary's sobbing stopped abruptly and she looked up at Dehan. "Rosario . . . ? She's dead . . . !"

"I know, Mrs. Irizarry. That house now belongs to Angela. Have you any idea why Luis and Sebastian would be parked outside Angela's house at three in the morning?"

Ed's eyes narrowed. "What are you implying?"

I put my elbows on the table and leaned forward. "It's a simple question, Mr. Irizarry. We are not implying anything. We know that at one time you were both friends with Rosario, and the boys used to play with Angela. So, have you any idea what they might have been doing there?"

He didn't answer. Mary shook her head. "I thought they had lost touch. When we moved out of the neighborhood, we lost touch with Rosario, Sue, Matt . . ."

I asked, "Sue and Matt were Sebastian's parents?"

She nodded. "Matt was ill. He died. Poor Sue, this is going to hit her so hard."

Dehan sighed. "Please forgive me, we have to ask these questions: Have you any idea, at all, however remote, who might have wanted to hurt Luis and Sebastian?"

Ed snorted. "You can spare us the phony empathy, Detective. The answer is no. And we will not collaborate in your transparent attempts to frame our son as being involved in drugs or prostitution. Whatever that loser Sebastian might have been involved in, I have no idea. But Luis had nothing to do with it!"

"*Ed!*" Mary's face was crimson and her neck taut and corded. She stared at her husband, and before he could answer she half-screamed at him, "*Can you not give it a rest for one single minute? Our son is dying in the hospital and all you can think of is scoring points off poor Sue! Sebastian is dead, for God's sake! Is there no trace of humanity in you?*"

He scowled at the table. The kitchen was strangely still and silent after her outburst. I looked at Dehan. She shook her head.

"Thank you, Mrs. Irizarry, you have been very helpful. We are very sorry to have brought you this news." We stood, and Mary stood with us. Ed continued to stare sullenly at the table, like it was the table's fault he was such an ass.

Dehan went on, "We may need to contact you again, but we'll try to trouble you as little as possible."

Ed snorted, and Mary showed us to the door through the dark house where dark blue light was beginning to tint the glass in the windows. We stepped out into the wild chatter of the dawn chorus. The door closed behind us, and I went and leaned on the car, gazing at the sleeping street under a sky that was turning from midnight blue to gray. The Irizarry house was the only one with lights in the windows. Unlike the squabbling birds, the people of Hering Avenue had not yet started stirring from sleep.

The car bleeped and flashed, and I climbed into the muffled dark. Dehan got in behind the wheel, fired up the engine, and switched on the headlamps. I said, "Evergreen Avenue. It's past the station, on the right, before the river."

"I know where it is." She pulled away. "Doesn't get any easier, huh?"

"Nope."

We drove in silence for a while. Then she asked, "Why do women stay with guys like that?"

"I've often wondered. If you asked her, she'd probably say, when he's nice he's great, and he makes her laugh. Maybe she figures the financial security makes it worthwhile. Or maybe it's some kind of Stockholm syndrome." Then I added with a sour twist, "Or maybe she wouldn't know who to be, if he wasn't there to tell her."

She was quiet for a moment, then said, "Wow."

"Mornings like this, Dehan, I wonder if Captain Jennifer Cuevas wasn't right when she advised me to take early retirement."

She looked at me like I was crazy. "Seriously?"

"If I am married to my job, my job is Ed and I am Mary."

She laughed, and we drove on in silence through the dawn, toward Soundview, toward a woman who was probably still sleeping, unaware that her life had, in the last few hours, disintegrated, unaware that her son was dead, unaware that nothing would ever be the same again.

Dehan's voice broke into my thoughts. "What do you think happened?"

"Hmmm?"

"Their group of *cuchi cuchi* friends. It broke up, they lost touch, stopped having *cuchi cuchi* parties . . ."

We pulled onto the Bruckner Expressway and started accelerating west. A hint of copper touched the sky from the east as the sun crept over the horizon. I spoke almost without thinking, expressing a feeling rather than an idea. I said, "Rosario was killed." I sighed. I felt unaccountably depressed. "That is the starting point. Rosario was killed. That spoiled their swinging scene, the Irizarrys moved, lost touch with their old *cuchi cuchi* friends. But the boys stayed in touch. Maybe they stayed in touch with Angela too. And now, fourteen years later, Sebastian has been killed, maybe twenty feet from where Rosario was." I looked at her face, and she glanced at me. I said, "And Ed and Mary know that's significant for some reason. This is a cold case, Dehan, no doubt about it. A cold case that just started getting hot."

Scan the QR code below to purchase UNNATURAL MURDER.
Or go to: righthouse.com/unnatural-murder

www.ingramcontent.com/pod-product-compliance
Lightning Source LLC
Chambersburg PA
CBHW020402210626
46816CB00006BB/2084